"I'm here for you, Mal."

Travis didn't wait for her response, but stepped inside, swung the door shut behind him and kissed her in one smooth move. She couldn't think, overwhelmed by feelings and emotions and Travis.

Always Travis.

She melted against him, into him. It had been so long. Incredibly long.

Mal had known before he'd kissed her that it would lead to this. She'd never have let him up to her apartment if she hadn't been willing to go there. Hadn't wanted to go there.

Oh, yes.

It would only be for tonight. Closure, a last goodbye, whatever she might decide to call it in the cold light of day.

Because tomorrow morning, she would be 100 percent, completely over this.

Dear Reader,

As I close the books on the Ford family, I'm reminded of my own family. The teasing, the laughter, the fight on top of the old rolling dishwasher that broke the kitchen door...

Mallory and Travis have a long history together. One that hasn't gone away even though they've been living miles apart. But they're back in the same city now and history seems to be repeating itself.

I've had a wonderful time sharing the stories of these three siblings, their lives and loves, and while I'm wistful about saying goodbye to them, mainly I feel happy that everyone (in their own unique way) got their happily-ever-after.

I hope you enjoyed your time with the Ford family.

Happy reading,

Jennifer McKenzie

JENNIFER McKENZIE

Table for Two

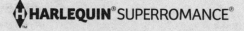
HARLEQUIN® SUPERROMANCE®

Recycling programs
for this product may
not exist in your area.

ISBN-13: 978-0-373-60926-0

Table for Two

Printed in U.S.A.

Jennifer McKenzie lives in Vancouver, Canada, where it rains. A lot. Which means she gets to purchase many pairs of cute boots without guilt. She spends her days writing emails, text messages, newsletters and books. When she's not writing, she's reading or eating chocolate and trying to convince her husband that it's a health food. He has yet to fall for it. Visit her on the web at jennifermckenzie.com.

Books by Jennifer McKenzie

HARLEQUIN SUPERROMANCE

That Weekend...
Not Another Wedding
This Just In...
Tempting Donovan Ford
One More Night

Visit the Author Profile page
at Harlequin.com for more titles.

This book is for Clark who makes me laugh
(even when he's wearing his grumpy face.
Okay...especially when he's wearing
his grumpy face), cheers me on, cheers me up
and is basically awesome.

CHAPTER ONE

THE LAST TIME Mallory Ford had seen Travis Kincaid he'd had his face buried in another woman's lap. That woman hadn't been wearing panties.

Normally Mal wouldn't have felt anything except embarrassment and foolishness for not knocking first. But Travis had been in his office with the door unlocked and they'd broken up only an hour earlier. Her overriding emotion had, therefore, been anger. And although that had been more than a year ago, she still hadn't forgiven him. She didn't know a person who would have.

Seeing him now, that same anger roiled up in her and made her want to dash the contents of her wineglass in his face and cut him down with some pithy commentary. The only thing that held her back was the fact that they were at her brother Owen's backyard wedding reception. That and the fact that she was too couth to lower herself to name calling and wine tossing. She hoped.

He looked good in his white shirt and pants. All the guests were wearing white, but Travis looked especially healthy, his tan a direct contrast to the pale clothing. Living in Aruba had clearly suited him. Mal fiddled with the hem of her own white dress—a lacy fitted number with long sleeves and a high neck—and turned away.

She'd known Travis would be in attendance, seeing as he was best friends with Owen, but that didn't mean she had to talk to him. Instead, she crossed the small patio to the side opposite Travis and joined a conversation with some old family friends she hadn't seen in a while.

The wedding and reception were about a quarter of the size of her oldest brother Donovan's wedding, which had happened in January, but the less formal event suited Owen and his new bride, Grace. Her parents owned the gorgeous farm they were on now. The ceremony had been out beside a small pond while the sun set and the reception was in their backyard, which felt as luxurious and stylish as anything in the city. The forest of trees behind them, the overhead heaters and the lights strung around the space created a magical environment. It helped that Grace was a professional wedding planner and her team had taken over all the decor.

The space felt warm and cozy. Welcoming. And it gave Mal the chance to chat with some of the people she'd missed at Donovan's nuptials.

That was until Owen came and dragged her away.

"Owen." She stumbled over a root as he sped up. "What are you doing? I was talking to those people."

"It's my wedding. I'm allowed to steal you." But he did slow his stride enough that she was no longer worried about breaking an ankle.

Mal glanced up from her feet, and immediately wished she hadn't. Owen was on a mission. With her. One that was leading straight toward Travis Kincaid.

She sucked in a breath and dug her nails into her brother's arm. No. No way.

Travis looked over at her, his expression a mixture of nerves and yearning. And hunger. Mal felt a shiver work its way over her body. She remembered that hunger, how it overwhelmed and devoured. How much she used to love it. She stopped walking.

Owen looked down at her. "I'd like to see the two of you talk."

Mal swallowed and shook her head. She didn't want to talk to him. But when she tried to take a step back, to return to the safety of her earlier conversation and location, Owen gave her a small nudge.

"You can do whatever you want after, but talk now."

Mal stared at him. How could he do this to her? He knew things were over between her and

Travis. Granted, he didn't know all the details because she'd never told anyone. She'd been too embarrassed at first and then she'd just wanted to forget everything. And, okay, she'd sent Owen to see Travis when he'd needed a friend, but that didn't mean she was fine with Travis, that she was ready for a nice little chat and all was forgiven.

Owen's expression softened, turned imploring. "Consider it my wedding gift."

"I already bought you something." A set of matching leather luggage packed with monogrammed robes and a trip to a weekend spa getaway in Napa Valley. Owen and Grace both worked long hours and Mal knew this was one way to ensure they'd take a few days for themselves when they needed it.

Owen put his hand over hers. "I'd rather have this. For both of you." He started walking again.

Mal was forced to walk with him or end up being dragged behind him. Not exactly the elegant and cool image she wanted to project. But she didn't feel cool at all. Not even the breezy spring evening helped. She felt the beads of sweat forming on her spine as they took the last few steps to come to a stop in front of Travis.

He reached up to loosen his collar. But his clear display of nerves didn't lessen her own or make her feel any better. Mal swallowed and blinked when Owen let go of her hand and started to walk away.

"Where are you going?" she called after him.

"I've got a date," he called back. "With my wife." Mal watched him cross the yard to where his lovely wife stood with a group of friends. He took hold of her hand and led her around the side of the house, out of sight.

Mal watched for a moment longer, waiting to see if Owen would reappear, this time with Grace to add a little social lubrication to ease the awkward situation he'd placed her in—but he didn't. She wanted to turn and walk away, too, to go anywhere, talk to anyone else, but good manners and her well-developed sense of pride compelled her to stay where she was.

"Travis." Even saying his name hurt.

"Hello, Mal." His voice was the same, that low blend of heat and roughness. It threatened to take her out at the knees. She locked them, determined to keep them firm beneath her. "Nice night."

She stared at him. Was that all he had to say? This was what Owen had dragged her over to hear? She nodded and waited.

"It's good to see you."

She didn't respond in kind—because it wasn't good to see him. She felt naked, exposed, as if everything she was thinking or feeling was bared for anyone to see. And none of it was anything she felt comfortable sharing. "Right. Well, if you'll excuse me." She moved to go, to leave and never return.

His voice stopped her. "Mal."

She closed her eyes and sucked in a deep breath of woods and earth. She didn't want to do this. Not even a little. She turned back and looked at him. "What do you want, Travis?" She saw no need to play coy or to act like things were anything other than they were.

"Just to talk." He took a step toward her, closing the distance between them. Distance that Mal liked right where it was.

She wrapped her arms around her body. "I don't think there's anything to say." Not on her end, at least. She'd said what she needed to over a year ago.

He ran a hand through his dark hair, a familiar gesture. He was upset and anxious. Well, too bad. So was she and she hadn't done anything wrong. "Will you at least let me apologize?"

"Why?" She steeled herself against the sorrow in his gray eyes—he'd brought it all on himself. "Why now? And why bother?" He'd had plenty of time to make amends, to atone. Instead, he'd left her alone—radio silence.

"Because I want to."

Because he wanted to? What about what she wanted? To be left alone to live her life without the painful memories that seeing him brought. She gave her head an airy toss. "I'm over it, Travis. You don't need to apologize." She held her body tight, her arms close, careful to let no part of her even hint at touching him.

But he didn't back off. "Mal, I know things ended badly."

She did not want to talk about this. Not at her brother's wedding reception. Not ever, in fact. "Travis, there's nothing to talk about."

In her mind, there wasn't. She'd needed to stay in Vancouver and help out the family after her father's heart attack—Travis had stayed in Aruba. They'd been living six thousand miles apart and there'd been no sign of their situation changing. Still, they'd tried. For a good four months they'd tried. They'd talked on the phone, texted, sent emails and connected through video chat via computer. But their lives seemed to be heading down different paths, and with no simple solution, the answer had seemed obvious. To end the relationship.

She'd flown down to tell him in person, feeling as though their relationship deserved that much, hoping things could end amicably as he was close with Owen. But he'd shot down that hope. He pinned the fault on her, calling it a choice, acting as if she'd chosen her family over him, which wasn't the case. She wanted to be together, but her family needed her at that time and Travis wouldn't give up the bistro in Aruba. In her mind, he was the one who'd said no to a future together. And had confirmed it by burying his face in another woman's lap.

"If that were true—" his gaze was hot "—then you wouldn't have spent the majority of this evening avoiding me."

"I'm not avoiding. I'm one of the hosts. I have guests to greet, mingling to do." Her chest felt tight, her cheeks hot.

"I'm moving back."

What? Okay, fine. Did he want a parade? "Congratulations."

"Aren't you going to ask why?" He cocked his head, that charming grin that used to make her weak in the knees playing around his lips. She hated to acknowledge that it still made her knees wobble slightly.

She locked them tight. "I'm sure it doesn't matter to me." Because they weren't together and whatever city Travis decided to call home had no effect on her life.

"My gram."

Those might have been the only two words in the English language to stop Mal from simply turning on her heel and exiting the conversation. She loved his grandma. Mildred Dawes was small and gray and, as she liked to claim, "full of beans." Her love of life and family touched Mal in a way she hadn't known before meeting the woman.

Mal swallowed the angry words, the hurt feelings, and looked at Travis. "Is she okay?"

Mildred was just one of the many things Mal had lost when she and Travis had gone their separate ways. Mal didn't remember any of her grandparents. Two had died before she was born, the others when she'd still been too young to form full sentences, but Mildred had acted as a pseudo grandparent, instilling common sense and downhome wisdom whenever she thought it necessary. And, according to Mildred, it was often necessary.

Travis smiled. "She's fine now. She had a little scare with her lungs that turned into pneumonia, but she's recovered. It'll take more than that to keep her down."

Mal reached out without thinking and put her hand on Travis's arm. The heat seared her palm and she jerked it back. "I hadn't heard. I...I'm glad she's okay."

"Me, too." He smiled. "It sort of brought home the truth about what I was doing with my own life."

She didn't want to know. She'd given up her right to curiosity about Travis's life when she'd walked out of his office and never looked back.

"And what was that?" She curled her fingers into her palms.

"I thought I needed the business, but it's not worth much without the people you love."

Her nails bit into flesh even as she told herself he wasn't referring to her. Even if he was, it was too late.

"I sold the bistro."

"What?" She blinked, glad she'd already locked her knees as it prevented her from reeling.

They'd opened the gorgeous beachside restaurant in Aruba together. Had planned to work there for a few years, watch it grow and enjoy the Caribbean lifestyle. And then her father had had a heart attack and Mal had been needed at home. When she'd explained to Travis, she'd thought he understood. Her family needed her. She had to go back. But he hadn't. Apparently he'd thought the business and his life on the beach were more important. Before she'd even gotten on the flight to go back home, he'd been consoling himself with another woman.

"I had some interest from buyers. Once things happened with my gram..." Travis shrugged. "I decided to take them up on it." His eyes caught hers, held. "I've missed you, Mal."

She swallowed, tried to breathe in some clarity and muttered, "Can't have missed me that much." Seeing as he'd never once contacted her since she left Aruba.

"I did." He reached for her hand. "I was just too stubborn to admit it."

She pulled her hand back. "Well, now I'm too stubborn to believe you."

He studied her for a moment, a smile spreading across his face. "I've *really* missed you."

Had he really? She looked at him, risked staring deep into those dark eyes she knew so well— had looked into so many times before. What she saw there scared her. Not the fallacy of a glib tongue or polite conversation. But naked honesty. Yet she just couldn't. She wasn't that Mal anymore. Couldn't be. "It's been too long, Travis."

"Has it?"

Mal didn't know what to say to that. Well, that wasn't entirely true. She knew what she should say, what her head told her to say, but there was that little matter of her heart. So she kept her silence, managing only a quick nod.

"Mal."

She shook her head so violently that she felt it in her temples. "No, Travis. I don't want to talk here."

"Then let's go somewhere else."

Mal shot him a look. "It's Owen's wedding. I'm not leaving."

But she should have known that wouldn't be

enough. Travis had grown up in a small paper-
mill town, a rough and tumble place where he'd
learned to push for what he wanted and fight
when necessary. Polite platitudes and dressed-
up words wouldn't put him off.

"Then we'll talk later. After the reception. You
tell me a good time and I'll make it happen."
He took a step toward her. "Midnight. Six in the
morning. Three days from now. I don't care. I'll
be available."

"Travis." She didn't finish. He didn't give her
the chance.

"I'm only asking for one conversation. Just one
and then you'll never have to talk to me again."

The old Mal would have agreed. Would have
heard him out. But the old Mal had been burned
by this man and she shied away from allowing it
to happen a second time. "I should go. Say hello
to the other guests."

She walked away before he could say anything
else. She couldn't listen to it, not now. And with
each footfall, the surprise and shock of Travis's
homecoming turned to something she could hang
on to. Something sharp and hot and angry.

Mal headed around the house, following the
same path Owen had earlier. Seriously, if it wasn't
his wedding she'd have had to kill him. In fact,
she might have to do it anyway. Grace would understand. There were certain behaviors that were

just not okay. Forcing your sister into a chat with her ex ranked right up there.

"What were you thinking, Owen?" She didn't care that she was interrupting him making out with Grace. They should be out mingling with the crowd, anyway.

"Busy here, Mal," Owen said, his eyes still on Grace. But then that was nothing new. When Grace was in the vicinity, Owen's eyes tracked her. Even now, when she was pressed up against the side of the house with nowhere to go and his arms around her, Owen's gaze shifted when Grace did. Mal pretended she didn't remember that Travis had once been the same around her.

"Yes, I can see that. But I'd like you to explain why you dragged me into a conversation with Travis." Even now, Mal could feel the flush of embarrassment warm her cheeks. She was glad the reception was outdoors, and although it had been an unseasonably warm March, it was hardly summer weather.

"Looks like you survived." He stroked a finger down Grace's cheek.

Grace caught his hand and turned her attention to Mal. "What did he do now?"

"Now?" Owen feigned shock. "You act like this is a common occurrence." He cupped Grace's face this time and she kissed him.

As Mal watched, her brother's entire body softened. A flicker of jealousy rose, but she slapped it down quickly. She wasn't jealous of her brother, not either of them, although they'd both gotten married within the past few months while she, the only one who'd even been in a serious relationship eighteen months ago, was flying solo. But she missed having someone. The companionship, the love, the sex. She pushed that flicker away, too.

"It was bad enough that he dragged me over, but it was the ditching me with him and coming here to make out. Did you really think that through, Owen?"

"So, things didn't go well?" Owen pulled his gaze away from his bride long enough to frown. "I thought you were okay with the fact that I'm still friends with him."

She was. She totally was. Hadn't she sent him off to visit Travis when he'd been in need of a friend and denying his feelings for Grace? "Your being friends with him doesn't mean *I* am." Could he not understand that?

Grace was giving her husband the same look Mal was. "Owen."

Owen turned back to her. "He misses her."

Mal felt a jolt rock her. She locked her knees again. Collapsing against the house in front of her brother and new sister-in-law would be as bad as falling prone in front of Travis. Well, almost as bad. "He doesn't miss me."

And even if he did, it didn't matter, didn't change anything. They were still broken up. She was still mad. And she'd still found him with his face buried between another woman's thighs.

"Did you even talk to him?" Owen was twirling the ends of Grace's hair through his fingers and the two of them were making googly eyes, which was to be expected, Mal supposed, considering it was their wedding day.

She swallowed. She should respect that this was a special day for them, a special day for her, too, since they were adding another wonderful woman to the family. No one needed to listen to her whine about Travis. Certainly not the bride and groom. "You know what? How about we just agree that you won't do it again and I'll leave you two to get back to your…" She waved a hand to encompass whatever they might get up to and then began walking away.

"Mal," Grace called to her over Owen's shoulder.

Mal turned around slowly. She really didn't want to get an eyeful of whatever Owen might be doing to Grace. "Yes?"

"Do you need us to come with you?" She elbowed Owen when he let out a groan. "You started this. We aren't going to let your sister go back out there alone if she needs support."

"I'm fine." Now she just felt foolish for having brought it up in the first place. Time and place. Neither of which were here and now. "You stay and enjoy yourselves. I'll be okay. Really." She even gave a brief nod to fully reassure them that she could handle herself and would not be in need of assistance. That would be assuming Travis kept his distance.

Too bad she couldn't get any reassurance about that.

TRAVIS WATCHED THE side of the house where Mal had disappeared. He made himself stay where he was rather than chase after her, even though it nearly killed him. He'd known he missed her, but actually seeing her in person, being close enough to touch, brought it all home. He'd been a fool to let her go. Yes, she'd caught him off guard when she'd suddenly sprung the news that she wasn't coming back to Aruba, but he'd handled it poorly.

He could see now that, in her shoes, he'd have done the same thing. In fact, was doing so now, coming back to be closer to his grandma and his family. Closer to Mal.

She was thinner than she used to be. She didn't fill out her dress the way she would have a year ago, but she still looked better in person than in his imagination. Her hair was longer, the dark locks falling halfway down her back. It suited her, filed away some of those hard businesswoman edges. And her eyes were the same deep brown; he remembered the way they'd darken when she looked at him, widen as she reached for him to touch or tease, to press a kiss to his cheek or shoulder. Damn, he missed those days. He wanted them back.

Maybe he should go after her. She'd disappeared around the side of the house, but there weren't that many places she could go. Not in those pale blue high heels that looked as if they could pierce a man's heart with one good stomp.

Instead, he gripped the bottle of water he held more tightly and told himself that he had time. He was back now. For good. He didn't need to rush things. He would take his time, show her that he meant what he said and then he'd slowly win her over. That was the plan. It was his only plan.

What he wouldn't give for a cold beer right now. But he hadn't had a drink in a year. Not since that night that Mal had walked in on him and another woman. It shamed him that he couldn't even remember the woman's name. She'd been a tourist, on the island for a vacation and looking for a little no-strings hookup that wouldn't follow her when she returned home. He'd been looking to lose himself. And he had, right up until the door

to his office had opened and Mal had walked in
to find him with his head up the other woman's
skirt.

He'd regretted it then, regretted it more now. If
only he hadn't let Mal walk away, hadn't grabbed
a bottle of whiskey and drunk until he could no
longer taste, hadn't let himself believe that he
could forget about her by filling the space with
someone else.

Travis took a swig from the bottle, letting the
cool water wash away the layer of bitterness coat-
ing his tongue. What happened was in the past
and he couldn't go back and undo it, but he could
try to make amends. Of course, that awkward
conversation mere minutes ago probably wasn't
how best to go about it.

Crazy. He'd not only spent the flight from
Aruba and ferry ride from Vancouver to Salt
Spring Island considering and planning what he'd
say when he saw Mal, he'd also thought about it
for many months prior. Hand hovering over the
phone or Send button on his email without doing
anything. He'd had the conversation a million
times in his head and heart. And still he'd choked
when the moment arrived.

Travis took another sip of water and rolled his
shoulders. He'd just have to try again.

But when she came out from the side of the
house she was clearly on a mission that nothing

and no one was going to interrupt. He knew that look, that strut. He enjoyed the sway of her hips as she moved across the patio and went through the back door, entering the house.

"Ahem."

Travis blinked and looked straight into the eyes of his best friend, the recent groom. "Ahem yourself." Then he clapped Owen on the back.

"You blew it," Owen told him, but he was grinning. "Pissed her right off."

"I didn't mean to." Travis's eyes darted back toward the door. But Mal didn't reappear. "How pissed was she?"

"Enough." Owen exhaled with the easy breath of a man who knew that his night would be spent in the arms of a loving woman. Travis tried not to be jealous. It had already been a year. What was one more night?

"Where's Grace?"

"She's gone to check on Mal." Owen nicked a skewer from a passing server and popped it into his mouth.

"They're friends?"

Owen nodded and finished chewing. "Yes, but don't ask her to get involved. You messed things up with Mal and you can fix them yourself."

"And here I thought you'd be eager to stick your nose in your sister's love life."

"I am. I said you couldn't ask Grace, but I am

amenable to being convinced. So go ahead, ask me to get involved."

Travis laughed. "Like I could keep you out of it."

"Well, I am a bit of an expert. I got Donovan and his wife back together when my brother screwed everything up." Owen sipped from his own bottle of water. His expression grew serious. "Listen, I love my little sister and I want her to be happy. She hasn't been happy since you broke up, so…" He trailed off with a shrug.

"I'll be honest, Owen. Things aren't off to a good start." Even *rocky* didn't cover it.

"Yeah, I caught that much. But if she didn't care, she wouldn't be mad."

Travis had picked up on that, too. Still it was good to hear from someone else. "I just need to get her to talk to me." Of course, that was easier said than done when she was slippery as an eel. "Any advice?"

Owen tilted his head, seeming to think about it. Then he shrugged again. "Put your head between your legs and kiss your ass goodbye?"

"Wow. You should charge for that insight. Brilliant."

Owen laughed. "Good to have you back, buddy."

Travis smiled, too. It was good to be back.

Even if he was pretty sure Mal was going to do her best to avoid the conversation they clearly needed to have.

CHAPTER TWO

RIDICULOUS. COMPLETELY RIDICULOUS.

Mal shook off the warm, caramel-y feeling that tried to melt the icy guard she'd placed around her heart. Travis hadn't missed her. Not really. No matter what he or Owen or anyone said.

She splashed some cold water on the back of her neck and stared at herself in the bathroom mirror. She looked tired. She *was* tired. But this was Owen and Grace's wedding and there was no time for a pity party of any sort.

She splashed a little more water. Her eyes tracked her hands, noticed the bareness of her fingers and not just because she was the only Ford child currently without a ring of commitment, but because seeing Travis reminded her that, not so long ago, she'd been the only one to have that symbol of a relationship.

Her stomach jittered and she pressed a hand to it, trying to take some slow deep breaths as she'd learned in Pilates. But the bliss of Zen never came. Maybe because Zen was more of a yoga thing.

Mal's eyes strayed to her bare finger again. She should have brought the ring with her. She'd known Travis would be in attendance. She should have placed it in her luggage, transported it here in her purse and then taken a quiet moment alone with Travis to return it to him.

The ring was his grandma's. A pretty, square-cut sapphire surrounded by diamond chips. Mal had been so thrilled when he'd given it to her. It hadn't been an engagement ring, not in the traditional sense, as they'd been too busy putting all their time and money, all their energy into the beachfront bistro in Aruba. But they'd talked about having a wedding once they were settled. Flying in their families and getting married with their toes in the sand and a starry moonlit night overhead, an ocean breeze blowing through the palm trees.

A ghost of a smile crossed Mal's lips before disappearing, much the way her dreams had. She needed to return the ring. Not just to Travis but to Mildred. It had been wrong of her to keep it as long as she had, sitting in her jewelry box so she looked at it every morning when she chose her accoutrements for the day.

She dried the water from her neck, pressed cold fingers under her eyes and, after a few deep breaths and a good roll of the shoulders, decided to head back out. She couldn't stay in the house forever. It might not be her wedding, but people would be looking for her. And it would be good to have something else to focus on, such as small talk and chatter about the family business—a string of wine bars, one fine dining restaurant and their recent expansion into the gastropub market with a single location. She would also be happy to talk about the charity event she was organizing to raise money for local food banks.

Mal made her way through the lovely farmhouse and out the door to the backyard. The party, though small, was still going strong. She glanced around for a group to join. She didn't care which one, so long as it didn't include Travis or her brother.

"Mallory." Her mother, Evelyn, swooped in like some kind of avenging angel or mother of the groom, as she was, and wrapped her in a tight hug. "I've barely seen you tonight."

"You saw me before the ceremony and sat with me during the ceremony. I've been around." *When she hadn't been doing her best to avoid a certain someone.* But really, aside from her quick chat with Owen and Grace around the side of the house and her short break to cool her nerves, she'd been in the backyard with everyone else. She'd tasted the food. She'd toasted with champagne. She'd mingled.

"You look tired." Her mother zeroed in with

the laser focus that she had for all her kids and brushed back a lock of Mal's hair. "Are you getting enough sleep?"

"I'm fine, Mom, and I'm getting plenty of sleep." And on those nights when she wasn't, she worked, so it wasn't as though she tossed and turned or lay on her back staring at the ceiling, contemplating sheep jumping a fence.

"You need to take care of yourself." Evelyn brushed back the lock of hair again. Like all guests at the wedding, Evelyn wore pristine white. In her case, a crisp white suit showed off her figure and demonstrated why she easily passed for ten years younger than the age on her driver's license. "I worry about you. About what happens when you don't take care of yourself."

Health was a newly discovered focal point for all the Fords, as it was just over a year ago that Mal's father, Gus, had suffered a heart attack. Suddenly eating reasonably well and exercising occasionally hadn't been enough. Mal had taken up Pilates, Owen had started running more regularly and was apparently eating egg whites, and Donovan had begun walking everywhere. Mal's father had taken up gardening while Evelyn had developed an obsession with making sure everyone ate their greens.

But the changes had been worth it. Her dad had bounced back with a new lease on life and a new attitude. One that he'd turned into a contract to do whatever he wanted. First, it had been his vegetable garden, then nosing around in his kids' personal lives, followed by the decision to hand over the reins of the family business to his three children.

Mal still wasn't sure her mother was over the loss of her flower bed by the side of the house—the once beautiful magenta peonies razed to make way for tomatoes and cucumbers. Or that's what Evelyn pretended, which Mal now suspected had just been a ploy to get the backyard greenhouse she'd been hinting at for the last five years.

"I'm taking care of myself," she told her mother. "I eat right and Grace and I still go to Pilates three mornings a week." Even on Saturdays, which had once been her day for lounging in yoga pants with a vat of hot coffee, a cinnamon bun, the crossword and a pen.

"I know." The line between Evelyn's eyebrows eased slightly as she nodded. "But it's a mother's right to worry about her children." She fussed with the high collar of Mal's dress, smoothing it down. "Have you spoken with Travis?"

Mal forced herself not to react, not to flinch or rear back, even though her bare fingers suddenly seemed to burn with the weight of the missing ring. "Only for a couple of minutes." Which had been plenty. Even if she still felt as if that final bit of closure continued to elude her.

"And you're okay?" Evelyn's dark-brown eyes, the same color as Mal's, darted up to meet hers.

Mal fiddled with her hair, the chocolate color, like her eyes, inherited from her mother. "I'm not going to throw myself into the Pacific Ocean, if that's what you're asking." Just how bad did she look, anyway? Travis was an ex and their breakup had been painful, but it hardly required the family to treat her as though she was glass—fragile, easily shattered. But then, there was Owen...

Mal felt the beginning of a scowl twist her lips. Owen and his ham-fisted attempts at creating conversations could definitely treat her more delicately.

Evelyn frowned. "That was certainly not what I was asking." She waved at her husband who was never far from his wife's side when they were in the same general area. "Gus. Come take a look at your daughter."

"Hello, love." Gus pressed a kiss to his wife's cheek, then his daughter's. "Hello, princess."

"I thought we agreed to call Owen princess."

Gus laughed long and loud. "We did. But not on his wedding day." Anyone who didn't know about Gus's heart attack would never guess he'd suffered one from looking at him today. He was tall and slim. He and Evelyn had recently taken up cycling and were talking about a trip to Europe to see the sights on a bike tour. He looked very much like his sons, with just a few more wrinkles and a little extra gray at the temples. "Exactly what am I looking at?"

Mal shrugged. "Mom's being crazy."

"She looks tired, doesn't she?" Evelyn said at the same time. She lowered her voice, though the other guests were far enough away that there was little chance of being overheard. "She talked to Travis."

The confusion on Gus's face cleared. "I see."

Mal just bet he did. That they all did. "As I already told Mom, I'm fine." Bad enough that she had to deal with her own emotions at seeing the ex she thought she'd left behind, but dealing with her family's concern on top of it was getting to be too much. And she was fine. So fine. Even if Travis was moving back.

She ignored the thump of her heart.

"Wasn't the wedding gorgeous?" Because Mal could think of no better way to change the subject than to do it herself.

But these were her parents she was talking to and they weren't so easily conned. "I think she's trying to pull a fast one," Gus said to his wife while Evelyn nodded.

"It's not a fast one." Mal held her hands out. *Nothing up my sleeves, folks.* "I'm simply commenting on the beauty of the day, which is what normal people do at a wedding."

"We're normal?" Gus feigned a shocked look. "Don't you remember when she was a teenager and she used to tell us we were from another planet because we didn't get her?"

"And how she used to make us drop her off a block from school if she couldn't get a ride with her cool brothers?"

"I was thirteen. It was a phase." Mal felt herself falling back into those old teen habits and stopped herself from rolling her eyes. Barely. She put her hands on her hips instead. "And I wouldn't have had to behave that way if you'd been able to *get* me and understand that climbing out of the family minivan on the first day of school would forever taint my chance of high school popularity."

"High aspirations," her mother said and pulled her into another hug. "I'm not sure how you managed to survive our parenting."

"Sometimes I wonder that, too." But Mal leaned into her mother's arms and rested her chin on her mother's head, which earned her a swat.

"You know I don't like it when you do that." But there was a twinkle in Evelyn's eye. "It makes me feel short."

"You are short," Mal and Gus said in unison.

"You should appreciate my height more." Evelyn straightened the cuffs of her winter-white suit jacket. "Who else would you find to lord your own height over if not for me?"

"Your mother has a point."

Mal nodded and followed her dad's lead when he curved his arms around his wife so that the two of them surrounded her completely. Their eyes met over Evelyn's head and without a word or even a signal, they both leaned forward to rest their chins on her head.

Evelyn might have been six inches shorter than Mal, and more than that compared to her husband, but her slight stature didn't stop her from being the bossiest member of the Ford clan. "Very funny." But even she couldn't help laughing.

The easy warmth comforted Mal. This was what she wanted out of life. A happy family and a devoted relationship. She let her parents wrap her up in the security of their love; she reveled in it. Just for a minute. And when they all stepped back, she felt better. Less fragile. "Thanks."

"For what?" Her mother reached up to pat her cheek.

"For being my parents." It was a little sappy. Okay, it was a lot sappy, but that didn't make it any less true.

Her mother hugged her again and her dad's voice sounded a little tight. "We love you, sweetheart. You know that."

She did, and it was good.

They chatted a few more minutes, talking about whether they should get up early and take the first ferry back home to Vancouver or stay a little longer and explore Salt Spring. The three of them, plus her older brother, Donovan, and his wife, Julia, were all staying in a huge farmhouse about ten minutes away. The place had eight bedrooms and an enormous kitchen that Julia had already called dibs on. Since Julia was a professional chef, and an excellent one at that, they were more than happy to let her take over the space.

When her parents headed off to go and talk to some friends, Mal was feeling much better. And when Grace slipped up to stand beside her, Mal felt better yet.

The two of them had become friends a few months ago. It was a friendship that Mal was grateful to have. Somehow, she'd allowed most of her personal life to fall by the wayside this last year. Instead of turning to her loved ones, she'd held herself apart, filling her time with work and not much else.

But with Grace it had been different. Maybe because Grace didn't know her from before and had no preconceived notions of what Mal should be like. Whatever it was, Mal appreciated what they had.

"Hello beautiful bride." She wasn't just saying it, either. Grace, with her long legs and silky blond hair was attractive at any time, but glowing with love and being loved? She was stunning.

"Everything okay?" Grace's tone was gentle. Obviously she was still concerned after Mal's little fit at the side of the house.

"Of course. A small overreaction for which I apologize."

"It wasn't an overreaction." Grace shook her head. "Your brother, my husband, doesn't always know when to mind his own business." But she smiled when she said it.

"Anyway, I'm fine." Mal pasted on a smile. Her issues were her own and not something she would unload on a friend on her wedding day. Talk about a downer.

But Grace merely lifted a pale blond eyebrow. "Right. So the way you're so obviously not looking anywhere to your left has nothing to do with the fact that a handsome and tanned man just happens to be standing over there studying you?"

"I don't know what you're talking about." Mal tried to lift her nose, but not before curiosity got the best of her and she risked a peek to her left. What better way to show Grace and herself that she wasn't afraid to look anywhere than by checking out just what Grace was talking about?

She immediately wished she hadn't.

Travis stared back at her, a soft smile that she remembered all too well on his lips and heat in his eyes. Even thirty feet away with small groups of other guests between them, Mal could feel the sizzle rock the length of her spine. She shuddered.

"That's what I thought." Grace's voice broke into Mal's thoughts. "You still want to tell me you're fine?"

"Yes." Because she sure wasn't going to admit that she wasn't. "What else would I be?"

"Upset, rattled, confused." Grace counted them off on her fingers. "I could go on."

"You could, but I'm fine." Though she'd been *more* fine before she became aware of Travis's eyes on her. Didn't he have somewhere else to look?

"Maybe you should talk to him."

"I have talked to him." Okay, so she hadn't unloaded the thoughts rattling around in her head, making her stomach tight. Thoughts like: *How could you not be there when I needed you the most? How could you choose the business over me? How could you let me go without a fight?*

Grace nodded, her eyes probing for another moment. "Mal, if you—"

"I'm fine, Grace. This is your day. You're not supposed to be worrying about me."

"Of course I'm going to worry about you. You're family and I love you." Grace put an arm around Mal. "And I just want to be clear that should you need to talk, I'm here. Or if you need a shoulder to cry on, mine are pretty big."

Mal smiled through the prickling behind her eyes. "Owen doesn't know how lucky he is to have you."

"He does." Grace leaned forward so their heads were nearly touching. "I tell him regularly."

Mal laughed. Grace had been good for her brother in so many ways. In fact, Grace had been good for her, too. "Thanks." Mallory felt a little better.

"And when you're up to it, remind me to tell you about my failed attempts at dating via matchmaker."

Mal craned her neck to look at her. There was a twinkle in Grace's eye, but not one that indicated she was joking. "Oh, I'm up to it, and that's an awfully juicy piece of intel to keep from me, one of your nearest and dearest friends. Tell me."

Grace smiled. "It was before Owen. Well, actually, it was between Owen. It did not go well. Except that it made clear to me that the only man I wanted to be with was your brother."

"Something I still don't understand."

Grace squeezed her. "Be nice, because I'm about to make you an offer you can't refuse."

"Shouldn't I hear it first?"

Grace gave her another hard squeeze. "Anyway, it was my failed attempt at getting over your brother. I only went on one date, but I'd paid for the full service. Social dinners, one-on-one dates, personalized matches."

Mal met Grace's expectant look. "Are you trying to gift me your matchmaking services?" Because while she was coming to the realization that her work-life balance was completely off, she wasn't sure she wanted to dive into the deep end of the dating pool. Maybe wiggle her toes around and wade in slowly. "I'm not sure."

"No pressure, but I think you should consider it." Grace slowly turned her head, shot a pointed look over Mal's shoulder. Mal knew she was looking at Travis. "Unless you've got your eye on someone else?"

"I don't." Mal felt she needed to be clear on that. "But not having my eye on someone else and joining a matchmaking service don't exactly go together."

But she'd be lying if she said she didn't feel at least a spark of interest. Even if it was just to show Travis how thoroughly she'd moved on. And it was probably time she started dating again. She hadn't been on a date in—she paused to mentally calculate—four years. Not since Travis had walked into her first year master's course, Foundations of Managerial Economics, sat down beside her and asked her to have coffee with him after class. The rest, as they say, was history.

Too bad it was a history she'd rather forget.

"I think it might be good for you."

"And it might not." But instinct had her head swiveling to look in Travis's direction again. Common sense had her stopping short and returning her gaze to Grace before she could embarrass herself. Again.

"You sure you don't have something or someone else in mind?" There was a teasing note in Grace's tone.

Mal gave what she hoped was an airy toss of her head. "I repeat, I don't know what you're talking about."

"Sure you don't." Grace didn't bother to hide her smirk.

Mal decided to ignore that. Not that Grace wasn't right. Nope, the problem was that Grace was right and Mal wasn't fooling anyone. She exhaled. Still, she wasn't ready to give in so easily. Because down that road lay danger. She'd be admitting her leftover feelings for Travis to Grace, who would mention it to Owen who, along with his warped idea that she and Travis might actually have a future together, would try to throw them together and then…who knew?

No, it was best to bury any lingering feelings she might have and move on. Maybe now, faced with the object of her discontent, she'd find it easier to work toward that goal. It was certainly no longer abstract.

"So, what do you say?" Grace gave her an encouraging nod. "You willing to give it a try?"

Mal knew she should say yes. Really, what could the harm be? That she didn't meet anyone? She already wasn't meeting anyone. That someone might break her heart? At this point, she wasn't sure it could ever be put back together again anyway. "I…I'm not sure."

Grace's eyes tilted down at the corners. "What about if I asked you to do it as my wedding present?"

What was it with Grace and Owen wanting her to do something as their wedding gift? "I already bought you something amazing."

But Grace didn't respond, just watched her with hopeful eyes. Mal couldn't deny those hopeful eyes.

She huffed out a breath. "Fine. I'll do it." And hoped she wouldn't live to regret it.

CHAPTER THREE

TRAVIS SPENT THE two weeks post wedding not in a state of wedded bliss. But since he hadn't been the one to get married, that didn't come as much of a surprise. The lack of other bliss was more disappointing.

Sure, it might have been foolish to think that simply by apologizing Mal might forgive him. But she wouldn't even agree to talk to him. He didn't count the few minutes of conversation at the reception because…well, because he didn't. He still had some things to say. Many somethings.

Fortunately, he had plenty to keep him busy so that he only spent half his time thinking about Mal, calling Mal and thinking about calling Mal. Okay, maybe a little more than half. Three quarters, tops.

He looked out the car window as Sara Thompson, his real estate agent, drove and chatted about the next potential bar location on the list.

The city hadn't changed much in the three years he'd been away. There was new construction, but that was the norm these days. A formerly derelict hotel had been torn down to make way for new condos, more coffee shops, another few sushi restaurants. One of the good things about the constant gentrification and renovation was that there was always property for sale, and property was something Travis needed.

He had no intention of returning to Vancouver to work for someone else. No, now he had a taste for ownership, for being the boss. And now he had enough money to qualify for a loan on his own and no longer needed another signatory or the financial backing of an investor. It was a good feeling. Proof that he'd made it.

The Kincaids weren't well-to-do. Travis hadn't grown up with much. A small house with well-loved furniture, two pairs of shoes, two pairs of jeans—one set for church, one set for everyday—and the knowledge that if he wanted more than the tiny town where he'd been born, he'd have to do it on his own.

But they'd had love. His mother and grandma were quick to shower affection and praise, even his father, in his own silent way, showed he cared. A small proud smile, a solid clap on the back and a grunt for a job well done. Travis knew he and his brother, Shane, had been lucky. Many of the kids they'd gone to school with hadn't been so fortunate as to have that love and support.

Until Travis, the Kincaids had always been

blue collar and they liked it that way. He was different. The thought of working at the mill, running the machines, driving the forklift, always with the worry of closure hanging over his head as more and more companies downsized or shut down completely just wasn't for him.

He much preferred the difficult and often back-breaking work of standing on his feet all day, handling customers with charm and overseeing the budget and obscenely thin margins that separated restaurant successes from failures. It exhilarated him.

The car slowed as Sara pulled into a covered parking garage still extolling the virtues of the space they were about to see. Travis already knew the details, but he listened because he didn't feel like talking. They exited the parking garage out onto the cobblestone streets of Gastown, the city's oldest neighborhood.

"I think you'll find this space has a lot to offer." Sara's heels clicked as they walked. "Don't expect it to be perfect. It's been closed for just over a year."

Closer to two years. Travis had done his homework. This place had been one he'd wanted back then, before he and Mal had decided to leave the country and try their hand in Aruba. But the old owners hadn't been ready to sell, and he and Mal hadn't been ready to wait. Now, it was as if the universe was correcting a wrong.

"There's a lot of charm under the dust and debris."

"Debris?" Travis's research hadn't turned up debris. Just that after many years of struggling, the restaurant that used to be here had finally turned up its toes.

"Nothing that can't be cleared out in a few days. A few weeks, at most."

Travis decided not to ask any more questions about debris that may or may not require a semi-trailer to haul it away, but to wait until he actually saw it. The fact that the building might not be as ready to move in as he'd hoped was a small obstacle in his path. Anticipation tingled over his skin. He just wanted to see it with his own eyes.

"The building was originally built in 1910 and the structure is sound. You'll note many of the original details have survived."

They clicked down the sidewalk, Sara still rattling off notes about the property. But Travis no longer heard them. He only had eyes and ears for his new bar. Or his soon-to-be new bar.

The door stuck even after Sara unlocked it and Travis had to lean his shoulder into it to open it, but that was all part of the charm. The interior was dim, only one of the overhead lights turned on when Sara flipped the light switch. There was dust everywhere and plenty of that debris Sara had mentioned, but Travis saw beneath it. Past the white paint peeling off the wood ceiling, past the scarred 36-foot bar and past the wicker chairs and round tables.

The space had once been a family dining establishment, one that provided a clean and cheerful ambience that particularly appealed to little girls. Or maybe it was the princess cakes they'd been known for. Mal had been wistful when she talked about them. She and her family had come to The Blue Mermaid for her birthday every year from the age of six on. Right up until it closed down two years ago. But the princess cakes and the clamoring little girls couldn't pay the kind of bills associated with a restaurant in the area. A bar could.

Travis moved farther into the room and ran a finger down the bar. It only needed a good sanding and a few coats of varnish to shine once again. The wood ceiling would need to be scraped, but the massive pillars remained unpainted, worn smooth by years of customers and no doubt little girls who hung on as they twirled around the bases. If they weren't part of the original structure, he'd be surprised.

The brick walls had been saved from paint, too, for which he was grateful. It was possible to scrape brick, but it was usually easier and cheaper to rip it out and start over. And since that was neither cheap nor easy, he was glad he wouldn't have to.

He could see damage in a few places, but the spots would be easy to replace with the same matcrials and maintain thc old-world charm that still permeated the space. He inhaled, sucking in some of that charm and the dusty smell of disuse. But there was no mildew, no dankness, no watery scent that indicated deeper, hidden problems that would be uncovered once he cleared out all the debris.

Sara had stopped talking and was just letting him absorb. Smart woman. There was nothing that needed to be said. This was his place. His paradise. His future. Okay, perhaps he was being a little melodramatic, but it felt big. He'd picked up and left home at eighteen. Did the same thing with Mal when they moved to Aruba. And now? He inhaled again. Third time was the charm. This was not a place he would be leaving.

He turned, his eyes searching for Sara in the low light, and as his gaze tracked across the room he could see what it would look like. The wood, polished to a perfect gleam so that it glowed, comfortable bar stools covered in leather, a mix of low and high tables, some couches. He envisioned something that looked as though it would be found in an English manor. A place where people retired after dinner for drinks and discussion.

"I'll take it."

TRAVIS LAY BACK on the bed in Owen's guest room, smiling at the knowledge that The Blue Mermaid would soon be his. Sara was writing up the offer and meeting with the owners to present it to them tomorrow morning. He had a feeling that it would be good news, or at least an opening to negotiations.

He would have to rename it. The Blue Mermaid was a name still known in the city and didn't indicate the kind of establishment it would become. But he had plenty of other things to do first. There were licenses to have approved, permits and renovations, staff and budgets and food and beer lists. Plus he had to find his own place to live, go visit his family, since he'd been back in the country for a few weeks now and still hadn't made the trip home, even though flights there, including check-in and disembarking, took under an hour. And then there was Mal. Always Mal.

The apartment was silent since Owen wasn't around. Travis never would have stayed if he had been. But Owen had moved into Grace's apartment after the wedding, so his place was sitting empty, and he'd told Travis it would be good to have someone there until he and Grace figured out what they were going to do with it. Sell it, rent it, keep it for no good reason.

Owen had told him to use the master, but Travis didn't want to get too comfortable and he didn't want to take advantage. It was more than enough that Owen had offered the space. But Travis needed his own place. His own bed. He made a note to mention it to Sara tomorrow. She specialized in commercial property but there would definitely be someone in her office whose focus was residential and he trusted Sara to steer him right.

He crossed his arms behind his head and exhaled. Things were coming together. Really, except for the fact that Mal didn't answer his phone calls, it was better than he could have expected.

His stomach growled, reminding him of the fact that there was nothing in the fridge but bottled water and he no longer owned a bistro where he could just wander into the kitchen and order something. But Vancouver was a city filled with great restaurants. All he had to do was push himself off the bed, head outside and go find one.

But he didn't. He lay there, staring at the ceiling and thinking about all the things he needed to do for his new bar until his phone rang, disturbing his planning. Travis smiled when he saw Owen's name on the call display.

"How was the honeymoon?" Owen and Grace

had spent the past two weeks in Fiji, no doubt having a lot more sex than he was.

"I am now officially a sex god." And there it was.

"I'm sorry I asked. Oh, wait. I didn't ask." Travis would have given Owen a punch in the shoulder if he'd been in the room, but he was happy for his friend. Owen had changed from the light-hearted guy Travis had once known, but he liked this slightly serious version even better. This was an Owen he could talk to about things deeper than sports, deeper than the mechanics of cars or their workout routines. "So, how was it?"

"Very, very good." Owen sounded relaxed. To be fair, Owen usually did, but this was a different kind of relaxed. A comfortable kind. "We're thinking of retiring tomorrow and then going back."

"Well, that does sound like you."

"Want to come with us and open a restaurant?"

"I would." Travis felt a burble of excitement. "But I've made an offer on a place here."

"Congratulations. Where? When?"

The immediate interest reminded Travis of why he liked Owen so much. No matter what was going on in his life, he always had time for someone else. Travis thought it was because Owen just really liked people, one of the reasons he was now in charge of managing all three wine

"That tacky place Mal always made us go for her birthday? Ugh. I think my teeth are still pink from the frosting on the princess cake."

"No, that would be because you don't floss. And it won't sell princess cakes on my watch." Though maybe he could do a bit of an honorific with some sort of drink—bright pink and sweet enough to rot teeth. He made a mental note to consider it later.

"Mal might like you better if it did."

"Well, then, princess cakes are back on the menu. If only I'd known it was so simple."

Owen laughed. "Speaking of, have you talked to her?"

"Not since you dragged her across the backyard during your wedding reception. I think she's avoiding me."

"You're probably right. She can be a little hardheaded sometimes."

"She's not being hardheaded." Travis had never told Owen what had happened between him and Mal, and he had to assume from the fact that he and Owen were still friends that Mal hadn't shared that piece of history, either. "I deserve it."

"Oh?" Another thing he liked, Owen would stop showing interest if Travis cut the subject short.

And he did so now. It wasn't his place to tell

Owen. Yes, Owen was his closest friend but Mal was Owen's sister. And if she didn't want him to know, Travis had to assume it was for a good reason. "If your sister wants you to know, she'll tell you. I'll only say that she's not out of line with her anger."

"Maybe. Maybe not." Travis could imagine Owen shrugging off the comment. "Mal can hang on to things too long."

"I hope I'm not one of those things."

"No, you're the thing she's trying to throw off the cliff, but you just keep hanging on." And Travis had no plans to stop. "Let's get together this week for dinner. We need to catch up and I'd like you to get to know Grace."

"Sounds great." It did. Travis stretched. His head bumped the wall, but he couldn't slouch down any lower unless he put his feet on top of the footboard. Just another reason to get his own space. A bed that fit. "As long as you keep your sex life to yourself—I don't think Grace would appreciate your sharing it."

"That's because you don't know her very well."

He didn't, but Travis had a hard time believing Owen's pretty blonde wife would find sex an appropriate topic for dinner conversation. "You willing to lay a bet on that?"

"No, but her mother did offer me condoms the

first time I met her. True story. I'll tell you about that over dinner. Sunday at eight? Elephants?"

"I'll be there." And not only because he had nothing else to do.

They chatted for a few more minutes, about the beaches in Fiji, the Vancouver hockey team and whether or not Travis was going to buy a car. Assuming he bought a condo in the downtown core, there was no reason he couldn't walk to work and everything else he needed. He could join a car co-op which allowed him access to a car a certain number of hours a week on those rare occasions that he might need one.

But then he wouldn't have his own car that was at his disposal any time he wanted it, wouldn't have the ability to pack a bag, toss it in the back seat and just drive somewhere else. He exhaled. There was something about the freedom of owning a car. The freedom to convince a certain brunette to hop in with him and go away for a weekend in Seattle or Whistler or to visit his family. And he'd need a car when he visited his family.

Buses in Duthie River were so rare as to be practically nonexistent, and his parents shared a car since his dad had to drive past his mom's hair salon on his way to the logging site. He could have borrowed his grandmother's Buick, but Gram had sold it last year when the doctor recommended that she stop driving. She'd turned around and given the money to his younger brother Shane.

Shane had used the car money to buy a new truck—one with four-wheel drive, undercarriage lights, a hemi engine and a custom paint job that Travis had been relieved to learn didn't include flames.

Travis didn't resent the gift. His grandmother had given him money for his education. She hadn't had much and he hadn't wanted to take it, but she'd insisted and it had motivated him not to waste her generosity. And Shane had never seemed resentful about that, so if his brother wanted to soup up his old truck, then Travis was all for it.

He added car shopping to his ever-growing list, then settled on the couch with a bag of chips and a soda and watched sports highlights for the rest of the evening.

His plans for the renovations, his own apartment and a car could take a night off.

CHAPTER FOUR

IT WAS EASIER than Mal had expected to transfer Grace's matchmaker package over to her. A phone call from Grace to authorize the switch and a confirmation number was all that was required to officially sign up Mal. She'd done it before she could talk herself out of it.

The time was now. Actually, the time was now past. She should have done something like this, taken control of her life, months ago. But Mal was a believer in better late than never, and she refused to beat herself up more than she already had. She was taking the next steps, moving on with her life and making a new start.

The matchmaking service was located in a tall building in the downtown business district. The lobby was elegant, polished and gated. Mal had to check in with the desk officer before she was given access to the elevators.

She appreciated that they took their safety and that of their clients seriously. She watched the ascending numbers as the elevator with an art deco style grille and marble flooring zipped upward.

The top half of the space was mirrored, so Mal checked her lipstick and smoothed her hair before she reached her destination.

Obviously she wouldn't be meeting any potential dates today, but she wanted to make a good impression on the matchmaker, Angela. When they'd spoken over the phone, Angela had explained that part of the service was image consultation and she'd advised Mal to dress as if she was meeting a date for a casual weekly lunch.

Mal had pulled out her favorite suit. Not her power suit, as that made her look intimidating and tough, but her favorite one. It was a soft dove gray skirt set; she matched it with a silk shirt in cream and T-strap heels. A statement necklace and matching bracelet in the same cream color finished off the look. Her makeup was muted and she left her hair down, feeling as though the loose waves helped promote the casual aspect. She wasn't tied back or pinned up, she was friendly and welcoming.

Her stomach jittered as the elevator reached its destination with a ding. She swallowed, rolled her shoulders back and stepped out into the hall.

The business took up the entire eighth floor, but rather than the elevator opening directly into the reception area, it opened onto a short hallway that led to a set of frosted glass doors. The business, simply named Vancouver Matchmaking Services, called itself VMS. The letters were printed on the doors in a rich charcoal shade, the effect one of professionalism and wealth.

As it should be. The service had certainly cost enough.

Mal pressed the discreet buzzer to the left of the door, as she'd been directed by the matchmaker, and waited for the young man sitting at the desk to buzz her in. His green eyes were friendly when she walked in. "Ms. Ford?"

"Yes. Mallory." She exhaled slowly and reminded herself that she wanted to do this.

"Wonderful, you're right on time." He rose from the expansive wooden desk that ran across a large portion of the wall to come around the side. "May I take your coat?"

Although it had been unseasonably warm for Owen and Grace's wedding, the typical Vancouver spring weather was back. Cold and wet. It wasn't raining today, but it was cool enough for a wool coat. Mal handed over hers, a military style in heather gray.

While the young man tucked her coat into a small closet, Mal looked at the gorgeous view provided by the large glass windows behind the front desk. The North Shore Mountains were shrouded in a low mist—any colder and it would be snowing up there—while the ocean looked dark and flat. As she watched, a float plane buzzed in to land.

"Would you like a beverage? Latte? Espresso? Tea? Wine?"

Mal turned her attention back to him. "An espresso, please." Her stomach probably didn't need the caffeine, but it would be good to have something to do with her hands, and since she had to return to her office at Elephants—her family's restaurant—after this meeting, wine was out. Not that Donovan would have judged her, but it sometimes made her sleepy and she had a meeting later on to discuss a charity event to raise money for local food banks.

"Single or double?" The man wore a slim-cut blue suit, plaid dress shirt and a sunshine yellow bow tie. His cheerful wardrobe and warm manner helped soothe her. Mal suspected that's why he'd been hired.

"Single, please."

"Great. I'll just let Angela know you're here and I'll be back with your espresso. Please have a seat while you wait."

The chairs that dotted the reception area were large and covered in rich fabrics—mahogany leather and ivory velvet. Gold brocade throw pillows tied the two disparate colors together. Mal took a seat on one of the leather chairs. Partly because it offered a better view and partly because she felt like playing against type. Clearly, the chairs had been selected with males and females in mind. But she preferred the leather. It set her outfit off better.

Mal double checked to make sure her cell was turned to silent while she waited. She imagined Angela would take the interruption about as well as any potential date might, which was to say not at all.

The young man was back quickly, carrying a steaming cup of espresso in delicate white china. "Angela is ready for you."

Mal followed him down another hall into a large office done in the same shades of rich brown and soft whites with pops of gold. A tall, slender woman with caramel-colored skin greeted her with a warm handshake. "Angela Wilson."

"Mallory Ford." She forced herself not to fidget as Angela gave her the once-over. The appraisal wasn't obvious, but Mal recognized it all the same. She'd expected it and gave Angela a covert once-over of her own.

The matchmaker appeared to be around Mal's age. Her simple black dress with a skinny red belt flattered her figure and was clearly quality material and tailoring. Her arms were toned, her hair was glossy and she wore a large diamond ring on her left hand. Mal thought she looked eminently qualified to find a suitable match.

"Have a seat." Angela gestured to a pair of matching ivory chairs in the corner of the large office. The young man had already placed Mal's espresso on the small wooden side table and shown himself out, so it was just the two of them. A couple of women having a get-to-know-you chat.

Angela had already explained to Mal what would happen. The interview would be completely confidential, hence the lack of any other client in the reception area. Mal suspected they were carefully timed to prevent any crossover. She appreciated their discretion. Although she wasn't embarrassed to have decided to use the service, she wouldn't have been thrilled to run into someone she knew, either. It was a matter of keeping her private life private.

Actually, it was a matter of *having* a private life, since her current life consisted of work and sleep. Mal was looking forward to having one again. A lovely private life with dates and dinner and sex. Which made her think of Travis, which made her hands clench.

She forced her fingers to uncurl as she sat down and picked up her espresso. There was no reason to be tense, nothing to get upset about. Plenty of people had a bad breakup in their past, probably most people, and they seemed to find love again. She could, too.

Mal took a small sip of the steaming coffee and resolved to be open and honest no matter what was asked. As Angela had explained during their preparatory phone call, this would make the entire process more efficient, more enjoyable and more likely to be successful and find her a match.

And so the chat began, and she thought she was doing a pretty good job, right up until Angela asked, "Have you ever been in love?"

Mal started. Fortunately, she'd finished the espresso so her sudden jerk merely caused the cup to rattle against the saucer. She tried to cover it by putting both pieces down quickly and adjusting them. As if the continued clink of ceramic would hide the fact that the first clink had been unintentional.

Angela simply watched, her long legs crossed, expensive pen poised over a leather-bound notebook. Mal had been admiring it earlier, now she wished Angela would put it away.

She swallowed, stopped fiddling with the espresso cup and sat back in the cushy seat. "No." Her pulse, already thundering, pumped faster. "I've never been in love."

For the first time since she'd sat down, Angela didn't make a note of Mal's answer. "I realize it can be a difficult question to answer."

There was no happy answer to be found sitting in the chair. She either admitted that she'd had her heart broken and the return of said heartbreaker was how she found herself here in the first place, or she lied. "I guess I just haven't been lucky."

Angela's dark eyes studied her. Mal knew she wasn't fooling the woman, but she did her best to meet the matchmaker's gaze. Really, why did it matter if she'd ever been in love or not? She wasn't interested in her past relationships—or relationship, as the case was. She was interested in meeting someone new, finding an as yet unknown individual to start a life with.

That was her story and she was sticking to it.

Angela slowly closed the notebook and put it and the pen down on the table beside Mal's empty cup. "Mallory, there are no wrong answers in this session. This simply provides a basis from which we can find your most suitable matches."

Mal wished her cup wasn't empty, even a drop would help the sudden dryness in her mouth, but only white china stared back at her. She folded her hands and hoped they weren't visibly shaking. And if they were, her knee provided a perfectly good point for grasping.

"I do have to tell you that if I feel you're not ready or that you haven't answered the questions honestly, we won't move forward in the process."

"Pardon?" Mal felt another jolt, though her healthy grasp on her knee helped to minimize it.

Angela nodded. She didn't appear upset, but

there was a serious look in her eye. "It's unfair to anyone you might be matched with. We pride ourselves on only matching those people we think have a viable chance of success."

"I'm ready to be matched." Hadn't she gone through the prescreening conversation on the phone? Worn an appropriate outfit? Arrived on time and with answers? Paid the expensive fee?

"Part of my role is deciding that. We find that often the reason people have been unable to find love is because they're not ready." Angela paused. "So I'll ask you one more time, have you ever been in love?"

Mal opened her mouth to repeat her fib and stopped. Why did she feel the need to lie? Angela didn't know her, didn't know her family. And *they* all knew the truth anyway. So who was Mal hiding from except herself?

"Maybe we should reschedule, Mal—"

"Once." Her throat felt tight even before she said anything. Where was the cute, hipster receptionist with access to the espresso machine when she needed him? "I've been in love exactly one time."

Instead of picking up her pen and notebook, Angela nodded. Mal was grateful for her discretion. This would be a hard enough story to tell out loud. She didn't need to watch someone write it all down. Immortalize it on paper forever.

"I thought we were going to get married." The image of the ring sitting in her jewelry box popped into her head. The ring she should have given back. The ring that still gave her a little start every morning. Mal shook off that tangent. She'd return the ring to Travis later. Soon. It was nothing she needed to share with Angela. It would only give her the wrong impression. "And then we didn't."

"How long ago did things end?"

Some of Mal's tension eased at Angela's straightforward and neutral tone. She didn't seem to think it was such a big deal. Maybe she was right. "A little over a year."

"And are you still in contact?"

"No." Mal shook her head. "I have no interest in seeing or talking to him." She didn't. The conversation at the wedding reception had been more than enough.

Angela did pick up the notebook now. "Tell me about your closest friends."

When Mal left the matchmaker forty minutes later, she felt both tired and exhilarated. Much the way she felt after a great Pilates session. Only less sweaty and better dressed.

Angela had stated that she thought there would be no problem in making a match and she would be in touch shortly. Mal didn't want to get her hopes up, but they were slowly climbing toward the sky.

A date. A real live date. Even just the idea of a night out with someone other than her family was enough to perk her up. Evidence that she really had let her hurt feelings linger far too long.

But now? Now things would be different.

She pulled the collar of her coat more tightly around her neck as a swift breeze swept off the water, but even the chilly air couldn't dampen her spirits.

AFTER SOME SCHEDULING, all done through Angela, who even set up the dinner reservation, Mal's date was set.

Josh. Mal rolled the name around in her head as she finished getting ready, spritzing on perfume and running a brush through her hair. It was a good first name. A solid first name. The name of a man who could be relied on to come home when he said he would, return phone calls and not have another woman's legs wrapped around his head. It was also one of the few things Mal knew about her date tonight.

VMS didn't share full names of their clients. They didn't share jobs, neighborhood of residence or anything else that might make it possible for someone to discover personal details, either.

Besides his name, all Mal knew about Josh was

that he was six feet tall, dark haired with gray eyes, had an athletic build and would be wearing a pale green shirt. All sounded promising.

She was meeting Josh at Chambar, a Belgian restaurant located in the gentrified Gastown neighborhood and known for its mussels. The restaurant was preselected by VMS, and Mal suspected it was halfway between both of their residences or workplaces. The taxi service called just as she was finishing getting ready to let her know her car would be there in one minute. She slipped into a coat and headed down to the lobby.

VMS advised clients not to share anything too revealing with their dates, including last names and work locations. With so much personal information available to anyone who could use a computer, it was far too easy for a person to get in touch when *touch* wasn't wanted.

Mal hoped it was wanted tonight. She wore a fitted knee-length dress in dark red, the color of a rich cabernet. The material was textured with small ripples inviting touch. She'd paired the dress with simple black heels and a black leather peplum jacket with suede panels on the bodice. The jacket dressed down the outfit, taking it from slightly formal to urban cool. Finished off with a gold three-tier necklace made of thick chains, she thought it displayed a note of badassery, as well. That she wasn't the type of woman who would be easily taken advantage of. Not the type of woman who put up with bad behavior.

Plus, it looked really cool. It was an outfit that should net a second date on its own, even if she wasn't completely charming and fun, which she would be.

Of course, there were no guarantees of a second date. No guarantees of anything. Not even the exchange of full names and phone numbers. Tomorrow, Mal would receive a phone call from Angela to discuss the date. Was she happy with the match? Was she interested in seeing Josh again? Would she like Josh to have her number? Mal hoped the answers to all questions would be yes. Or, at least, maybe.

The familiar sign of the restaurant glowed as they turned onto the street and Mal's stomach tightened. She shoved down the worried thoughts that attempted to rise and smoothed her skirt.

She hadn't been on a date in four years. What if it wasn't like riding a bike? Well, she might be in trouble. But she refused to think about that or the reason for her long dry spell. She would focus on the positive, on the promise of a future. Maybe her future was waiting in the restaurant.

Her stomach knotted again, but this time with anticipation as much as nerves. She stepped out

of the cab into the cool April night and prepared
to meet her destiny.

At worst, she was in for an excellent bowl of
mussels.

THE MUSSELS WERE excellent, as was the company.

Mal laughed as Josh finished his ridiculous
story about how he'd spent his Sunday. It had
started with waking up at four and going on a
run to the Seawall, then whipping up a gourmet
breakfast, kayaking, climbing the Grind—the
long and winding trail up Grouse Mountain—
paddle boarding, shopping at Granville Island
Market, seeing a local band at a club, visiting
a food cart, traversing the Capilano Suspension
Bridge, holding a dinner party for twelve and finally finishing the crossword puzzle. In ink.

"All right, you got me. I actually believed you
for a minute. Right up until the crossword puzzle."

Josh laughed, too. He had a nice laugh, a nice
smile. "Ink was taking it too far? Would you have
gone for it if I'd said pencil?"

"Absolutely." She appreciated his humor. It
made her feel more relaxed and made it easier
to share her own stories. "Just like I'm sure you
buy that I spent Sunday riding the Sea to Sky
Gondola, eating dim sum, checking out an indie
flick at 5th Ave, completing a mini-tri, meeting

friends for beer on a heated patio and finishing the crossword puzzle. In ink."

Josh's already big grin widened. "I see what you mean about the ink part. Makes the whole thing unbelievable."

"Exactly." Mal nodded. She was enjoying the banter. In fact, there had been quite a number of enjoyable moments this evening and they'd only just finished dinner. Mal still had half a glass of wine in front of her, Josh had three-quarters of a beer.

"So, tell me." Josh leaned forward and reached for her hand. His fingers were warm as they curled around hers. "What did you really do on Sunday?"

Mal resisted the urge to pull her hand free. She was doing nothing wrong. Hadn't she wanted touch? And Josh was polite and funny and very good-looking. It wasn't inappropriate to hold hands in a public setting, and she reminded herself that it only felt odd because she was out of practice. There was only one way to fix that. She curved her fingers around his. "I went to Pilates in the morning, did a bit of work and had dinner with my family."

"Was there beer and a heated patio?"

"No. But there was a view of my parents' garden and wine paired with dinner."

"Fancy. Consider me duly impressed by your

knowledge of wine." A dimple twinkled in his cheek. "I'd bow to your superior knowledge, but then I'd have to let go of your hand."

"Right." Which made the whole hand-holding feel horribly awkward and made Mallory self-conscious. It was all she could do not to rip her fingers free. She settled for giving him a gentle squeeze and then picked up her wineglass, so it wasn't as though she didn't want to touch him, she was merely thirsty. But she was careful to put her hand in her lap and out of holding range once she let go of the glass.

Still, she was having a nice time and resolved to continue doing so. Josh appeared to be everything she was looking for. He told her he was a lawyer, though she didn't ask which firm, and that he lived downtown, though she didn't ask which neighborhood. Mal, in turn, informed him that she had bought her own little slice of heavenly real estate last year.

"We could be neighbors and not even know it," he said. The downtown core was so densely populated that it was possible to live next door to someone for years and never see them.

"Maybe. Do you like to practice guitar on Thursday nights?" Her neighbor did. But aside from that, Mal knew nothing about him or anyone else in her building. She seriously doubted she could pick any of them out of a lineup.

"No, that's on Mondays."

"Well, good. Because my neighbor is pretty bad." Or maybe it was just that she didn't love his music choices, which seemed to consist of him strumming the same chord over and over and over. "If it had been you, I'd have had to pretend I enjoyed it to spare your feelings."

"So thoughtful." His dimple winked again. "But then, you haven't heard me play yet."

"There is that." She cocked her head, feeling some of her earlier fear recede. See? She could do this. She could date and flirt. Totally like riding a bike. She even left her hand on the table the next time she sipped her wine and was rewarded by Josh picking it up.

"So, I was thinking." He leaned closer. He had very pretty eyelashes, long and dark and lush. "I'm very much enjoying this date and you." He gave her hand a gentle tug, pulling her closer. "And I'd like to continue it. If you're interested."

Mal hesitated. She should be interested. Josh was a good-looking guy with a good job. He was very much her type and what she'd told Angela she was looking for. And yet…

"I'd like that very much." Mal said the words quickly before she could change her mind. She could figure out later if it had been a good idea or not.

"So where were you thinking?" Mal asked

once the bill was paid—split between them—
and they were on their way toward the restaurant's lobby.

"What about Elephants?"

Mal stiffened. Really? Of all the places in the
city, he had to choose the one owned by her family? And the one that housed her office upstairs?
Her eyes darted to him. Did he know? Had he
somehow uncovered who she was and this was
a little test to see if she'd explain?

But Josh merely looked back at her with an
open smile and nothing in his eyes resembling
guile. Still, she trod lightly and chose her words
carefully as they entered the lobby. "Have you
been there before?"

"I have." The hostess had their coats ready and
Josh helped Mal into hers. She shivered when his
knuckles brushed across the back of her neck. She
wasn't sure what it was from. Fear that he was
possibly toying with her? The fact that his hands
were cold? Attraction?

"A lot?"

"Once or twice. It's nice, but if you'd prefer,
we can go somewhere else."

Mal looked into his eyes again. She saw no
sign that there was any hidden agenda. And really, why wouldn't Josh suggest Elephants? It
was a great lounge in a great location, perfect
for extending a date, and she didn't think that just

because it was owned by her family. She made a snap decision before things got awkward and Josh started thinking she wasn't interested.

"I think Elephants sounds great." And Owen wasn't working tonight, so there was no chance of him horning in and embarrassing her, accidentally or otherwise.

Maybe being on her own turf would help ease some of her unsettled feelings about reentering the dating arena. She had no reason to feel unsettled. She was single, with no lingering strings that needed to be severed, the ring in her jewelry box notwithstanding. Josh had a lot going for him. She wanted to be attracted to him. She *should* be attracted to him.

They shared a cab as it only seemed sensible since they were heading to the same place, but Mal wondered what Angela would say. She decided she wouldn't tell her—what Angela didn't know wouldn't hurt her.

Conversation flowed easily during the brief ten-minute trip across the downtown core. Josh had one brother and was in a men's hockey league.

Mal admitted to having two older brothers, though she definitely thought herself the wisest of them all, and a newly discovered affinity for Pilates. "I think part of it is just the opportunity to spend time with friends."

Josh nodded. "Friends that Pilates together and all that."

When the cab pulled up outside of Elephants, Josh paid the fare and helped her out. He didn't let go of her hand after he closed the cab's door. Didn't let go when he pulled open the heavy wooden door of Elephants, either.

Mal had a quick internal discussion with herself over whether to break the contact or not before deciding to roll with it. But, once again, she was glad Owen wasn't in—because holding hands with a stranger was the kind of thing he'd bring up for years after the fact. In truth, it was nice to have the human contact. So what if Josh's touch didn't give her butterflies? That part of herself had been shut down for so long that she probably just couldn't feel the butterflies fluttering around. They might very well be flapping away in there and she just didn't know it.

She wrapped her fingers more tightly around his, which earned her a smile as they stepped into the wine lounge. And though it was a Monday, the tables at Elephants were already full. Even the actual bar itself had a full house of people bellied up to it.

"Busy place."

Mal tried not to shy away at the fact that his mouth, which was bent close to be heard over the noise, had practically brushed her earlobe. "Do you see any seats?"

She was tall, made more so by her stiletto heels, but Josh, at just a shade over six feet—according to Angela—was taller. "Nothing except a man waving his arm like he's trying to get your attention."

Mal's first thought was that it was Owen. That her dear brother, after taking two weeks off for his honeymoon, was making up for the time away by working on his one off night. But when she followed Josh's pointing finger it was much, much worse.

Travis. He was sitting in a large booth with both of her brothers, Donovan and Owen, and their two wives, Grace and Julia. All were staring at her with a range of expressions from surprised to sad. As though what she did on her own time was anyone's business but her own.

Mal put on a smile she didn't feel, reminded herself that she wasn't doing anything secretive or illicit and turned to Josh. "I realize it's a bit rushed, but how would you like to meet my family?"

She could only hope that her parents weren't going to come sauntering by next.

CHAPTER FIVE

TRAVIS WATCHED MAL move toward him, hips swaying, hair bouncing, hand held by another man. He fisted his own hands beneath the table and hoped what he was feeling wasn't written all over his face. But it probably was.

She wasn't supposed to be dating other men. She was supposed to be with him.

He'd called her three times since the wedding. Every Tuesday to ask if they could talk. Every time she'd claimed work or other activities filled her schedule so completely that she didn't have time. He'd suspected she hadn't been entirely truthful with him and now he had proof.

Mal wasn't too busy to go out with some preppy guy in a suit—she was just too busy to go out with him. And even though he'd already figured it out a few weeks ago, the confirmation still stung. As if he wasn't good enough for her, wasn't worthy of forgiveness.

Which felt really crappy. Even if he might have deserved it.

"Who is she with?" Owen didn't bother to keep his voice down.

"I don't know. She's still not talking to me." It didn't feel good to say it, but Travis saw no point in lying as they'd all know the truth as soon as Mal reached their table.

Donovan and Julia both agreed they were equally uninformed on the subject of the stranger holding Mal's hand, but Grace was noticeably silent.

Travis looked at her. She gave a jolt when she caught his eye and then hurriedly looked away. Busted.

"Grace." Travis had only known his best friend's wife a short time, but he already liked her and felt at ease around her. "Anything you'd like to add to the conversation?"

"Not particularly." She ran a finger around the stem of her wineglass without looking up.

Owen jumped in at that comment. "No secrets. It's my number one rule for a happy marriage."

Grace shot him a private look. "Really? That's your number one rule."

"That and…" He leaned over and whispered something in Grace's ear that left her half blushing and half laughing.

"Hey." Bad enough that Travis was about to make polite conversation with the man touching Mal. He didn't need his painfully single status pointed out, too. "Are you going to tell us who he is or not?"

"Well…" Grace's blush deepened. "I might have sent her to my matchmaker."

"You have a matchmaker?" But Owen looked amused rather than upset. "How is this the first time I'm hearing of it?"

"Because I was mad at you when I signed up." She leaned over to give her husband a peck, which turned into a kiss, which Travis put a stop to, asking his next question before Mal reached them.

"So she's on a date?" He glanced over, noting that Mal wore a dress and kick-ass heels. Definite date wear. The water he'd been enjoying earlier now tasted sour.

"I'm not sure." But the sympathy on Grace's face looked sure.

"It's a date." Julia nodded when she said it. Travis appreciated that she didn't dance around the obvious. "But you could always ask if you want to be certain."

"Right," Travis said while Owen snickered. "I'm sure that'll help convince her to talk to me."

He'd have said more but finally Mal was at the table, giving them all a tight smile. "Everyone. This is Josh. My date."

And then there was no reason to ask at all.

Travis thought he put on a pretty good face,

maintaining a polite glare instead of the vicious one that he wanted to emit. "Josh." He held out his hand. If he happened to squeeze the other man's hand a little harder than necessary, it wasn't because he was trying to indicate superiority of mate. Okay, it totally was. And if he got a small curl of pleasure when Josh attempted to out-squeeze him and failed, well, he was only human.

He caught Mal's look and pasted on an innocent face. *Nothing to see here but a bit of chest-thumping.* "Mallory."

"Hello, Travis." Her voice was clipped, indicating her lack of interest.

Travis hurriedly shifted to his left to make room in the booth, effectively shifting everyone else to their left so that the only place to take a seat was next to him. He patted the seat when she didn't immediately drop down beside him. "Join us?"

Mal's lips pressed together. "There isn't room," she pointed out.

"We can fit." He patted the space again. "I'm sure Josh doesn't mind grabbing a chair to join us, do you?" Travis certainly didn't mind, so long as it was Josh on the outskirts instead of him.

"We'll find our own table," Mal said. "We just wanted to say hello."

Travis didn't want her to go. He drank in the sight of her. The sexy dress and heels, the flip of her long hair. He longed to reach out and run a hand up her neck to cup the back of her head and claim a kiss from her soft lips. He swallowed. Hard.

She'd been out of his life for a year. A year during which he'd thrown himself into his business in an attempt to move past their breakup. An attempt that had failed, which had become shockingly clear when Owen had come down to Aruba for a visit and dropped the little bomb that he didn't think Mal was as over their relationship as she claimed. And a seed of hope had been planted.

No, that wasn't true. It had been planted all along, just waiting for that ray of sunshiny hope to urge it free, to reach for the light and bloom. He swallowed again.

"If you'll excuse us," Mal said, and Travis noticed she was careful to meet everyone's eyes except his. He watched her take Josh's hand and tug him in the opposite direction. A stone dropped into the pit of his stomach.

What if he'd made a mistake? After Owen's visit, Travis had taken some time for self-reflection, to consider what he really wanted out of life, and when he'd looked around the beachfront bistro that he'd worked so hard to make a success, he'd been faced with the reality that it didn't mean a whole lot without someone to share it with. Without Mal.

But what if she didn't feel the same? What if Owen was wrong? Maybe she really was over him, over them. The squeeze of his lungs put his hand-shaking to shame.

"Okay, they're gone," Owen said. "You can stop glaring."

"I wasn't glaring."

But the rest of the table just looked back at him.

"I wasn't." Travis ran his thumb back and forth along the edge of the table.

"You keep telling yourself that." Owen reached over to punch him in the shoulder. "But I'm really hoping that's not your A game."

Sadly, it was. "Of course not." Travis punched Owen back and was rewarded by seeing him wince, which he deserved. "But if you want to throw a guy a bone," he included everyone at the table, "I'd certainly be willing to listen to ideas."

But the table remained silent. He'd have been upset if they hadn't all looked so sympathetic. The realization was almost enough to make him laugh. As a teen, he'd accepted sympathy with a pair of flying fists. But he was older now and wiser.

Okay, older.

"Buddy." Owen clapped him on the shoulder.

"I think this is something you need to figure out on your own."

Travis looked at him. "In case you haven't noticed, I haven't been too successful on my own."

"Oh, we've noticed." Owen snickered, which was a damn sight better than the earlier pity. But only just. "And I, for one, am going to enjoy watching you figure it out."

"You're assuming I will."

Owen shrugged. "Misplaced though it may be, I have faith."

"That makes one of us." Travis said it quietly, more to himself than any of his table companions, and though no one should have been able to hear him over the ambient noise of the bar, it was Grace, Owen's new wife with her soft smile and calm manner, who reached across the table to give Travis a supportive pat.

"Don't give up. You know Mal. She plays her cards pretty close to the vest."

She did. Travis had had firsthand experience of that when she'd walked into his restaurant to tell him that she wasn't coming back. Ever. No conversation, no discussion. Just that her family needed her and she was out of there.

It still hurt. Though he better understood her perspective now, having experienced the fear of nearly losing a loved one himself and being too far away to do anything about it. When his gram had fallen ill and been confined to the hospital where doctors could closely monitor her vitals, he'd been stuck in Oranjestad, Aruba, waiting to catch the next flight out. By the time he'd actually gotten to his small hometown, more than a day had passed.

It had scared him, badly. Knowing that if bad had turned to worse, he might never have seen his gram again. Might never have gotten a chance to make her laugh, tell her he loved her and say goodbye. Mal would have felt the same when her dad had been sick.

Maybe if she'd explained, had let him know her own fears, what she was feeling. But she hadn't. And he'd responded by explaining that he couldn't leave the bistro. Not when it had only been starting to flourish, becoming a popular destination with profits rising.

Travis sawed his thumb along the table edge again and looked in the direction that Mal and her date had headed. Her date. That guy was not her type at all. Too slick. Too polished. Too pretty.

"Did you see that guy's nails? I think they looked better than Mal's."

Owen let out a supportive chuckle and Donovan smiled, but neither Grace nor Julia looked amused.

"Why are you two laughing?" Julia gave her husband a quick poke with her finger. "You've both been known to attend the spa to maintain your pretty-boy appeal."

Grace nodded. "You don't get hands that soft without professional help."

Donovan frowned. "I only went because you told me the massage would relax me."

But Owen wrapped an arm around his wife and whispered something in her ear. Then he kissed her while she blushed. "I plead the fifth."

"You would." Julia gave him a poke, too.

"Hey." Travis drew the conversation back to him and his so-far weak attempts to win over Mal—if trying to talk with her at the wedding and a few phone calls could be considered attempts. "I'd go to the spa for Mal. Mud mask, apricot scrub. The works."

Owen stared at him. "Who *are* you?"

Travis shrugged. "Just a guy trying to have a conversation with your sister." A guy who was going to have to step up his game if he wanted to succeed. "So, you think I should invite Mal to the spa? Or maybe just casually show up?" When they all just stared at him, he shrugged. "Too creepy? Not creepy enough?"

"Just the right amount of creepy." Owen leaned against the padded booth back. "But that won't work with Mal."

No, it wouldn't, but it was better than doing nothing. Travis rubbed his thumb along the edge of the table again. Thinking. At one time, he'd have instinctively known what to do, how to get back in Mal's good graces, back in her life. But that was before. This new Mal was cooler and yet more fragile. As though she might shatter with a careless touch.

"I do have one suggestion." Owen sipped his water instead of revealing his thought, clearly enjoying the moment. "Since you're just a guy who wants to have a conversation, maybe you should have this *conversation* with her instead of us? Not that I don't love your wallowing."

"I don't wallow," Travis said, feeling the need to defend himself.

He was met with silence, but suddenly he didn't care, his gaze caught on the sight of Mal coming toward them, toward him. His heart lodged in his throat. Had she ditched the pretty boy? But she bypassed them with a nod and headed down the short hall that led to the washroom.

Travis was pushing out of the booth before she was even out of sight.

"Where are you going?" Owen called after him. Travis merely waved him off, eyes focused on the path Mal had taken. This avoidance of hers had gone on long enough. They needed to talk. He needed to know.

He picked a spot in the hall, leaned his shoulder against the wall and waited. A few other patrons passed him, barely flicking a glance his way as they went about their own business, but for the most part the hall remained empty, which suited him just fine.

His pulse jumped when Mal reappeared. Even when she scowled at him. "Travis. I don't have time."

"Make some." He straightened up. "We need to talk."

Her eyes darted past his shoulder, but she didn't move to go around him. "I'm on a date."

"I'm aware of that." His entire body practically strained at the idea. At how wrong it was.

"Then I don't see what we have to talk about." She crossed her arms.

"We're in the same city. We work in the same industry. We're going to continue bumping into each other." He still wasn't sure how she would feel when she found out he'd purchased The Blue Mermaid. Happy that it was going to receive the love and attention it deserved? Or upset that it was him giving the love and attention?

"So?" Mal put her hands on her hips. Her red lips pouted at him.

"So I want us to…" He trailed off, unsure of how to finish the sentence. The truth was he wanted them to be okay, but that was only part of it. He wanted much more than that. "I want to apologize."

"Travis."

"Hear me out." He'd just keep talking until she did. "I understand now why you had to come back. I should have supported you." He saw the dip in her shoulders. "I'm sorry I wasn't there for you."

There was only silence. He heard her breath hitch and then sync with his, instinctively they mirrored each other, finding common ground in their bodies while they struggled with their emotions.

"Why are you telling me this?" She looked up at him, her eyes huge and pained.

Travis wanted to cup her cheek, wanted to stroke away the hurts with the rub of his thumb, but the moment felt too delicate, too fragile. "Because I'm back." And she was a big part of the reason why.

She blinked and then straightened. Away from him. "You figured we could just pick up where we left off?"

"No." He hadn't thought that. Maybe hoped, but logically he understood that notion wasn't based in reality. "But whatever was between us, it's still there, Mal. You can't deny that."

"Not for me." He noticed she didn't quite meet his eyes this time.

"Do you mean that?" He kept his tone low,

private, and didn't reach for her, though his arms longed to wrap her up and pull her against him.

Her throat bobbed and she swayed on her heels. Her long lashes fluttered down against her cheeks. When she looked up her eyes were empty. It hit him right in the gut. That blank look of indifference. "I have to."

Which was not the same as saying it was true. "Mal." He did reach for her then, longing for the familiar feel of her body, the scent of her skin.

She sidestepped away. "I'm on a date, Travis. I have to go."

His arms dropped to his sides. Trying to force the conversation now wouldn't get him anywhere. He knew that. "We still need to talk." He knew he'd been wrong about some things, but she'd been wrong, too. She shouldn't have made the unilateral decision to relocate to Vancouver without talking to him. He'd thought they were a team, a united pair who looked out for each other. They *needed* to talk.

She didn't respond, merely ducked her head and moved past him back down the hallway toward her pretty-boy date.

His eyes tracked her until she was out of sight. Then he took a few deep breaths before following the same path. Her citrus scent tickled his nose and his memory. The way she used to smile at him as if he was the only person in the room, the way her body melded to his when he kissed the side of her neck, the bond that seemed to flow between them no matter how far apart they were.

As he stepped back into the main room of the lounge, his eyes found her. As he sat back down in the booth, he saw her looking back before she turned around and said something to the man sitting across from her. And Travis knew, no matter what she said or didn't say, the bond was still there.

And they still needed to talk.

Travis kept an eye on Mal, and the door, taking note when she finally left with her date. He waited another few minutes, long enough not to seem obvious, before he pushed himself out of the booth and pulled a few bills out of his wallet to cover his meal.

"Your money's no good here," Owen called after him as he walked toward the exit, but Travis wasn't listening. He had something more important to do and it didn't include wallowing.

He'd barely closed the door of the cab behind him before he dialed Mal's number on his cell. She'd gotten a new number once she'd returned to North America, but Owen had given him both the phone number and her address, with the understanding that Travis would say it had been Donovan who'd spilled the beans. He didn't expect her to pick up and she didn't. So he left a voice mail.

"Hey, Mal. It's me. Travis." God, he hated saying that. Like he was so far gone from her life that he was no longer known by voice recognition alone. "Listen, we need to talk. I'm on my way to your place. If you'd rather not talk now, call me back."

He clicked off. He didn't expect her to call back because he didn't expect her to listen to the message. Which made it cowardly and a little dastardly to say that she should call back to cancel, but things were nearing a level of desperation.

Hell, who was he kidding? He was already desperate.

Desperate to see her, desperate to talk, desperate to make up. His stomach tensed as the cab neared her apartment in the downtown core. He could probably walk there from Owen's place in Coal Harbour, which was good to know because there was a strong possibility she wouldn't let him into the building at all.

But he'd deal with that if it happened.

A chill wind cut across his body, tugging at the edges of his shirt as he climbed out of the cab. Travis shivered. The months in Aruba had made him sensitive to the cooler weather in the Pacific Northwest. Before he'd moved there, he'd been known to wear short sleeves year round and only in the coldest, wettest months did his jacket make it out of the closet. As for a scarf or gloves? Forget it. Unnecessary. But now, he could do with a scarf. Except he really didn't want to look like a hipster. Or wear skinny jeans.

He strode to the building, feeling the twist in his stomach, knowing there was a chance she'd turn him away or wouldn't even answer when he buzzed. There was a fancy touch screen glowing beside the building's front door—into it he punched the numbers that would call Mal's suite. Owen had coughed up that information, too, as well as the fact that Mal—like many women who lived alone—didn't post any personal information that could be tracked back to her. Protection from stalkers, weirdos, ex-boyfriends.

The system rang, that computer-generated double ring. *Brrp-brrp. Brrp-brrp. Brrp-brrp.* She didn't answer, and for a moment Travis wondered if she was home. His stomach grew tenser as did the muscles in his neck, his legs, his hands. If she'd gone home with that slick-looking guy, he was going to...well, he'd do something. Something he'd have to figure out, but breaking something or punching a wall sounded like a good start.

"What do you want, Travis?"

He blinked and stared at the computer screen, which was still glowing but no longer ringing. "Mal?"

"Why are you here?" She didn't sound welcoming, but at least she had answered.

Travis glanced up the side of the cement building, past the rows of windows reflecting the city lights. Was Mal behind one of them? Phone pressed against her ear looking down at him?

"You're on camera," she said, as though she'd read his mind.

He blinked again. Of course. A place like this would definitely have a camera at the front door to allow residents to see who was calling before they decided to pick up or let someone in. He should have figured that out on his own. "Can I come up?"

"Why?"

Which was better than a no. "I'd like to talk." He waited, and when she didn't refuse, he pressed a little harder. "Come on, Mal. I've been calling you for weeks. I just want to talk." He didn't just want to talk, but he didn't want to scare her, either. The simple fact that she'd answered and hadn't yet hung up on him was an improvement on past interactions.

"Travis. It's late." But she didn't sound sure or maybe that was wishful thinking.

"It's not that late." It was, but he wasn't about to admit it, wasn't about to let her shuffle him off so easily. He reminded himself that in the old days, they'd often worked until closing on Sundays and then gone out to an after-hours place. It wasn't even midnight yet. "Mal?"

"I have to get up early in the morning. Why don't we meet for coffee tomorrow before I head to work?"

Travis might have agreed a few weeks ago, before Mal had become a professional avoider of him, but now he knew what would happen if he agreed. She wouldn't show up. The excuse would run along the lines of she was running late and was so sorry but they'd have to reschedule, a surprise morning meeting had been called and she couldn't miss it so they'd have to reschedule, there were no cabs, the buses were full her shoes weren't made for walking so they'd have to reschedule. Regardless of the reason, the result would be the same. Him and no Mal. "I'm here now."

"Travis." But this time she didn't follow up with any good reason or any reason at all.

"Just to talk." He spoke slowly and calmly. The way he would to a disgruntled diner or one who'd imbibed one too many and required soothing. He heard Mal exhale, that soft waft of breath that used to waft across him. He could practically feel it and felt his response come unbidden. To reach for her, gather her close and kiss her until they were both breathless. God, he missed that. "So? Am I allowed in?"

She answered by pressing the front door's buzzer. Travis didn't wait for her to change her mind. He grasped the handle and was in the elevator in under sixty seconds.

MAL STARED AT her apartment door. It was fully bolted. Double locked with both the door handle and deadbolt. But she still didn't feel safe. No, that wasn't it. Not exactly. She still felt exposed. Even with the nearly two inches of steel between them, plus however far away he still was, she felt as though she was on display, bared, and that with one glance he'd see everything.

All those things she tried to keep hidden, even from herself.

Why had she agreed to let him up? Why had she buzzed him into the building? For that matter, why had she picked up when he'd buzzed? He wouldn't have known she was home. She could have still been out with Josh. Maybe they were having a nightcap somewhere. Maybe she'd gone home with him. Maybe.

Mal swallowed. Maybe she was an idiot.

At least she looked good. If she had to face her ex-boyfriend—again—she was glad to be wearing a woman's armor of a great outfit. She even slipped her heels back on. She'd still be shorter than Travis's six-foot-three-inch frame, but four extra inches was four extra inches.

She didn't even consider not answering the door when he knocked. Okay, briefly, but since she rejected the thought almost the moment it popped up, she was counting it as no consideration. He knew she was here. He knew her phone number. And it was clear that even if she didn't deal with him now, she would have to deal with him at some point. Better to just get the whole thing over with.

But her well-thought-out, well-reasoned plan didn't stop her heart from trying to pound loose or keep that niggle of panic from making her spine tingle or a low ringing from filling her ears. She swallowed, wished she had something stronger than white wine to drink and that she had time to uncork the bottle and take a swig. And waited.

Fortunately she didn't have to wait long.

The knock came at her door a couple minutes later at most. Mal focused on that as she went to answer the door because it was easier than thinking about Travis on the other side of it.

It was late, she had to get to work early and he wouldn't be staying longer than two minutes, three tops, she consoled herself.

She wiped her palm on her skirt, flipped the deadbolt and pulled the door open. "Travis."

He stared back at her. For a moment neither of them moved, their eyes locked. Mal's pulse picked up in tempo. She wanted to pretend she didn't know why, wanted to act as if she was simply glaring at him, letting him know that his presence was not required or appreciated. She wanted to think she was staying quiet because she was waiting for him to say something first.

But it was more. It was always more with Travis Kincaid. With his dark hair, broad shoulders and muscled arms that could throw a punch as easily as defend one. Her fingers itched and she curled them against her palms. He wasn't hers to touch anymore.

Mal sucked in a small breath but didn't move, fearful it would be construed as weakness or an invitation, unable to decide which would be worse. She shouldn't still want him, shouldn't care how he looked or what he said. She felt herself rocking forward, toward him, getting closer. "Why are you here, Travis?"

He rocked closer, too. So close that she could feel the night air wafting off him and smell his clean woodsy scent. "For you."

Mal didn't want to hear that, couldn't. She curled her fingers more tightly into her palms until she felt the edge of her nails mark the skin and closed her eyes. But when she opened them, he wasn't gone, hadn't disappeared in a puff of smoke or slunk away like an unwanted stray.

No, he stood closer, so close that she couldn't take in any air without smelling him, tasting him, wanting him.

"I'm here for you, Mal." He didn't wait for her response, but stepped all the way inside and swung the door shut behind him.

She shouldn't have let him in. Her head was quite insistent on that, even as her body softened, yearned to touch him and to feel him touch her.

He leaned against the door, all hot eyes and bad-boy tattoos. "You still going to tell me there's nothing between us?"

Mal dragged in a breath. She should tell him that whatever they'd had was gone, explain that her hurt had gone so deep it had cauterized all feeling, leaving her a numb shell. But she didn't feel numb. Her senses felt sharpened, alive. "What do you want me to say, Travis?"

"I want you to be honest." He pushed himself away from the door and came toward her. She felt the heat rolling off his body, swarming and surrounding her. "Why did you let me up here if there's nothing between us?"

Mal's mouth felt dry. She swallowed. "I'm not sure." Maybe because she hadn't been able to stop thinking about Travis during the rest of her date. Maybe because she'd already decided that she wasn't going to see Josh again. Maybe because she worried that until she got Travis completely out of her system, she'd never be able to move on. She looked up at him. "I don't want to feel like this."

"Like what?" He leaned closer, his breath whispering across her ear, making her shiver.

Like she was stuck. Living a half life, neither here nor there.

"Mal?"

But she wouldn't tell him that. She reached up, stroked the side of his face, felt as well as saw the shudder that rolled through him. Felt an answering one roll through her. It would simply be a final goodbye. A way to exorcise his memory, to push him out and make space for someone new to slip in. "This doesn't change anything," she said. Then she rose onto her toes and kissed him.

"Yes, it does." He slid his hand up her back, cupped her head, captured her mouth more firmly under his.

Mal melted against him, into him. It had been so long. Incredibly long. The entire length of the written history of time long. And she was so lonely.

A little gasp built up in her chest, but she shoved it down. Cold and ruthless. She did not have room in her life for gasps. Not for sighs or moans, either—though she wasn't as successful in stopping those.

Her hands tangled in his hair. He hadn't been to get it cut and it was still too long to be considered businesslike, even in laid-back yoga-pants-at-the-office and jeans-at-the-theater Vancouver.

But she liked it. Heat built through her. She liked it a lot. Tugging her fingers through his hair, she grabbed on and twisted it around and around as her head spun from his kisses, from the fact that he was back and here for her.

Mal had known before he kissed her that it would lead to this. She'd never have let him up to her apartment if she hadn't been willing to go there. Had wanted to go there.

She pressed her breasts into his chest. Despite the weight she'd lost, she still had breasts—Travis had always loved them. As if on cue, he groaned, his free hand moving between their bodies, sliding up her stomach to knead her breast through her dress. Her nipples rose. Both from his attention and knowing the effect it was having on him—on both of them.

Oh, yes.

It would only be for tonight. Closure, a last goodbye, whatever she might decide to call it in the cold light of day. What she wouldn't call it was a new beginning, a reminder of how good they'd once been and could be again. Because tomorrow morning she would be one hundred percent completely over this.

But for tonight, tonight Mal just wanted to be in this with Travis.

She stopped playing with his hair, mourning the loss even before she slipped her hands free.

She could go back later, investigate the change, let her hands run through it, shape it and see how it felt pressed against her cheek, her wrist, the inside of her thigh. She stroked his chest through his T-shirt, splaying her fingers to feel everything he had to offer. His heart thumped beneath her touch, made hers skip a beat in return.

They'd always been like that, in tune with each other even when she didn't want them to be. She fisted her hands in his shirt instead of thinking about it.

He hadn't stopped kissing her, hadn't let her catch her breath and she didn't want him to. Didn't want to think beyond getting into her bedroom, removing her clothes and having her way with Travis Kincaid.

He went where she followed. His mouth fused with hers, one hand glued to her breast, rolling her nipple back and forth and back and forth until her knees grew weak and her steps began to stutter. But she didn't care if she fell, not tonight. Travis would catch her and she wouldn't mind being swept up in his strong embrace. Feeling his bulk wrap itself around her, cocoon her as though she was delicate and breakable. Precious.

This time it was her heart that thumped. Hard.

She told herself it could be anything. Her family had a history of heart disease. Maybe it was lack of oxygen. Or she was tired. There was no proof that the cause was anything out of the ordinary. That it had anything to do with the big, sexy man currently making her remember in exquisite detail how much she'd missed this. With him.

Travis put his hands on the doorjamb as she led him into her room, pulling them both to a stop. Rather than separating and allowing the cool rush of sanity to flow between them, she stayed plastered to him. Her feet paused when his did, his body curved to fit hers, their mouths teasing, tongues tangling.

"Babe?"

Her breath shuddered. No one had called her babe since Travis. She wouldn't have allowed it if they'd tried, but the simple fact was that no one had tried. She hadn't let anyone get close enough to even consider it.

"Only if you want."

Only if she wanted. Mal paused, still pressed up against him, fingers wrapped in his shirt. Oh, she wanted. She wanted so badly that her entire body shook with it. Despite everything that had happened between them, everything that still needed to happen.

"Travis?" She could feel the puffiness of her lips, already responding to his touch and wanting more. She rose onto her toes, so they were nearly eye to eye.

He reached out to brush a lock of hair away

from her face. She felt the softness of the strands and his touch. His eyes stayed on hers. Open, warm, hopeful.

She could choose. She could choose just for tonight. She leaned forward, so he had to bear the majority of her weight or send them both tumbling. She wanted someone to carry her, just for a little while. "Yes." Her voice was more breath than sound. "I want this."

Which she'd known before she even answered the door.

"Mal." His arms tightened around her, squeezing the air from her lungs. The hope flared brighter in his eyes, making them more silver than gray. She would have to tamp that down. But not tonight. Tonight, she needed this, needed him. And she was going to take it.

Travis started moving again, faster now as though the brief pause at the door had taken a millennium instead of a minute.

His hands were everywhere, sweeping along her shoulders and down her back, pulling her close and tangling in her hair, sliding over the delicate curves of her hips and thighs. And where his hands weren't, his lips were. Trailing a line from the hollow of her collarbone up to her ear, licking a path to her jaw, taking her mouth and demanding more.

Mal barely noticed when they reached her bed and dropped onto the soft, silky comforter.

It shouldn't have felt familiar. She hadn't seen him in more than a year, hadn't been intimate in longer than that. And yet, everything slipped so easily into place. Her body in lock step with his, the way he tumbled them to the bed, careful to protect her so that she landed with barely a bounce, their fingers, mouths, everything back in sync. As though they'd never been apart.

Travis shifted his attention to the hem of her dress, sliding it up her legs, his fingers cleverly stroking her thigh at the same time. Mal released a low, shuddering breath. Even as she ached for more, she wanted to enjoy every moment, roll it around in her mind and wring every bit of pleasure from it. Make it take as long as possible, keep Travis here as long as possible.

"Babe?"

Mal squeezed her eyes shut, and then her heart. She would not be done in by an easy endearment. She would not be so weak. She spread her legs and pulled him closer, so he was cradled between them. "Stop talking."

She felt as much as heard his surprised laugh, the rumble that crested from him to her, linking them, and felt her emotions shake. She refused to give in to them, to let the little voice that wondered if maybe, just maybe, she wasn't being honest with herself and what she wanted. This was only for tonight and it was a release, closure. It wasn't more. It couldn't be.

Mal gripped the back of Travis's head, letting the long strands of his hair slide through her fingers as she pulled his mouth to hers. She wanted to stop thinking and wondering—wanted only to feel.

Travis seemed happy enough to oblige, turning his attention to thoroughly exploring the inside of her mouth, his tongue darting out to swirl and circle in the way she knew so well. His hands shoved her dress up to her waist. Mal lifted her hips to help.

Her shoes slipped off, landed on the floor with a thump that barely registered. His hands were rubbing her waist, sliding around to dip into her navel and then around to cup her butt. His long, gentle fingers that had played with every inch of her body. Mal shuddered again.

This time Travis didn't say anything, just pulled back slowly. Mal tried to stay with him, leveraging herself up and clinging to his biceps. But she was no match for his determined movement. Then he looked at her, just looked, smoothing her hair off her face.

She swallowed and wanted to close her eyes, afraid he would read something in them that didn't exist, that she didn't want to exist. But she feared it would make things seem more important than they were, that he'd imagine it to mean something other than that she didn't want to talk.

She stroked a hand down his biceps. She'd always loved his arms and shoulders. Powerful, capable of swinging her up without effort, of protecting those he loved and carrying heavy burdens. Mal saw his eyes darken, knew he remembered her touch as well as she remembered his. And just as he knew her body, knew the sensitive spots, she knew his, too.

She knew that he liked it when she rubbed her nipples against his chest, when she swirled her tongue around the edge of his ear and massaged his inner thighs.

Mal pushed herself into a sitting position, not breaking eye contact. She yanked off her dress, not bothering to evoke images of a striptease or any slow and sexy unveiling, then tugged off Travis's shirt, too, rubbing her hands over his chest and around his back. Her fingers unerringly dancing along the series of tattoos he had. She'd never liked a lot of tattoos on a man before Travis. Hadn't liked them on anyone since Travis, either. But on him? Her whole body quivered and begged him to press those tattoos to her naked skin, marking her.

She rose onto her knees, so she could push against him. True, her nipples were still covered by the silk bra she wore, but it was closer to naked than they had been. She lowered her mouth to his ear and licked.

She heard his sharp inhalation and his hands came to her hips, gripping, holding her against him. Mal licked again, feeling a mix of power and surrender, twisting and turning until she didn't know which held sway. Until she didn't care.

She might regret this later, but later didn't matter. Not right now.

She pressed closer, looping her hands around his neck, feeling the bunch of his muscles as he lifted her up, placed her closer to the edge of the bed. Mal didn't worry about falling. Travis was there and he'd never let her fall. She didn't think too deeply about that little realization.

"Mal." Her name was a breath on his lips. She felt her heart stutter and put her finger against his mouth.

"Stop talking." But this time her words came out as a whisper, too. This was not how it was supposed to go. He was supposed to throw her onto the bed and take her. Their bodies were supposed to come together like thunder and lightning. She was supposed to feel drained and sated when it was over, with her heart firmly intact. It was not supposed to be like this, where her pulse kept hiccuping. A series of tiny questioning beats that could, if she weren't careful, crack through the guard she'd built up around herself.

Travis's hands came up to cradle her face, so light, while he carefully explored her lips. Every touch was thoughtful, attentive. No, it wasn't supposed to be like this, either. Mal didn't want a cradle. She didn't want soft or gentle. She wanted demanding, devouring. She took his hands in hers and put them on her butt.

Better.

She reached behind her back to unhook her bra and felt Travis's fingers tighten. Better yet. She shimmied the tiny scrap of red silk off and dropped it on the floor, then pressed her now-bared chest to his. He sucked in a breath through his teeth as she rubbed against him. Oh, yes. He liked this a lot. Another rub or two and she should be getting that toss on the bed she wanted.

But after another squeeze of her behind, Travis slid his hands up her back, cradling her again, but this time her whole body, his hands holding her head safe while he kissed her. A tender kiss, one full of feelings and emotions that Mal didn't want to feel. Not from him or from herself.

She should take control here. Shove her tongue in his mouth, unzip his jeans and shove them down his legs, push away all these unwanted thoughts pounding in her head. Instead, she rocked back on her heels, letting Travis come with her, his added weight dipping the mattress while he gently laid her back on the bed, watching, always watching, so cautious with her, making sure she was taken care of.

Mal felt the shiver start in her chest and work its way through her entire body until she felt fragile, delicate. Afraid.

She looked up at Travis.

He ran a thumb across her eyebrow, down her cheek, along her jawbone. "Are you okay?"

Was she? Mal didn't know. Which meant she probably wasn't. But she felt herself nod. She would be okay, which was almost the same thing.

Travis stretched out beside her. The rough weave of denim scraped against her thigh and she shivered. He tugged her into his arms, warming her with his body, but it wasn't cold Mal was feeling. She shivered again and turned into him, burying her face in the curve of his shoulder and her hands in his hair.

If they could just get down to the sex, she'd be fine. But she didn't push again, didn't put his hands on her or demand that they get things moving with her lips or tongue. She remained in the circle of his arms, their bodies remembering, twining together in a familiar knot.

Travis didn't say anything, didn't rush or push. He simply ran his hands up and down her back in long sweeping motions. Mal felt her worries begin to drift and recede like the tide. Tomorrow would provide plenty of opportunity for wondering what had come over her, what had made her retract her previous thought that the seas would run dry before she'd ever let Travis Kincaid touch her again, let alone touch her in her bed, not even half dressed.

She tilted her head back, her lips searching for his. But he was already there, waiting, knowing what she'd be looking for. They kissed slowly, barely brushing their mouths against each other while their hands roamed, rediscovering each other.

Mal had forgotten how much she loved the feel of his skin, the smoothness over his muscular body. She relearned it now, taking her sweet time as she stroked, dipping her fingers beneath the waistband of his jeans and then back out.

She wanted to think that it was only because she hadn't been with anyone since Travis, that she was so primed for human contact that anyone could have had this effect on her, but she knew it for the lie it was. It was Travis. Always and only.

She traced the outline of the Celtic knot on his chest with her fingers. In an easy, familiar motion, her hand slipped from point to point and then followed the circle in a long, slow sweep. She heard his intake of breath, saw the way his stomach sucked in.

Looking up into his eyes, she saw him smiling down at her, and remembered how she used to trace his tattoos after sex while they talked. She yanked her fingers back.

"Hey." Travis caught her hand before she could bury it behind her back like the bad hand it was. "You don't have to stop."

Mal knew she didn't have to, but she needed to. Just as she needed Travis to put his clothes on and leave. But she didn't say anything. And she didn't stop him when he drew her hand back to his chest, placed it on top of the knot, the symbol of something without end.

She felt the steady thrum of his pulse against her palm, saw the question in his eyes and made her decision. If only for tonight, she would enjoy this, enjoy him.

Mind made up, she returned to her slow exploration, rediscovering the planes of his body, the velvet feel of his skin.

His breathing came sharper, faster, and Mal felt the strain of his body as he battled not to overpower, to take control of the situation and her. The guard around her heart slipped just a fraction. She shored it up by kissing him hard in an attempt to remind herself that this was only physical.

Emotions weren't required and, in fact, she preferred they not make an appearance at all.

But they kept rearing up when she least expected it. Like when he stroked the side of her neck before kissing it and the way he rocked his body into hers twice before settling her against him. Little reminders, the routines they'd long ago established that she'd forgotten about until now.

He ran a hand down her side and stopped on the curve of her hip. Mal felt the warm press of his hand, the heaviness and strength, and felt her body rise in response. Whatever problems continued to exist between them, they weren't an issue now.

Travis fingered the edge of her panties, slipping the silky material down and then back up. Running it back and forth along her skin so that even the lightest touch left her breathless and aching for more. She buried her face in the side of his neck.

"Please." It was a whisper, barely heard over the rustle of covers and exhale of breath. Mal was embarrassed that she was so responsive with someone she claimed to be over, but her need to be held and touched and taken overcame that. She pushed against him, feeling the rub of her nipples against his chest. "Please."

Travis didn't answer. At least, not in words. With a low growl, he flipped her onto her back, loomed over her. Mal felt another rush of longing, gave a low moan of her own when he slipped a hand inside her underwear and stroked.

"Mal." Her name was another moan as he lowered his forehead to hers. His finger stroked again, beginning a sure rhythm that her body remembered. She clutched at his shoulders, his arms, grappling for something to hang onto, something to keep her grounded while he brought her body to the heights of pleasure.

Her legs fell open, spread wider for him, not only granting access but begging him to take it. She wanted him naked, too, but the signal from her brain to her body got muddled in the pleasure and all she could do was lie back and enjoy.

He slipped her underwear off, a quick flick of motion, then ran his hands up the insides of her legs from her ankles to her inner thighs. "You are so beautiful."

She blushed, though it probably wasn't visible in the dim light. "Travis." But his name was lost in another moan as he pushed her legs farther apart and shimmied down the bed to pay proper homage to her nudity.

She jerked at the first flick of his tongue. Her mind suddenly filled with the unbidden image of the woman in Aruba whom he'd pleased in the identical fashion. "Stop." She gasped when he licked again, the edges of the image beginning to shimmer. "Travis. Not this."

He stopped where he was. She tried to close her legs, but he was nestled between them, the flat of his tongue still pressed against her. When he removed it, the stroke was long and slow and nearly sent her reeling. "You love this." His voice was sure, the tone of a lover who knew his partner's favorites well.

It was true. She did love that. But that other woman...

She squeezed her eyes shut, tried to catch her breath.

"Mal?" His breath whispered against her skin, sending another pulse of pleasure rolling through her body.

"I just..." She swallowed. Was he going to make her say it? Force her to relive the humiliating scene in living color? Some of the heat leached out of her body. Maybe this was a mistake. Maybe she should stop him now and ask him to go before things went any farther.

Travis's hands rested on her thighs. His thumbs rubbed in small, soothing circles. "It's just us, Mal. You and me." He pressed a kiss to her inner thigh. "Nothing else matters."

"We don't live in a vacuum." Although wasn't that what she'd wanted? To encase herself in the thick folds of fantasy just for the night, to have her last goodbye. She sucked in a breath.

His thumbs circled higher. Mal felt her body

respond, eager for his touch. He stroked her thighs and bent his head again, but didn't touch this time. "Just us," he repeated.

Mal nodded slowly and reached for his hands, pulling him toward her, until the lengths of their bodies were pressed together. "Then let's just be us." She dug her fingers into the waistband of the jeans he still wore. "Without these."

Travis disposed of his jeans and boxers in a flash and settled his big, hard body between her thighs.

Mal wanted to wrap herself around him. "I don't have condoms," she said. There'd been no need, seeing as she hadn't even dated in recent memory. Until tonight.

"Good."

Mal was so busy kissing him, running her hands up and down his back, over his thighs, desperate to get closer, to feel more, that it took a second for his words to register. "Good?"

"Yes." Travis was kissing her back, but his movements were measured and controlled, sucking every drop of feeling from the moment. "Because it means you've been waiting for me."

"I have not." Her defense was automatic. But even as irritation rose at his cockiness, his high-handed explanation for why she might not have felt like throwing herself into bed with someone else, she wanted him. Her hands continued to roam, her mouth to taste, though she did give him a little bite on the shoulder, just to show that he didn't know everything.

He laughed. "Deny it all you want. Your lack of protection speaks for itself. Not to worry. I came prepared."

"I'd say you shouldn't have bothered, but…" But she'd have been lying, and they'd both have known it.

Travis lifted his head and ran a finger down her cheek. "I'll always take care of you, Mal."

The overwhelming urge for more now came to a sudden halt. She felt exposed and not because she was naked. "I never asked you to take care of me." She wanted to sound strong and assured, the kind of woman who knew what she wanted and demanded it without fear.

"That's what you do when you love someone, you support them. You care for them."

"No one said anything about love." Her lungs struggled for breath and her limbs felt heavy, but she didn't push him away.

"You didn't have to." He kissed her then, a light press of lips that started slow and built.

Mal didn't stop him and didn't find the words to respond. She didn't know how she felt. Or maybe she did and it was something she wanted to keep to herself.

When he kissed her deeper, his tongue sliding

between her lips, she welcomed him. The obliter-
ation of thought and truth, replaced by the sweet
release of touch.

And when he put on a condom and slid inside
her, she was pretty sure she'd forget everything,
including her own name. But as the yearning for
more grew and filled her, she realized there was
one thing she still hadn't forgotten. This feeling
that had only ever been provided by this man.

"Travis." It was a benediction on her lips, a sigh
of approval and gratitude. And as he rocked inside her, arms wrapped around her body, holding
her close, the motion slow and steady as opposed
to hard and fast, Mal felt everything break. Her
body, her emotions, the carefully erected wall
around her heart.

And worried she wouldn't be able to put herself back together again.

CHAPTER SIX

YES, THIS WAS how it was supposed to be.

Travis cupped a hand over Mal's hip and pulled her more firmly into his body. He'd missed spooning, matching his breathing to hers, slow and even. Feeling the way she shifted and shifting in return until their limbs and torsos were melded together in a tangle of unity.

Together, like they were supposed to be.

He exhaled softly and lifted her hair off her neck so he could press a kiss to that warm, scented skin. He'd be lying if he said that he'd known this would be the end result of his visit. But Travis wasn't one to question his good fortune. He would just appreciate it and do everything in his power to make sure it lasted. He kissed her neck again, finding it impossible not to taste and touch. He had a lot of months to catch up on and a lot to make up for.

"Travis?" Mal's voice was thick and dreamy, and her eyes remained closed.

"Yes?" he whispered, not wanting to break the moment.

Her hand found his, laced her fingers through his and dragged his palm to her chest. She wriggled back, snuggling against him more completely. "I'm glad you're here."

He felt the lift of anticipation, the bloom of hope rise in his chest and played it cool. "Me, too." He felt anything but cool, and not just because they were naked in bed.

He heard her breathing even out, grow deeper, felt the slackening of her body as she fell asleep. He closed his eyes, shifted just a little closer and for the first time in a long time felt content. He wrapped his arm around her more fully, blanketing her, not wanting any part of them to be separated. They'd been separated too long already.

A few hours later, Travis awoke slowly, each part of his body rising to alertness while his mind swam through the slumbering fog. He felt good, rested, fulfilled.

Mal lay beside him, still dead asleep, her hair fanned out on the pillow. Travis felt one more part of his body rise to alertness.

His hand was curled around hers and wedged between her breasts. She'd slipped one leg between his while they slept, creating a knot of unity. Good. He liked it this way.

The sky was still dark, no hint of sun peeking through the blinds in her room, and the clock told him that most people wouldn't be up for a couple of hours. Travis could go back to sleep, too, but he wanted to enjoy every moment of being exactly where he was. With Mal.

Travis pressed more fully against her, smiling when she exhaled softly and wriggled closer. She murmured something, but since the words weren't along the lines of, "What are you doing in my bed?" or worse, "Oh, Josh, Tom, Harry, some-other-man's-name," Travis was content. He didn't move. Not even when his left shoulder began to ache and his right hand went to sleep.

He'd love to take Mal out for breakfast and then walk her to work before he met with Sara to discuss final concerns about the property. He hoped they might sign the papers today. He couldn't wait to show Mal. She'd loved The Blue Mermaid and Travis had no doubt that she'd have some thoughts on the changes he should make as he renovated it into a fresh, new spot in the city's night scene. His lips curved up as he thought about Mal and the bar and the new life he was starting.

The first fingers of light began to creep into the room, but Travis still didn't move. Not until Mal started, her entire body jerking against his.

"Good morning." He nuzzled the side of her neck.

She didn't move right away. For a full thirty seconds, they lay there in peaceful silence, then she slowly rolled over, looked him in the eye and said, "I think last night was a mistake."

Travis wasn't surprised. Mal wasn't one to back down from a decision lightly, and despite her body's desire for his, he knew her head needed to catch up.

"Oh?" He kept his tone light and undemanding, sensing if he pushed too hard she'd feel backed into a corner and would stand firm there even when it became obvious that she was punishing herself.

"Yes." She nodded as though to further strengthen her statement, but the effect was lost since she still wouldn't look at him directly. "I was, well… I was something and now I'm not."

"Now you're not," Travis repeated. He noted that Mal still held his hand in hers, keeping it close during her movements.

"Right." She nodded again. He doubted she even realized she was still clinging to him, her fingers tightening around his even now.

"I don't think it was a mistake."

"Maybe that's your mistake." She kept her eyes down.

Travis shrugged. "Maybe it is." But he didn't think so and he didn't believe that Mal did, either. He reached out with his free hand and tilted her face upward. There was a small wrinkle between her eyes and a small frown on her lips. "Babe?"

Her head snapped up without help this time. "Don't call me that. It makes me do things I shouldn't."

Travis allowed himself a small smile. "I'm not sure you should be telling me that."

Her eyes met his. "Good point."

"Like I might ask you to kiss me good morning, babe."

She scowled. "It's not a form of hypnotism."

"I don't think we've had a large enough sample to prove that." He could think of plenty of ways he'd like to test his hypothesis, though. "How about I take you out for breakfast so we can discuss further?"

"I don't think so."

"You need to eat, don't you?" He knew how cranky Mal got when she missed a meal. From the looks of her thinner figure, she'd been cranky on a number of occasions this year.

"I can get by on coffee."

"Since when?"

"Since always." Her glare dared him to contradict her. Travis never had been able to ignore a dare, even when it was in his best interest to do so.

"What about that time in Whistler—"

She put her free hand over his mouth. "One time. And you never let me live it down."

He kissed her palm and said around her fingers, "You tried to steal my doughnut."

She whipped her hand behind her back, but not before he got in another kiss. "A gentleman would have offered."

"As I recall, I did." He remembered very clearly.

"You squeezed the filling onto your chest."

"You seemed to like licking it off."

"I was starving!"

"Are you starving now? Because I'm sure I can find a doughnut shop nearby."

The corners of her mouth flickered, but stayed down. "No, I don't want a doughnut."

"An omelet? Pancakes? Toast? I'm a champion toast maker and I have a chest that likes crumbs."

She pressed her lips together and shook her head. "I need coffee and I broke my coffeemaker."

"How?"

Mal shrugged. "I was hungry. It was between me and the toaster. It had to go."

Travis snorted. "Well, then let's save the rest of your small appliances and have breakfast out. Do you want to shower first or should I?"

"Travis." Her mouth was making that down arrow again.

"Okay, okay." He lifted a hand in compromise. "You win. We'll conserve water and shower together." He paused. "Babe."

Mal did her best to keep her scowl front and center, but he saw the edges quiver, threaten to turn upward into an actual grin. "I don't think so."

"I can be very convincing." He leaned forward, kissed the side of her neck. "Very convincing."

He felt her shudder, heard the little sigh escape her mouth. "Travis."

But she didn't say no and didn't push him away. He trailed the kisses upward, taking a moment to explore the soft curve of her ear. He would totally forgo the shower if they stayed right where they were.

"No." She pulled back. "I can't do this. You should go." She glared when he didn't immediately leap out of bed and start hunting for his clothes, tossed around the room in their haste last night. "Well?"

"You've got my hand." He glanced meaningfully at the appendage, which remained cushioned between her breasts.

"Oh." She let go and Travis instantly missed the connection. "Well, now I don't."

No, but she had his heart. "Mal." He took a deep breath. "I—"

She cut him off before the second word. "Don't." She turned her face toward the pillow and pulled the cover over her body, depriving

Travis of the glorious view. "I can't do this, Travis."

"Do what?" He honestly wanted to know. Couldn't forgive him? Couldn't be with him? Because she'd certainly seemed capable of both of those things last night.

She stared at the pillow. "This. Us. Whatever you want to call it."

Travis swallowed his hurt. He'd thought after last night that they'd be able to move forward. He hadn't expected things to revert to how they'd been before, but he'd thought they could at least start fresh. Or, if not fresh, over. "Why?"

"Because." Her eyes met his. He saw the swirl of confusion and concern in them. "Just because."

"I've got to tell you, that's not a very convincing argument."

She didn't laugh at his little play on his earlier comment, didn't smile either. "I know. But it's all I have."

"Mal." He reached out to rub her shoulder. When she didn't shrug him off, he continued. "I know that what happened damaged us, but we can get through it."

"You can get through it."

His fingers went icy, but he maintained his calm tone. "You can't?"

Her chin dipped again and she busied her

hands fussing with the edge of the bedcover. "I don't know."

Definitely not saying no.

Travis wanted to reach for her, kiss her, hug her, reassure her that this could work. That *they* could work. Instead, he rolled onto his back and put his hands behind his head. "Whatever you want to call last night, it wasn't a mistake."

He felt the bed dip when she shifted, felt her eyes on him, trailing along his body and up to his face. "What would you call it?"

"A beginning."

A BEGINNING?

A jolt rocked Mal right down to her toes, followed by a beam of hope she pretended not to notice. It was one night, just to get him out of her system and that was it. "Be serious."

"I am serious." Travis swiveled his head to look at her. Mal had to admit, he certainly looked sincere.

She dropped her gaze, but that only put his tattooed chest in full view. Her cheeks warmed as she remembered how she'd traced his tattoos last night with her fingers and her tongue. Not a memory she should be appreciating if she wanted to steer this conversation. "It can't be a beginning," she told him.

"Why not?"

"Because we've already had our beginning." And their ending. Her chest squeezed and she had to focus on drawing in a breath.

"We can have another one."

Mal glanced up, saw the hopeful smile on his face and felt the answering return on her own before she frowned it away. They couldn't. She'd made her decision and she planned to stick to it. Wavering and wondering had no place in her life. And if Travis felt otherwise, he'd had an entire year to do something before now.

"Give me a chance, Mal. I promise I'll make it all up to you."

She wished that could be true. It would be so easy to nod and agree, to slide back into his arms and let him kiss away her fears. But it couldn't last. She couldn't trust him and every time he was late or didn't answer his phone or had to cancel plans last minute, she'd wonder.

She didn't want to wonder.

"I'm sorry, Travis." And she was, even before his expression fell. "But I can't."

"Then what was last night?" He didn't sound angry. She would have found it easier to handle if he had.

"It was goodbye." She pulled the bedcover more tightly around her as though she could hold herself together with a 600 cotton thread count.

"No." He rolled on his side to face her. "I don't believe that."

"You don't have to because I do." She heard her pulse give a loud thump, as though asking if she was sure. She was. For the sake of her poor, battered heart, her broken dreams and her now innate trust issues, she had to be.

"I don't believe you." Travis's brow wrinkled. "Because if you really wanted to say goodbye, last night wouldn't have happened."

"It was goodbye whether you believe me or not." She forced her gaze to his. Her reasoning was twofold, both to ensure that he knew she meant what she said and to remind herself that she still had her pride. She had no reason to hide, no reason to tuck herself away and avoid him. She had nothing to be sorry for or embarrassed about.

Travis's frown deepened. "Really."

She heard the note of disbelief in his voice. She'd have to be deaf not to. "Yes, really." And if she sounded a tad more strident than she meant, it was only because he wasn't accepting her pronouncement.

"And there's nothing I can do to change your mind."

Mal shook her head, but disappointment twisted through her relief. It wasn't that she wanted him to fight her decision, but it would have been nice to know he cared—that he thought she was worth fighting for.

"So, then, we're just lying here naked for our own enjoyment?"

"I don't know why you're lying here." She clutched the edge of the cover. "But I'm lying here because I always take a few minutes to plan my day before I get up."

Now Travis shook his head. "No, you don't."

Her pulse skipped. Why wasn't he getting up and getting out of her bedroom? "I do."

"No." He rolled forward. Mal could feel the warmth of his body through the covers and shivered. "You wait until you get into the office to plan because you want to make sure nothing's come up before committing to your schedule." He reached out to stroke her cheek and Mal felt her pulse skitter. "You forget that I know you and I know when you're lying."

"I'm not lying."

"About the planning or the goodbye?"

Her tongue froze and she had to take a few quick breaths before she could speak. "Both." He stroked her cheek again. She wanted to close her eyes and revel in the touch, but she couldn't. "So if you don't mind, I need to shower."

"Is that an invitation?"

"Yes, to leave." Because she wasn't getting out of this bed until he was gone. She considered wrapping the sheets around herself and dragging them off the bed, but that would leave Travis completely naked and that might prove to be just as dangerous as exposing herself. "I have to work, Travis."

"I know." He cupped her cheek. The familiar touch almost undid her. Almost. "So I'll go, but this isn't over."

Mal watched as he slid from the bed, his tight ass winking at her as he stretched and then bent to retrieve some of his clothing. She watched as he stepped into his jeans and slipped his shirt over his head, the edge of his Scottish Cross tattoo peeking out beneath the cuff.

Her breathing stilled when Travis walked around the bed and turned toward her instead of the door. No, he was supposed to walk out the door without a backward glance, without another word or touch. He wasn't supposed to watch her, emotion coloring his eyes a lustrous gray. He wasn't supposed to give her that little smile that made her insides feel melty.

His head dipped, his face lowered to hers. Mal knew why. Everyone knew why. And yet neither she nor anyone else stopped him. She simply stared at him, feeling her eyes widen and then slip shut when his lips brushed hers. Her heart beat harder, then faster, but their kiss remained light, lips skimming more than pressing. She clutched the sheet, her fingers burrowing into the soft material. Oh, she shouldn't be enjoying this at all, period, let alone as much as she was.

He needed to go, she needed to forget him and get on with her life. It wasn't healthy, this half-life she'd been living. She knew that and yet here she was, all growing heat and whispering need, feeling her entire body arch toward him.

Why had he come back? Why couldn't he have stayed in Aruba? Or, if he'd had to come back, why did he insist on re-inserting himself into her life? Her grip on the sheet loosened as his hand came around to support the back of her head and lift her closer. She felt the material slide down her body, but rather than pulling it back into place, her hands lifted to circle Travis's neck. So much for showing him that this was it, that she was done.

Why couldn't she just move on? Why couldn't he?

A small sob rose in her chest. But she didn't know if it was sadness or something else, simply a surfeit of emotion that needed an exit.

"Mal." His breath kissed her lips. "I need to tell you something."

She squeezed her eyes shut and dropped her hands back to her sides. It wasn't that she didn't want to hear it, it was that she didn't know if she could handle it. Not when she was naked in her bed, her entire body imprinted with memories of his. But rather than finishing his thought or lowering himself onto the bed with her as she'd expected, Mal felt a rush of cool air as Travis stepped back.

Her eyes popped open. He was leaving? Without telling her what was so important that he'd had to stop kissing her to voice it?

"Travis?" Even as she told herself that he was leaving and she shouldn't stop him, that she should just let him go, she couldn't help asking. "What did you want to tell me?"

He smiled and stopped moving, staking his place in her bedroom. "This isn't goodbye, babe." Staking his place in her life.

Mal knew she shouldn't have let him upstairs last night, but by the time she gathered herself to say so, he was already out the door, closing it behind him with a light click. And it wasn't as if she could run after him to insist he listen to what *she* had to say. Not even with a sheet wrapped tightly around her. Not even if she was fully clothed and in her highest, most kick-ass heels. Not even if she had a suit of armor. Because she had a feeling that armor would be nothing when faced with the onslaught from a determined Travis Kincaid.

So she'd just have to be stronger. Which meant no more late-night visits, no more inside jokes and no more access to her bedroom. No matter how much she might want to grant it.

CHAPTER SEVEN

TRAVIS STOPPED FOR coffee and a muffin at a shop half a block from Mal's. What could he say? Their conversation had put him in the mood for breakfast. Of course, he'd have preferred a doughnut, but in yoga-pants-wearing, running-up-mountainsides-for-fun Vancouver, a muffin was easier to come by. Especially if you were willing to entertain a healthy option.

According to the young woman at the counter, this one had been made with applesauce in lieu of butter. It was actually quite tasty. No comparison to cardboard or birdseed or dust, except in his head before he'd actually taken a bite. The fair trade organic coffee was pretty good, too. He could learn to make the small, steamy café his regular morning stop.

He downed the muffin in three bites, but lingered over the coffee, enjoying the dark-roasted flavor as he made his way along the empty sidewalks, most residents still in bed, catching those last minutes of sleep before they had be up and getting ready for work. It suited him, the quiet of the city, the stillness. It allowed his mind to wander freely. It wasn't a bright day, but Travis felt plenty cheerful, so the lack of actual sun didn't bother him.

Things were looking up. He had his potential bar site, he had his health and friends. And he had hope. A whole lot of hope.

He grinned as he let himself into the tall building he currently called home and downed the last of his coffee. He wanted to call Mal. To see how she was, ask if he could see her tonight. His fingers actually flexed in preparation for pulling out the phone and doing so, but he stopped himself.

She needed space, a little time to think about what had happened—and about him. And now that he was back in Vancouver to stay, there was no need to rush. He had plenty of time to win his way back into her heart. So long as he could stave off his natural inclination to push harder and faster.

Travis waited until he was in the apartment before he pulled out his phone and looked at the blank screen. Just a few quick swipes and he could be hearing Mal's voice on the other end. He paused. Maybe she needed a push, a little nudge to prevent her from building up that protective wall again, convincing herself that she was over him, that they were finished.

He woke up the device, keyed in the password

and studied the brightly colored screen. *Just a few quick swipes*. His thumb had a mind of its own. One touch here, a scrolling down the screen, another touch there and the familiar click of the line connecting followed by two rings.

"Do not tell me you're calling to say you burned down my apartment."

Travis snorted. "No, just trashed it throwing a raging party."

"And you didn't invite me?" Now Owen snorted. "That's grounds for eviction. What's up?"

"Invite me to the family dinner on Sunday."

Owen laughed. "Mal shut you down hard and you're trying to find another angle?"

Travis thought about Mal, all rosy and warm and naked between the sheets when he'd left. "Something like that."

"I don't know. I probably shouldn't get involved. It'll be good for your character to figure this out on your own."

"My character doesn't need help." He'd had more than a year to reflect, recognize his flaws and get to work on them. Now he just needed the chance to let them shine. "And, anyway, maybe I want to see your parents. I didn't get a chance to catch up with them properly at your wedding."

Owen huffed in a way that indicated he wasn't convinced. Travis didn't really care, so long as the invite was forthcoming. "Fine. Consider this an official invitation."

"How kind of you to think of me. I'd love to come to dinner on Sunday. Seven?"

"Don't be late."

As if. He'd probably spend the afternoon twiddling his thumbs and checking to see if it was time to go yet. But he didn't tell Owen that.

They chatted a few more minutes, before hanging up. Travis looked at the face of the phone again. Sunday seemed so far away. A whole six days. Did he really want to keep his distance that long? Would it backfire by wrongly indicating a lack of interest? He tapped the phone so his list of contacts showed up. It was a short list. He'd purged most when he'd moved back, wanting to leave his old life and his old contacts in the past. Only those who were truly important had remained. He scrolled down the list until he found the one he wanted and selected it.

"Hello?"

"Mom?" Travis smiled. "What are you doing today?"

TRAVIS STEPPED OFF the short forty-minute flight home to Duthie River right into a rainstorm. He swore under his breath as the drops pelted his face and bare arms. Of course he hadn't brought a coat. Not because he'd gotten rid of all his winter or rain-protective outerwear when he'd moved to Aruba, but because he hadn't thought he'd need it.

When he'd left Vancouver, after a quick shower and a quicker packing job, the sky had been gray but clear and he'd figured a coat would be unnecessary. He'd forgotten how quickly the weather could and did change in the Pacific Northwest. Well, he'd just have to spend the extent of his visit indoors or borrow a coat from his father or brother.

He brushed at the drops clinging to his arms and hurried toward the covered terminal. The plane was small, carrying only about twenty people including crew. Most headed straight through the terminal to the parking lot on the other side, stepping into the oversized trucks and SUVs that the majority of residents chose to drive in order to deal with the rough terrain and generally wet weather.

But when Travis looked for Shane, whom his mother had promised would be there on time, there was no one in sight. He sighed. He should have expected this. His younger brother wasn't what anyone would call reliable, but he'd turn up eventually. And hopefully sooner rather than later after Travis left a terse message on Shane's voice mail.

With nothing to do but wait, Travis settled on one of the metal benches and mowed through a bag of chips from the vending machine. He'd left the city early, too early to feel hungry, but now with merely a few hours of sleep to his name and only a muffin to his belly, his stomach let him know that it needed food. Fast.

He ate a second bag of chips followed by a chocolate bar, and washed it all down with a soda before his brother finally rolled up out front. On the plus side, it had stopped raining. On the negative, Travis had been waiting nearly an hour.

"Thanks for showing up on time." Travis tossed his bag into the middle of the vehicle's bench seat and climbed into his brother's bright red truck. The rain might have stopped falling, but there was a chill damp in the air that a belly full of chips did little to combat.

Shane only laughed, clearly unbothered by the less than friendly greeting from the brother he hadn't seen in over a year. "I aim to please." Then he squealed the tires on the expensive vehicle as he pulled away from the curb and out of the parking lot.

Travis felt the edges of his mouth quirk up. Shane could be a pain in his ass—he was rarely on time for anything and often in need of a loan to pay his rent. But he always paid the money back and his charm generally made up for his tardiness, so Travis couldn't remain mad at him for long. Or maybe he just appreciated the ease that Shane brought to his life.

"Not working today?" Travis asked as they headed away from the airport and into the town. Like many people in Duthie River, Shane worked at the local paper mill.

"I'm on swing shift this week." Which meant he didn't start until three in the afternoon.

Shane was following in their father's footsteps by working at the mill. In fact, Travis was the only male in a long line of Kincaid males not to work at the mill, which at its height had employed more than half the town in one form or another. But in recent years, the demand for services had declined and many legacy employees had been forced to find work elsewhere. Travis considered Shane one of the lucky ones. Though he considered himself, and his choice to pursue a different career path, even luckier.

"No Mal?" Shane asked as he accelerated onto the highway.

"Not this time." The deception tripped easily off Travis's tongue. It had to, seeing as he'd never told his family that he and Mal were no longer together, though he had high hopes for changing that soon.

He probably should have come clean months ago, simply explained that he and Mal had broken up and dealt with the fallout then. But every time the right opportunity arose, he found he just wasn't ready. Wasn't ready to face their disappointment and his fault in the matter.

Travis had been the one to leave—the first member of his family not to stay in the small paper mill town in generations. It was a lot of pressure to live up to. Perfect business. Perfect girlfriend. Perfect life. Or what passed for perfect in his mind. A breakup followed by a sordid hookup was far from perfect.

Travis shoved the thought out of his mind. That was in the past and he was moving forward, which, at least at this point, did not include talking about the breakup. He didn't see the point, not when he was hopeful that his separation from Mal would also soon be a thing of the past.

Sure, she'd sent him on his way this morning, but he knew Mal. She didn't do one-night stands, didn't do casual sex—as evidenced by the lack of condoms in her apartment. The fact that she'd been so willing, even eager, to allow him access to her, to share such an intimate act with him, spoke volumes.

He settled back against the leather seats of the truck, glad that the interior was warm and dry— Shane's previous vehicle, a rusted-out muscle car, had never been able to make the same claim— and watched the scenery flash by.

It was a quick jaunt to the home that Travis

had grown up in. But Shane piloted them a few blocks farther to their grandmother's house. Mildred Dawes was 81, five foot one and the only one of his grandparents still alive.

She was waiting on the porch of her house when they pulled up, a frilly apron on over her dress, a huge smile on her face as she waved. Travis felt his already buoyant spirits lift a little higher. It had been too long since he'd seen his family. He would have to make a point of visiting regularly now that he lived closer.

"Oh, Travis." His grandma, who only came up to his shoulder, reached out to pull him into a warm hug. It always made him feel like a little boy, back when he'd only come up to her shoulders and she'd fed him cookies even though it would spoil his dinner. "I'm so happy to see you."

He hugged her back. "I'm happy to see you too, Gram." She smelled like perm solution even though she'd given up working at the salon years ago. The scent seemed to have infused itself into her and despite the caustic nature always made Travis feel content.

"Well, don't just stand there, come in. I made cookies for you boys."

"I can't stay, Gram." Shane gave her a quick hug and a kiss. "Got a hot date."

"For lunch?" Mildred Dawes frowned at her

youngest grandchild and then grinned. "Maybe you'll introduce this one to me?"

"Maybe." Shane flashed his get-out-of-jail smile. It had literally gotten him out of jail when he'd been picked up for public drunkenness as an underage teenager, which only Travis knew about. "But I'll be here for dinner on Sunday."

It was a family ritual to get together for dinner every Sunday. They always had the same meal—pot roast, mashed potatoes and canned corn. Travis was looking forward to it, despite his more refined palate. There was something about the food of childhood that just tasted good. Even if it did come from a can.

"Maybe you can bring your lady friend."

Travis hid his grin. His grandmother would keep asking and Shane would keep acknowledging her question without agreeing. It was a well-choreographed routine that the two had worked out years ago.

"We'll see how today goes." He looked at Travis. "Mom's going to swing by after work to pick you up."

"Or you can stay here." His grandmother put a hand on his suitcase and tried to lift it. He hadn't packed heavy, but then his grandmother was a small woman who couldn't lift much. Travis took it from her hand before she threw out her hip.

"I've got it, Gram. You handle the cookies."

Even though he was full of chips and soda, he always had room for his grandmother's peanut butter cookies. He could be stuffed with three turkey dinners and an entire cheesecake and still find room for her cookies.

"You always were a good eater." She patted him on the cheek and turned to go back into her little house.

Travis waved at his brother, who gunned the engine before peeling out of the driveway, and followed his grandmother inside.

"Do you want coffee?"

"That sounds great, Gram." He placed his bag by the front door and went with her into the kitchen. It was warm and a little steamy, and a sheet of cookies cooled on a rack on the counter. Travis popped one into his mouth and then breathed in and out quickly when it burned his tongue.

His grandmother clucked her tongue as she poured the coffee. "You never did have patience."

"One of my best qualities," Travis said around the cookie, which was still trying to adhere to the roof of his mouth. He'd have gulped down some coffee, but the liquid would be just as hot as the cookie. Maybe hotter.

"Well, sit down. Let the cookies get a chance to cool and tell me what you've been up to." She carried the cups over to the table.

Travis couldn't help but notice the shake of her hands. Guilt swept through him. He didn't usually think about it, but his grandmother was getting old. Her hair was grayer than last time—or she'd just stopped coloring it—and she moved more slowly. Not to mention the shaking. But he didn't say anything. He knew she was still more than capable of giving him a swat and wouldn't hesitate to do so.

"Not much new to share. Just uprooting my life." He told her about the move and the place he'd put an offer on.

She smiled the entire time, wrapping her hands around the coffee cup. "Well, it sounds wonderful and it'll be nice to have you closer."

Travis agreed. Although life was going to be hectic, renovating and starting up a new business, there was no reason not to reestablish their weekly phone call. And once his business was up and running, he wouldn't be able to visit on a regular basis. "How have you been, Gram?"

"Oh, you know." She waved a hand. "I'm an old lady. Not much new happens at my age."

But Travis noticed the way her gaze darted to the side and she didn't meet his eyes. "No new beaus?" He always teased her about her love life. Widowed at a young age, Mildred had never remarried though she claimed to have been asked many times. Travis couldn't blame her suitors.

His grandmother was still an attractive woman and one of the kindest people he knew. Not that he was biased.

"I'm too old for that. But you..." Her gray eyes, the same shade as his, gleamed as she looked up. "Where's that gorgeous girl you're engaged to?"

Once again, not the right time. Spilling the story now, before he'd even had a second cookie, didn't seem ideal.

"She had to work," he found himself lying. Actually, that might not even be a lie. Mal probably was working. "But she says hello."

"I'm sorry she couldn't make it." His grandmother nodded. "I always like it when she's here. She adds a certain spark to the family gatherings."

Mal always brought great wine, too, which his grandmother also appreciated. "She was disappointed, but promises she'll visit soon." Travis also hadn't told anyone in his family that Mal had returned to Vancouver over a year ago *or* that he'd bought her out of the bistro. But maybe that was another thing he wouldn't have to share...if things worked out. "So tell me what's been going on, catch me up."

And his grandmother's eyes gleamed again as she launched into stories about people Travis had known all his life. He settled in on one of the flowered kitchen chairs for a nice, long listen. It was good to be back.

CHAPTER EIGHT

MAL STARED HARDER at her computer screen. The words were all there in their itemized glory— the event title, the mission statement, the budget, the communications plan. All the pieces that, when pulled together, provided the overview of the charity event she and other local food and beverage insiders were putting on to benefit the homeless. And Mal didn't actually need to read anything on the screen since she'd drafted the first version of the document, sat in on every meeting and knew all the details by heart. But it annoyed her that she couldn't.

Well, she could. She just couldn't guarantee that she'd retain any of it.

"Mal?" Donovan stuck his head into her office. "Got a minute?"

She had more than a minute, she had the rest of her day, seeing as she couldn't get anything done. "Sure. Come in."

He took a seat, but studied her instead of launching into whatever had brought him to her office. She shifted, but stilled once she realized she was doing it. "Are you feeling okay, Mal?"

"I'm fine." The words shot out of her mouth, no doubt proving just how not fine she was, but Mal rode it out, even nodding and folding her hands on top of her glass desk as though she hadn't a care on her mind.

"Right." Donovan, who was the oldest and, in his mind, most responsible Ford sibling, didn't even bother disguising his disbelief.

"I am." Mal, as youngest and, in her mind, most *together* Ford sibling, felt obligated to defend herself. "Why wouldn't I be?"

Donovan merely continued with his brotherly look of disbelief. Mal tried to look offended, but it was tricky when he was right. Still, it was her sisterly duty to try. Otherwise, Donovan might start thinking he was right all the time, then the ailment would pass to Owen and soon anarchy would reign. So, really, it was for the sake of the family's well-being that she maintained her pretense of fine-ness.

"All right." Donovan gave in with a brief shake of his head that told her he wasn't fooled but was willing to let it go for now.

Mal exhaled silently, grateful that his interrogation had been short-lived. "What's up?" Maybe he'd give her something new to focus on.

"What's going on with you and Travis?"

And maybe not.

"Nothing." She kept her voice steady, her tone measured. "Why would you think something's going on?" Aside from the fact that he'd spent the night in her bed two days ago. But Donovan didn't know that. No one except she and Travis knew that.

"Because of the way you didn't stick around at Elephants the other night."

"I was on a date." She spoke each word clearly since he needed reminding. "And hanging out with my brothers? Not exactly helping me get to know the guy."

"So you wouldn't have stayed for a drink even if Travis hadn't been there?"

"That's right." And what Donovan didn't know wouldn't hurt him. She kept her gaze on his, willed her bubbling emotions to flatten.

"Oh. Because it seemed like something was going on." Donovan shifted forward in his seat. "And when Travis left, he said he was going to talk to you."

"Did he?" Mal wasn't about to confirm anything. Not about to deny it, either, afraid that might give even more away.

"Yes, and he seemed serious. He didn't stop by?"

Mal went with an airy wave in place of a verbal response.

Donovan's brow smoothed. "I see." And Mal feared that he did. "Mal." His empathic expression almost undid her. Almost.

"Yes, Donovan?"

He stared at her with his patented I'm-older-and-know-better stare and then conceded. "Fine. We'll pretend everything is normal."

"Good." Mal did her best to ignore the internal voice that wondered why she still felt the need to hide what had happened. To protect herself? Her pride? Travis? "Because everything *is* normal."

"I'm so glad you said that."

"Why?" And why did she suddenly feel as if she'd been had?

"Because Owen invited him to join us for dinner next Sunday."

Mal wondered if she could come up with a sudden emergency or come down with a sudden illness.

"And if you don't show up, I'll know that everything *isn't* fine."

She planted her hands on the desk. "I'll see you there."

"Good."

"Good." She didn't move until he was gone and only then did she suck in a calming breath.

Not good. She'd intended to keep as far away from Travis as possible until she figured out how best to deal with him. Seeing him at a family gathering wasn't what she'd had in mind. No, not good at all.

Also not good? The handprint on the glass top of her desk. And the smear she left when she tried to scrub it off with a tissue.

She blamed her brother. In fact, she blamed both of them. Donovan for trying to make her talk and Owen for inviting Travis to dinner.

And she blamed Travis. For coming back to Vancouver. For knocking her off balance. And for refusing to let the little spark of their former relationship burn out.

At least she still had her charity event. Assuming she could concentrate long enough to focus.

"SWEETHEART." EVELYN FORD greeted Mal with a hug and a kiss as though it had been months since they'd seen each other last rather than days.

All the Ford children had made a concerted effort to stop by the house regularly when their dad had first been released from the hospital last year. Now they just stopped by because they liked it.

For Mal, it was a place to hang out that wasn't her lonely apartment. Sure, she and Grace got together after Pilates once in a while, but that was usually in the morning and Grace was a newlywed, so much of her free time was spent with her hubby. Plus, Mal didn't feel like doing much besides having a quiet dinner these days. Which was why she was forcing herself to go on another date next week.

She followed her mom into the house, listening with half her attention while Evelyn talked about planting for spring and her ideas to switch up the flower beds to let the soil rest.

The rest of Mal's attention was focused solely on sight. Was Travis already here? How did he look? How would he look at her?

She straightened the hem of her simple black blazer, making sure her slouchy cream-colored top didn't slip below it and that her sleek black jeans were straight, no unfortunate wrinkles or other lumps ruining the clean lines. She'd dressed to prove something, or so she'd told herself when she'd pulled her very strappy, very high black heels out of her closet and slipped them on. They weren't exactly ass-kicking moto boots, but they were pretty close. They were don't-mess-with-me-because-I-can-do-damage-with-more-than-just-these-stiletto-heel shoes.

Just in case.

It annoyed her that she was concerned at all. She doubted she'd have worried about it before she slept with him— or wouldn't have worried as much. At least, no more than any person running into an ex thought about such things.

There was no sign of Travis in her dad's study where they often tended to congregate as a family. Of course, no one else was in there, either, so that didn't mean much. Mal exhaled slowly, hoping to still her racing pulse.

It was a trick she'd seen Grace pull many times, mimicking the steady in and out championed by their Pilates instructor, but Mal always struggled with the simple exercise. She found it far easier to maneuver her body into the necessary shapes and control her muscles through the movements than manage the breathing portion. Too bad she couldn't drop into an Open Leg Rocker right now to unfurl the tension tightening her back.

Moving into the living room Mal heard his voice before she saw him. That low, familiar rumble that sent a shiver through her already tense spine. She swallowed. Of course, she'd known he'd be here. Had been given plenty of notice, but that didn't erase her growing nerves or worry about what she'd say when faced with him.

"Mal." Grace saw her first and rose to greet her with a warm hug. Mal hugged back, reminding herself that Grace would understand and man the door in the study if Mal needed a minute to practice her Open Leg Rocker, after all.

By the time Mal had greeted her brothers, her sisters-in-law, her mother again and been treated to a bone-cracking embrace from her father, she felt almost normal. And then she looked at Travis.

He looked back and while his mouth seemed

perfectly normal, she saw the secret smile in the depths of his gray eyes. "Mal."

"Travis." She was grateful that her voice didn't shake, though she couldn't say the same for her knees. She lowered herself into an empty seat before they gave her away as she tried to pretend that it didn't bother her at all to see her family welcoming Travis back into their warmth. That it was her fault they did so didn't make it any easier to swallow.

Mal was the one who had encouraged Owen to maintain his friendship with Travis, convincing herself that Travis was good for Owen and she shouldn't damage that relationship. She reminded her lesser self—the part of her that wanted to rage and throw things and call him every name in the book—that just because she and Travis were no longer together didn't mean that her family should have nothing to do with him ever again, either. Of course, back then she hadn't expected Travis to return to Vancouver and get himself invited to family dinner.

Why wouldn't he stop looking at her?

Mal felt a delicate flush begin to rise, knew that if she looked in the mirror her cheeks would be a rosy pink that she never managed to achieve with blusher. But she refused to look his way, as though if she kept her gaze averted he'd follow suit. She should have known better. Travis wasn't the type who followed the crowd or did what was easiest. It was one of the things that had drawn her to him. Here was a man who'd broken free of his family's expectations, someone who set his own goals and went after them no matter what anyone around him said. He treated criticism and praise with the same casual disinterest.

Her mother suggested appetizers and bustled back to the kitchen to prepare them. Although she was surrounded by her loved ones, Mal suddenly felt exposed. Probably because Travis was still staring at her. "I think I'll give Mom a hand." She rose from the sofa, her face set in a polite smile while she hurried after her mother.

She reminded herself that walking too fast would only give rise to questions she had no interest in answering. So she kept her gait steady, the calm click of her heels across the hardwood floor marking her path, the overly tall heel announcing what she might do to anyone who questioned her intentions. Which didn't stop Travis from joining her.

Mal heard his voice as he explained he'd help, too, felt the shake of the floorboards as he caught up with her and endured the rush of nerves that accosted her. She shot him a look as she picked up her pace, hurrying the last few steps to the kitchen.

"Oh." Evelyn looked up when the pair of them

entered the kitchen and smiled as though it was eighteen months ago and they were still together. "Travis, why don't you take care of the drinks." She gestured to the built-in wine fridge. "The pinot noir, please."

Travis nodded and went to the fridge. Mal looked at his butt in his suit pants.

"Sweetheart?"

Mal dragged her eyes away and pretended she hadn't been looking.

Evelyn's face wore a knowing smile, but much to Mal's relief she didn't mention it. "Will you make the glaze for the Camembert?"

Mal slid behind the stove, taking over from her mother, adding diced pear to the melted butter in the skillet and gently stirring to coat. The double wheels of Camembert topped with a pair of glazes was one of her mother's go-to appetizer recipes and Mal had made it herself many times.

She waited until the pears had softened and added a splash of brandy and a bit of fresh, chopped rosemary. The woodsy, almost pine-like scent of the herb tickled her nose.

"So?"

Mal looked over her shoulder to see Travis standing there, wine bottle in hand, his front looking as good as his back. Another quick glance told her that her mother had slipped away—very likely on purpose, having sensed Mal's discomfort. She'd never been able to hide much from her family, which was both great and annoying. Though, at this particular moment, she definitely leaned toward annoying. She turned back to the stove. "So?"

"How are you?"

Really? They'd slept together, she'd kicked him out, he'd retaliated by not calling her for days and then getting himself invited to her family's house for dinner where she had to pretend that it didn't bother her, and he wanted to know how she was? "Fine." She was fine. Just fine.

She pulled the glaze off the stove and poured most of it over the first wheel of cheese, putting a little aside for garnish, then returned the skillet to the stove and added some balsamic vinegar and honey, heating it to a simmer. She could feel his eyes on her back.

"What do you want, Travis?"

"Just to talk."

"You had plenty of days to call me and talk. You didn't." She winced even as the words poured out. She shouldn't care that he hadn't called. Scratch that, she didn't care.

"I went to visit my family." Mal felt him move closer. She stirred the mixture and didn't ask how it had gone, even though she wanted to know. "They're good. They asked about you."

She wanted to shrug that off, act as if it had

no bearing on her life. She and Travis weren't together, and as much as she liked his family, they were no longer in her circle. But it wasn't that easy. Things with Travis never were. "I hope you told them I was fine."

"I did." This time she heard his footstep as well as felt it. She was sure if she turned to look he'd be right behind her. All gray eyed and dark haired, that luscious body barely contained by his charcoal dress pants and dove-gray button-down shirt. She could probably see the edge of the Celtic cross tattooed on his chest peeking past the shirt edge if she craned her head to the left and looked directly down the open neck. Which she was *so* not doing.

"They're well. Shane has a new truck and my mom is still working too many hours. Dad looked good."

Mal nodded but didn't turn around. "How's your gram?" She liked Travis's entire family, but there was a special place in her heart for his grandmother. Kind and open, but quick to tell people exactly what she thought and why she was right, Mildred didn't let things happen to her, not without her permission. Mal missed her.

"She's good, too. Still the same old Gram. Don't tell her I called her old." Mal could hear the smile in his voice and the answering one on her face. "You should visit her."

Her own grandparents had died when she was still in elementary school so she'd never known them as an adult, but Mildred had shown her what it might have been like. "I don't think that would be appropriate." But maybe she could send a letter. Mildred had often bemoaned the loss of letters in the new millennium.

"Why not?"

Mal stirred the glaze, decided it was ready and pulled it off the heat. She fussed with the cheese though there was nothing to do until the balsamic and honey mixture had cooled. "Because we're broken up."

"We are." He paused. "But I'm here, at your parents' place."

As though that was a ringing endorsement, as though his presence wasn't in the least bit inappropriate or weird. Mal decided to ignore her urge to tell him exactly that. They were at her parents' home and an argument, even if done out of sight of everyone else and in hushed tones, was more inappropriate than his being here. "I'll think about it." She wouldn't, but it would put a stop to whatever else he might have to say.

"She'd love to see you."

"I'll think about it." There was absolutely nothing to do to the cheese until the glaze was no longer simmering, but she did her best to look busy with it anyway. "You don't have to wait for me."

"I want to wait. I'll always wait for you."

Mal had only meant he could take the wine out. Her chest grew tight at his words, which most certainly had to do with something bigger than wine. "Don't, Travis."

His voice was easy. "I'm not leaving, Mal."

"You didn't leave last time." No, that had been her. Humiliated and deeply hurt. Scared that her father wouldn't get better, afraid that her life would never get put back together again. "Which isn't the point."

"I think it's exactly the point." He laid a hand on her shoulder. Mal felt the strength and the heat of it, knew just how good it would feel to let herself sink into the feeling. "I should have come back sooner. But I want you to know that I'm staying now."

She shrugged his hand off and moved back to the stove, checking the glaze again. "Stay, go, whatever makes you happy."

"Are you happy, Mal?" Travis moved with her. He didn't touch her again, but she knew all she had to do was reach a hand out and they would be connected. She could feel that warmth and heat surrounding her from all sides. She needed to stay strong. On her own.

"I'm fine."

"Fine isn't happy."

Mal picked up the second glaze. She didn't

care that she normally would have let it sit another couple of minutes. It was cool enough. She poured it over the first wheel and then placed the second wheel on top. Another drizzle of the honey glaze and the remainder of the pears for garnish and the cheese plate was done. Just like this conversation with Travis.

"Mallory."

She squeezed her eyes shut, tried to close her emotions off, too. "That is my name." Which would have sounded a whole lot cooler had she been able to bring herself to look at him.

"We need to talk."

"We just did." She wanted to look, wanted to see his expression. She opened her eyes and her gaze made it as far as the cheese plate before stopping.

"There's more to discuss. Things I need to tell you."

Mal could hear the sincerity in his tone, but she wasn't up for more talking. Her knees felt weak enough without any talking. "Later, Travis."

He moved in front of her when she turned. His gray eyes locked with hers. "When?"

"Later."

He inhaled and it felt as though he sucked all the oxygen from her lungs. Or maybe it was the sight of his tattoo, not quite fully covered, that did it. "You wanted me to call. I'm sorry I didn't."

Her fingers curled. "I didn't want you to call." Right. Just like she hadn't wanted him to come over to her apartment or take her to bed.

"I'm sorry," he repeated and cupped her face. Mal had to work to keep her guard up in the face of his onslaught. The fact that a light touch seemed capable of bringing down the walls she'd worked so hard to build was not a good sign. "I promise I'll call every day from now on."

"Not necessary." She shook off his hand and the part of her that whispered to trust him. He'd betrayed her once, which meant there was every chance he'd do so again.

"I want to." He angled his body so they were facing each other once more.

Mal didn't move. She just stared into his face. "Travis."

"That is my name." But when he said it, the words sounded sexy, as if he was whispering them across her bare skin.

She shivered. It would be so easy. So, so easy to let herself go and fall back into what they'd had. But Mal Ford didn't follow the easiest path unless there was good reason and Travis had yet to give her one. Not that she hadn't enjoyed the sex. She'd enjoyed it very much, but it was hardly sufficient to act as a base to rebuild what they'd lost.

"I'm not letting this go so easily again," he said before she could say anything.

Her heart thumped, just once, but it was enough to send a flood of endorphins and emotions running through her.

"I made that mistake before." He reached out and stroked her cheek. Just one stroke, but that was enough to have her knees threatening to buckle. "I won't be making it again.

"Mal, I—"

She cut him off. "Later, Travis. I need to take the appy in before it gets cold."

Mal could feel his frustration, the nearly tangible urge to reach out and stop her. She was glad he didn't. Her knees were shaking plenty without adding any further touching to the mix.

When she carried the still-warm cheese appetizer out, she was purposeful in taking a chair, so as to prevent Travis from sitting beside her. But that didn't stop him from taking a seat across from her, his eyes boring into her every time he wasn't directly involved in the conversation.

She managed only a bite and a half of cheese and was grateful when dinner was served and she was able to seat herself diagonally from Travis. Though the seating arrangement didn't eliminate his watchful gaze, it did mitigate it and that was better than nothing.

If only she could deep breathe like Grace or find a private place for her Open Leg Rocker.

TRAVIS STARED AT Mal across the table. He'd been staring at her all night. And she'd been avoiding his looks. But he noted the surreptitious peeks she sent his way every so often, and the way she averted her gaze when she saw he was completely non-surreptitiously watching her. He could have been less obvious, but he didn't want to be. All he wanted was Mal.

He waited until coffee and dessert were served and boisterous conversation about gardens and cooking began to wind down. "Remember The Blue Mermaid?"

All faces swiveled toward him. Grace looked oblivious and Julia had a small furrowed line between her eyebrows as though she'd heard the name but couldn't quite put her finger on why he was bringing it up. But the Fords all watched him with equal parts understanding and interest. Except Mal. Mal looked down at her coffee cup, slowly swirling her spoon through the liquid.

"I bought it."

Travis sensed the reactions around him. Grace turned to Owen for an explanation. Julia asked Donovan if that was the place in Gastown or something else. The Fords all looked at Mal. Mal swirled her spoon a little faster. She still didn't look up.

"Travis." Evelyn was the first to speak, her innate good manners shining through. "That's wonderful. Congratulations."

"That's a good site." Gus reached out to shake his hand. "I always knew you had an eye for those things."

"I couldn't have done it without Mal." Which had the intended action of getting a response.

She frowned at him. "Me? How? I mean, I'd heard that the owners were putting the property up, but I didn't say anything to you."

"No, but it was your favorite restaurant in the city."

Julia cleared her throat. "I'll pretend I didn't hear that because we all know that La Petite Bouchée is Mal's favorite restaurant."

"That's right." Mal was quick to jump in. "The Bouche is my favorite."

"I'm sorry." Owen shook his head. "When did we start calling it The Bouche, and why?"

Travis sipped his coffee. He knew he could bring them back around to topic, but they'd get there on their own eventually and he enjoyed being part of the general merriment. He'd had a good staff back in Aruba, but he'd been more boss than friend—and they definitely hadn't been family.

"I just thought I'd test it. Marketing purposes. So, no go?" Mal said.

Owen and Julia shook their heads though Donovan seemed to be considering it. Grace appeared to be watching and absorbing everything, but rather than the Fords, her attention appeared to flick between Mal and him. Travis wondered what Mal had told her...

Grace wasn't glaring, there was no sharp twist to her lips that announced she knew about the woman in Aruba, but Travis still wondered. Owen had mentioned that Mal and Grace were friends and had only grown closer over the past couple of months. Travis would have expected Mal to tell her everything.

Shame washed over the back of his neck at the thought. He pushed it away. Tonight was about moving forward, not looking back.

"I think The Bouche has a certain ring," Donovan said.

"You are not renaming my restaurant." Julia turned to scowl at her husband.

Donovan grinned back. "Not officially."

Since his return, Travis had noted the change in Donovan—his attitude was far more laid-back than it used to be. Owen, on the other hand, was more serious. Their parents had changed, too. Gus was pretty much out of the business and had a new interest in growing vegetables, while Evelyn made sure those veggies didn't take over the entirety of her flower beds. But what about Mal? How had she changed in the preceding year?

Her dark eyes snapped as she jumped in to take Donovan's side in the restaurant name issue. This made it a fair fight since Julia and Owen were standing strong. He saw a flash of the Mal he remembered, the humor that glinted around the corners of her mouth, the flush of confidence that colored her cheeks.

She was still beautiful. But then Travis had always thought she was. He noticed she hadn't taken any of the cheesecake topped with raspberries made by Julia, who was now arguing that though she may only be half owner of the restaurant, she was full owner of the name.

Gus cleared his throat. "All right, that's enough." He might not have the bulk of the Gus of five years ago, but his authority still rang true. "You're upsetting my Julia."

"You're just taking her side because you're afraid she'll stop cooking for you," Donovan said.

Gus nodded. "Exactly right. Now stop fighting and let's hear about Travis's new restaurant." He nodded at Travis and then stole a bite of dessert off Evelyn's plate. Though he was now a year past his heart attack, the family remained vigilant so that he wouldn't experience another one. Which meant his serving of a sliver of cheesecake had resulted in a gruff complaint and this pilfering of the considerably larger sliver on Evelyn's plate.

"I take possession at the end of the month." Which was only a couple of weeks away. Just long enough to have the inspector write a report and confirm that the space was safe for use. "You're all welcome to come see it anytime."

Travis meant the offer. He'd be happy to show any one of them the property if they were interested, but his eyes landed on Mal. And stayed there.

Gus insisted on opening champagne for a toast and then there was coffee and tea. When they finally wrapped up the evening, the summer sun was beginning to set. As everyone wandered to the front, slipping on shoes, making sure they had purses and keys and wallets, Travis pulled out his phone to call a cab as they left the house.

"Put that away," Owen told him. "We'll give you a lift." He looked at his sister. "You drive right by my old place on your way home, don't you?"

"No." Mal pinned him with a look. "You know that my route home goes nowhere near your old apartment."

"Huh?" Owen faked confusion. "I would have sworn that—"

"Drop it, Owen." Mal looked at Travis. "It's fine. I'll give you a ride."

Travis paused, phone still in hand, "You sure?" He felt as though he'd made some good headway tonight. He didn't want to risk wrecking it all for an extra ten minutes together. Even if she would be in the car, unable to avoid anything he might ask.

Mal simply headed down the front steps and signaled him to follow. Travis didn't waste any time doing just that.

He kept his silence until they crossed the Granville Bridge that took them into the downtown core. Then he turned to look at Mal. "You didn't tell them, did you?"

"Tell them what?" Mal's eyes stayed on the road, but her fingers on the steering wheel tightened—the only indication that he was making more than idle conversation.

"About us." He'd known she hadn't told Owen and could extrapolate that meant Donovan didn't know, either, but he'd assumed she'd told her mother. But it had been evident from the moment he'd stepped through the door that Evelyn had no knowledge of exactly what had happened between them.

"I told them that we broke up."

"But you didn't tell them what happened." She hadn't told them what he'd done. "Why?"

A small, barely there shrug. "It didn't seem important."

"It seemed pretty important that night."

Mal brought the car to a stop at a red light. "It was important that night." She didn't say anything else and she didn't look at him either, keeping her face forward.

"And now?"

She didn't answer.

"Because I can't help but think that you didn't tell them because you hoped we'd get back together and you didn't want them to hate me."

That drew a reaction. She pinned him with a long look, which he greeted with a smile. Yes, he was trying to rile her, but there was truth behind his words. And hope. If she was truly over him and them, she would have told someone, right? Taken his name in vain, cursed him to the high heavens and boiled an effigy in oil. Something.

"I didn't see the point." The light turned green and she accelerated through the intersection. "And I thought you were good for Owen, but I'm beginning to see the flaw in that plan."

Travis leaned back against the seat. "And now I'm back and ready to make it up to you."

"There's nothing to make up." The scenery began to speed by a little faster.

"There's everything to make up and I plan to do it."

Mal pursed her lips and drove faster.

"Mal." But she didn't look over and her spine was ruler straight.

"Why didn't you tell me about The Blue Mermaid?"

The question caught him off guard, but he rolled with it. "I tried to tell you in the kitchen, but you had cheese to get out."

She did shoot him a look this time. "You had opportunity."

"I did." He couldn't deny that. "But I felt like it needed a moment. I'd have preferred to pour us each a glass of wine and make a toast, but I took what I could get." He paused. "You didn't seem that interested over dessert, anyway."

"Only because I couldn't believe you bought it."

Travis blinked. "Why? We always used to talk about buying it if it came up for sale."

"That was before." She zipped around a car going the speed limit. "Things are different now."

"Not for me."

His words only caused her to drive faster, but Travis didn't say anything. Mal was in control of the vehicle. "Just because things aren't different for you, doesn't mean they're the same for everyone."

"I'm just asking for the chance to make things right."

"There's nothing to make right." She steered around the corner.

Travis could see his building ahead of them. He

only had a minute to make his case. "I'd love for you to come and see it." He knew she wanted to. She'd loved The Blue Mermaid and the opportunity to get behind the scenes and see every part of it would be tantalizing. When she didn't jump at it, he added to the temptation. "Maybe you could give me some advice on the renovations?"

She pulled up curbside and stomped on the brake. "Don't think you can win me over with renovation talk."

"But it was your favorite restaurant."

"I know it was my favorite restaurant." She mimicked his tone. "But it's you. It's us."

"Ah. So you agree there is an *us*."

"Travis." He knew she was going for a withering tone, but it just came out tired. His heart ached. He didn't want her to be tired, didn't want to be the cause of her sleepless nights unless he was lying in the bed beside her and they were only going sleepless for a good cause.

"Just come by and see the place. You can keep your opinions to yourself, if you want."

Mal exhaled. "I'm busy."

"I'll work around your schedule. I'll even promise to feed you."

She looked at the steering wheel. "You should go."

Travis remained seated. "I'm not going anywhere."

"You're just going to sit in the car all night?" Her hair swung as she turned to face him.

"That's not what I meant." Which he was pretty sure they both knew. Was assured of when she lowered her eyes. He was close, so close to convincing her. He knew it, he could feel it. "Just come and see it. You know you want to."

Her chin stayed tilted down. "This isn't about what I want, Travis."

"Why not? It doesn't have to be difficult."

"But it is." Her dark eyes met his. "It is difficult." He saw the jagged rise and fall of her chest. "I don't want to ruin your relationship with my brother. You're friends and I respect that, but I have to ask you to respect my relationship with my family."

"Which means?"

"Which means you don't come to family dinner. You don't ask me to come and give opinions on your new property and you don't keep showing up in my life."

Another man might have felt beaten down, certain that this was it. Their last goodbye and that after tonight he would never see her again, except accidentally, at which time they'd both pretend not to see each other and would change direction to ensure avoidance was complete. But Travis knew Mal better than that. "I'm scared, too."

"I didn't say I was scared." But she was holding onto the steering wheel as if it was a life raft. "And what do you have to be scared about, anyway?"

"I belong to you, Mal. Whether you like it or not."

She took a deep breath but didn't say anything.

Travis reached out to touch her cheek. Her skin was so soft. He could stroke it all night. He satisfied himself with just a moment. "I'll call you later."

She still didn't say anything, but he felt her eyes on him as he exited the car and entered the building.

SHE WASN'T SCARED. And she wasn't going to go and see The Blue Mermaid no matter how curious she was. At least, that's what Mal kept telling herself.

And what did Travis mean he *belonged to her*? Ridiculous. A person couldn't own another and even if that were possible, she'd claimed no ownership. And she most certainly didn't belong to him, if that's what he'd been subtly implying. She was her own person and under the ownership of no one.

But his words stuck with her and no matter how hard she tried to shake them, they kept popping up. She tried to go back to sleep, but it remained elusive, sliding just out of reach whether she tried grasping for it, squeezing her eyes shut and counting her breaths or attempting not to think about it at all.

Finally she gave up and just went in to the office. If she was going to be awake anyway, she might as well put her time to good use. The building was quiet. No one else was in yet. As they worked in the food and beverage industry, the office kept slightly later hours than a traditional office. She probably had at least another hour before anyone else showed up.

In previous months, she might have found Donovan in his office crunching numbers, but since his marriage he'd changed his hours to sync with his chef wife. So it was just Mal and her computer for now. She sipped the coffee she'd grabbed at the café near her building and battered at her computer keyboard, hitting the keys so hard that her fingers practically bounced. It didn't make her feel any better. Her shoulders hurt and she swore she could count the knots along her spine.

Not good.

Once she heard the first sounds of other people entering the building, the ding of the elevator and low hum of conversation, Mal gave up trying to pretend that everything was fine and called Grace. Grace was generally at work early and Mal needed to talk to someone. She eased out a breath when she heard her sister-in-law's calm greeting.

"Are you calling to let me live vicariously through your exploits last night?"

"No." No, Mallory was not. There were no exploits, though her thighs trembled at the memory of Travis between them. "I was just wondering if you were working tonight."

"Oh." There was a wealth of questions in the brief interjection.

"Yeah." And a wealth of answers in the brief response.

"Then I am definitely free if you need some girl time." Mal loved that about Grace. No doubt she had her evening scheduled, but she would rearrange if she was needed, without a question.

"I wouldn't say need." Mal *would* say need, but it sounded so…needy. "I thought maybe we could go to an evening Pilates class and then dinner?"

The pair often did so, though their schedules hadn't meshed in the preceding week. Grace had been honeymooning and then making up for the work she'd missed, and Mal hadn't wanted to intrude on her newly wedded bliss. But she needed to intrude now.

"Of course." Mal could hear the light tapping and knew Grace had entered the notation in her computer calendar. "See you at six."

"I'll be there."

Mal was about to hang up when Grace asked. "Mal, is everything okay?"

It wasn't, but she wasn't sure she wanted to tell Grace that and she really wasn't sure she wanted to talk about it over the phone. "I'll see you at six, okay?"

"Call me if you need anything. Anything."

"I'll meet you at class." Just knowing that Grace was only a phone call away helped ease some of Mal's tension. Enough that she was able to concentrate a little and answer the emails that had been sitting in her inbox since this morning.

A few hours later, Grace was waiting for her outside the locker room, her blond hair pulled back in a sleek ponytail, her gym clothes looking like they just came from the dry cleaner. Even the piping on her shoes matched her outfit, a pale blue with touches of grass green.

Mal's outfit reflected her own current mood. Unrelieved black from head to toe. Even her shoe-laces.

They left their shoes along the edge of the Pilates classroom and unrolled their mats without talking. Mal felt some of her nerves abate as she stretched, hearing the familiar murmurs of the class settling in around her, knowing that some of the tightness in her body would be gone by the end of the class.

It was a hard session, but just what she needed,

so when she and Grace changed back into their street clothes Mal was almost looking forward to the talk. It would be good to share, to get it off her chest and stop feeling as though she had to hide the truth from everyone.

They headed to a restaurant nearby. They could have gone to La Petite Bouchée, the fine-dining restaurant owned by the Ford Group, or Elephants, or one of their other establishments, but Mal was taking no chance of running into anyone she knew. Most especially any other family.

She barely waited for Grace to take her seat before she opened her mouth and said, "I slept with Travis."

Mal hadn't meant to blurt it out quite like that. Too late now. Grace stared at her, the only indication Mal hadn't been making banal small talk was a single elegant eyebrow quirking up.

"So, yeah." Which was really just a stellar follow-up to her blurting. Was it any wonder she handled all the media, marketing and other PR for the Ford Group brand?

"And?"

"And what?" Did Grace want details? Her cheeks flamed.

"I assume you're telling me this for a reason. Or are you just bragging?" Her blond eyebrow shifted higher along with the corners of her lips.

Was she smiling? "Are you smiling?" Mal

goggled. "This isn't a smiling matter. It's bad. Very bad."

"Bad." Grace seemed to ponder the meaning. "Is that why you broke up with him?"

"Not bad in bed." Oh, no. "He had moves, has moves," she corrected, and then wondered why she bothered. Travis's prowess in the bedroom or lack thereof wasn't the point. "It was an accident."

Grace nodded knowingly. "So you two just happened to be naked and he slipped and you just happened to be in the right position, so that his—"

"Bad choice of words." Mal stopped that line of conversation. It wasn't that she was against girl talk, but this thing with Travis wasn't just girl talk. She didn't know what it was. "I meant I didn't intend for it to happen."

"What did happen?"

"Well." She swallowed and reminded herself that she'd been the one to bring it up. She'd been the one to decide to share and Grace's questions were perfectly reasonable. "After I ran into all of you last week…"

"With your date," Grace added.

"With my date," she confirmed. "My perfectly lovely, handsome, smart date."

"Who you clearly didn't find that lovely, interesting or smart," Grace pointed out. "Or you wouldn't have dumped him to sleep with Travis."

"I wouldn't say dumped." Dumped sounded so harsh, as though she'd actively broken his heart and left him shattered, when in reality she'd simply told Angela that they didn't click. "We'd have to be going out for any dumping to occur. The point was, Josh was a great guy and instead of appreciating that and setting up another date with him, I had sex with my ex."

"Maybe Travis isn't your ex."

"He's an ex." Mal was firm on that. She had to be.

"Then why did you sleep with him?"

"That's an excellent question." The server appeared at their table then and they paused their conversation to place their dinner orders. When he left, Mal returned her attention to Grace. "I was hoping you might help me figure that out. The why."

"Of course." Grace nodded knowingly and Mal immediately felt better.

She'd been right to share with Grace, to get the other woman's opinion and see if together they couldn't figure out the best way for Mal to navigate the potential minefield.

Grace leaned forward as though to impart some extremely important information. "Now, I understand there was some accidental nudity, which might have resulted in the situation."

Mal tried to frown, but she could feel the corners of her lips twitching. "You've been spending too much time with Owen."

"I know." Grace's words were practically a sigh, all filled with newly wedded bliss. "Isn't it great? But enough about me. Why is Travis an ex?"

Now it was Mal's turn to sigh, but there was no bliss in it, newly wedded or otherwise. "I'd say it's a long story, but the truth is, it's embarrassingly short." And just flat-out embarrassing. Mal took a sip of her water and reminded herself that there was no shame in her story. It was the story of many breakups. Of course, that didn't make her feel any better. She put down the water, the lone sip already sloshing away in her stomach. "He cheated on me. I left. That's it."

Grace froze with her own water halfway to her mouth. She put the glass back down without sipping. "He cheated on you?"

Her appalled tone filled Mal with the warmth of righteousness, which lasted about two seconds. "Well, we weren't exactly together when it happened." If she was going to talk about it, she had to tell the truth.

"Meaning?"

"Meaning, it was just after my dad's heart attack. I was living back here and he was down there. In Aruba. Things were a struggle." It had been hard, incredibly hard. She'd been worried about her dad and sliding into her new role with the family company. Travis was alone in Aruba handling everything on his own when she was supposed to be with him. And it all got to be too much.

"It got to the point where I just didn't see the point. I loved him and I know he loved me, but it wasn't working. We were living two separate lives. So I flew down to see him, and we talked and we agreed that it was better to part before things turned ugly."

"Seems very mature."

"It does." It hadn't been. Mal's attempt at a factual, clinical recitation of events only served to remind her of how painful it had been. How she'd questioned every word, every thought and even as they'd been agreeing to remain friends another part of her had been screaming to keep trying, keep fighting, that Travis and their relationship were worth it. "I gave him the bistro, had the papers drawn up and notarized and left them in my hotel room safe. I didn't realize until afterward, so I went back to the bistro to deliver them in person. He was in his office."

Grace was nodding along now. She was a smart woman and had clearly seen enough Lifetime movies to know where this was going. "And he wasn't alone?"

"He was not. I knocked, but he didn't hear me

since he had another woman's thighs clamped around his head." There. Now it was out. Mal waited for the humiliation to wash over her.

Instead, Grace laughed. "You're kidding."

"I'm not." Finding Travis like that, as though their relationship had meant nothing, less than nothing since he'd already found someone else, had nearly broken her. She'd dropped the papers on a chair by the door and fled. But now, well, with the passing of time, she could see how it might seem funny to an outside observer. "Right there in the office with the door unlocked. It was almost like he wanted to get caught."

"Maybe he did," Grace mused.

Mal blinked. "No, I'm pretty sure from the shocked look on his face that he didn't."

"Subconsciously he might have. Sparrow would say he was in search of his profound truth." She smiled. "You know my mother."

"I do." And Mal quite liked her. While on the surface, Sparrow Monroe and Evelyn Ford seemed to have little in common, they were both family oriented and fiercely protective of those they loved. They also always thought they were right.

"Did you talk about it?"

"No. Crazy as it might seem, I didn't really feel like standing around and having a chat at that point." She hadn't felt like standing at all, which was why she'd left and ignored Travis when he'd followed, trying to explain. Really, what was there to explain? She'd seen it in live color. No explanation necessary.

"I didn't mean at the time. I imagine you were in shock. He probably was, too."

"Don't go feeling sorry for him." Mal narrowed her eyes. "I invited you here to listen to my side of the story and decide that I'm perfect and he's the jerk."

"Done. So did you ever talk to the jerk about it after?"

Mal exhaled. She'd thought calling Travis a jerk would help, but it just made her sad. "I didn't. I asked the hotel to hold all calls, turned off my cell and changed my flight to leave the next morning. Then I left." She shrugged. It had seemed like a good idea at the time and she still thought it was. She'd been too upset, too tender and distraught to talk then.

"And once you were back here?" Grace's blue eyes were sympathetic. Mal had known she would be, which was why she'd decided to confide in her. Unlike her family, who would jump to quick conclusions good and bad, Grace was unbiased. She hadn't known Mal and Travis as a couple. "Did the jerk call you then?"

Okay, maybe not completely unbiased.

"He did, but I refused to take his calls." There

had been a lot of nights when she'd questioned her decision, when she'd wondered if she was being too harsh or cutting herself off from possibilities. But there were more nights when she was warmed by the knowledge of her own virtuousness. She'd been hurting that night, too, but she hadn't grabbed the first good-looking man she'd seen and pulled him into her room for a quickie. "Finally he stopped calling."

"So how did he end up in your bed?"

"If I knew the answer to that, we wouldn't be having this conversation."

The waiter interrupted again, bringing the bottle of sparkling water they'd ordered and a pair of goblets. Mal watched the fizzing water, feeling the unsettled movement mirrored in her stomach.

"I don't even know why I'm telling you all of this when it doesn't matter."

"Of course it matters." Grace reached out and patted her hand. "It mattered then and it matters now. Thank you for trusting me with it."

Mal hadn't fully grasped that aspect until Grace said it. Trust. She trusted Grace. Trusted her opinion, her kindness, her ability to keep things confidential. Mal's lungs grew tight. Sure, she trusted her family and loved them deeply. But there were certain things you just couldn't talk about with your brothers or your parents.

She started to thank Grace, but her throat had

closed up and all she could do was flip her hand over and squeeze her dear friend's fingers.

Grace seemed to understand. "You can tell me anything. I'll still love you, no matter what."

"Great." Mal sniffled. "Now I'm going to start sobbing like a baby."

"I have tissues and a shoulder, so we're all set."

Mal gave a watery laugh and squeezed Grace's hand again, then let go to dab at her wet eyelashes with her fingertips. She'd had many close friends growing up, but over the years she'd let those friendships drift. It made her relationship with Grace all the more poignant. "Thank God Owen didn't mess things up with you."

"Thank God I didn't mess things up with him." Grace's face softened. "It was close."

"Not *that* close." Mal still remembered her surprise when she discovered that her playboy brother had fallen in love with a woman who wouldn't fall at his feet.

"Closer than you might realize. I did go on a date at Elephants with another man," Grace said.

"I remember." Mal had sent Owen off to lick his wounds and get his head on straight a few days later. Seeing as she'd sent him to Aruba to do it, she supposed she had Travis to thank for her brother's happy ending. "And it all worked out."

"It did." Grace still had that just-married glow, which made sense since her marriage could be counted in days instead of years. But Mal had a feeling Grace would still have that same glow a decade from now. She wasn't jealous of her friend's happiness, but she wanted that glow, too. "Can you forgive him?"

Mal blew out a breath, wishing the answer was easy. "I don't know. I don't think so."

"Then why did you sleep with him?" Grace's gaze was firm but not judgmental. "It wasn't an accident. I know you, and you don't do accidents."

"I guess I thought it might bring me some closure." But that whole riding off into the sunset while a cheerful tune played and the credits rolled thing didn't seem to be happening. "And now I think that was a mistake."

"Why?"

Mal exhaled again. "Because it didn't feel like an ending. It felt like a beginning."

MAL WAS WORKING in her office when her cell phone rang in her purse. She blinked. Her phone didn't usually ring in the evenings unless it was Grace or her mother, which was a truly sad statement. She knew it was unlikely to be Grace as they'd said goodbye only an hour earlier.

The phone rang again. Mal dug it out of an interior pocket and felt her heart skip when she saw Travis's name. She should really set his number up with its own ringtone so it wouldn't catch her off guard. Maybe Taylor Swift's "We Are Never Ever Getting Back Together." Of course, every time she heard the ooooh-ooh-ooh-ooh-ooh, it would have the same effect. And would probably ruin her enjoyment of the song entirely.

She ran her thumb along the touchscreen to accept the call. "Travis, I'm really not—"

"My gram's dead."

"What?" Mal shook her head and blinked hard. But he didn't take back the words and she knew he'd never joke about something so serious. Her hand holding the phone began to shake.

"She just…died." His voice sounded thick, as though he'd been crying.

Mal blinked back a sudden wash of her own tears. She couldn't believe it. "Travis, I'm so sorry."

She heard him swallow. "My mom just called me and… I can't get out there tonight. The next flight isn't until tomorrow."

"What about by ferry?" It took a lot longer, but Mal knew that wouldn't matter, not if it got Travis there sooner.

"I won't be able to make the last connection, so I'll be stuck midway." There was only the sound of his breath, harsh and rasping. "Can I see you?"

She hesitated. She wasn't ready to see him. She hadn't figured out her own feelings, the lingering emotions that rose to the forefront and swamped her when she was in his presence. But he needed her. She couldn't turn him away in his moment of need.

"Of course." She made her decision. She'd just suck up her own confusion. It didn't matter now. All that mattered was supporting Travis. "I'm at the office, but I'll leave now."

"I'll come to your place. A walk in the fresh air…" His voice trailed off.

Her heart went out to him. He sounded so lost, so helpless. She knew the feeling, remembered well how powerless she'd felt when her father had been in the hospital just over a year ago, the family waiting to hear how the surgery had gone, waiting to hear if he was going to be okay. "I'll be there in ten minutes."

"Thanks, Mal."

She was already heading out of the office, purse slung over her shoulder, leaving papers on her desk. The mess wasn't important. Not tonight.

She got to her building before he did. Instead of going upstairs, she waited out front, not wanting him to be alone any longer than necessary. The evening was warm and balmy, though Mal was in no mood to appreciate it.

The news that Mildred was gone hadn't quite sunk in. She'd always been so full of life. Mal had just assumed she'd always be around. Or at least long enough that she'd see her once more.

Tears pricked her eyes. But she'd never see Mildred's cheerful face, eat her cookies or sit at her kitchen table over a long chat again.

Mal brushed at the wetness rolling down her cheeks. She needed to be strong for Travis. This wasn't her time to fall apart. She swallowed and took a few deep breaths until the sob in her chest eased. By the time Travis started up her block, she had the crying under control.

"Mal." He hugged her so tightly, lifting her off the ground, that she lost her breath. She hugged him back just as hard. They stayed that way for a moment, two people clinging to each other while the world spun on without them.

His grip loosened only slightly when he set her back on her feet and he continued to hug her. Mal inhaled his scent, the night, the moment and closed her eyes. This felt right. She still wasn't sure she wanted to admit that, but it was hard when it was staring her in the face. She wanted to be here, wanted to be the one Travis turned to when he needed someone. And she wanted him to do the same for her.

"Let's go inside," she said gently, smoothing his hair back.

"Just a minute." He pulled her against him again. "I just need another minute."

Mal understood that he was gathering his own strength, steeling himself for the next step, because at a time like this even breathing could feel like too much. She stroked a hand up and down his back in a slow, soothing rhythm and felt him relax. One incremental movement at a time the tension left his body. She smoothed his hair again.

He pulled back just enough that their eyes met, held. Mal saw the sorrow in them and the need for human connection. He was looking to her, counting on her. Her heart thumped. "Travis."

"Will you come home with me? Tomorrow?"

The earlier hesitation returned. What would she be telling him, telling herself, if she agreed? And what would she be saying if she declined? She hovered on the precipice of indecision for what felt like forever, but it lasted no longer than a blink as she watched Travis's lashes sweep down and then back up.

And she knew that whatever came out of this next step, she wanted to see it through to the end. Knew that she was never going to shed the chains of fear or her own inability to let go of the past and move forward unless she did. "I loved her too, Travis. I'd be honored to go with you."

His hard squeeze and slow shuddery exhale told her just how much he'd been counting on her answer. And the guard around her heart dropped a little further.

TRAVIS SLEPT AT Mal's that night, though they didn't have sex. He wanted to, but more than that he wanted the closeness they shared. Their bodies pressed together, hands clasping as they talked. He craved her gentle touches, the light press of her lips to his forehead, the trail of her fingers along his arm, the simple caresses that spoke of love more than straightforward sex ever could.

He'd booked them on the first flight out, which took off just after eight in the morning. She went with him when he returned to Owen's place to pack up a few things, never more than a few steps away from his side. He was incapable of telling her how grateful he was, how much this meant to him. But he hoped one day he'd be able to do the same for her—be there for her when she needed him most.

He held her hand tight after they parked the car at the airport, made their way into the terminal and walked through security before boarding. The other passengers on the flight were cheerful. On their way to visit friends or family, maybe have a wilderness experience or go fishing at one of the lodges that dotted the coast near Travis's hometown. He barely noticed them.

As the plane lifted into the air, the loud buzz of the propellers made conversation near to impossible, so Travis just stared out the window. He usually enjoyed the scenery, the majestic show of old-growth forest and the islands that dotted the ocean when they got farther out. The proud mountains, still snowcapped even in the heart of summer. But today he didn't see any of it. His head was filled with memories of his grandmother. And Mal.

His grandma had loved coming to the city though she preferred the ferry, claiming that she liked to stay as close to the ground as possible. She had loved taking him with her. He could remember being a little guy, carefully boarding the ferry, his hand wrapped in his grandma's as she pointed out things his five-year-old eyes didn't notice. They used to visit the city at least once a summer, though the trip had been too much for her in recent years. Travis felt guilty that he'd only been back once since his return to Vancouver.

Mal seemed to sense his sudden emotion and rubbed his back. He leaned into her, let his head rest against hers. She hadn't asked how he was doing, if he was okay or if he wanted to talk about it. She was just there. He was grateful. He wasn't ready to put his feelings into words. It would make it too near, too real.

When she slipped her hand into his and held tight, he felt some of the pressure in his lungs ease. At least, enough so he could take a breath.

Travis didn't let go of her the entire trip.

They rented a car at the airport. Mal took on driving duties while he stared out the window. He should have come back before. The time he'd spent away, the two years in Aruba living out his dream of business ownership, seemed so unimportant now. He'd thought he had years left with his gram. She wasn't young, but he'd still believed there was time. Time for him to get married, have kids, tell her how much he loved her. And now it was all too late. He let his head thunk against the passenger window.

He felt Mal's eyes on him. "I'm fine," he lied.

She patted him on the thigh. "No, you're not. But that's okay. You don't have to be fine. You be whatever you need to be."

Travis turned his head, still maintaining contact with the cool glass. "You mean that, don't you?"

"Of course." She gave his thigh another pat before putting both hands back on the wheel. "I wouldn't say it if I didn't mean it."

Travis reached a hand out and touched her arm. A light brush of contact just to confirm that he could, that she was there beside him. "Thank you."

"You don't have to thank me. I want to be here." She put her hand over his and left it there. Another subtle moment of bonding.

CHAPTER NINE

"MALLORY." MAL FOUND herself enveloped in a tight hug the moment they entered the house where Travis had grown up. She hugged Donna Kincaid back just as tightly. She could feel the older woman's body shaking and she rubbed what she hoped was a soothing hand up and down her back.

"Donna." She didn't say anything other than her name. There was nothing she could say, nothing that could ease the pain of loss the Kincaids were feeling so deeply. All she could do was be there, a calm and steady port in their storm of sorrow.

"Well, now that I've embarrassed myself." Donna stepped back and brushed at Mal's shoulder. "I cried on you."

"I'll dry, and you didn't embarrass yourself." Mal caught Donna's hands and gave her a reassuring smile. In fact, she thought Donna was holding up well. Better than Mal would have in the same situation. Better than she had when her father had been in the hospital. Oh, she hadn't cried. No, it had been much worse. She'd buried. Buried her fears and feelings, all the things she wasn't ready to bring into the light of day, down deep and pretended that they didn't exist.

She'd succeeded in that nothing had boiled over, but Mal wondered now if that was truly a success, if turning away from all those feelings had damaged her in some way. She squeezed Donna's hands and then released them so the woman could greet her son.

They clung to each other, not saying anything. Mal let them have a moment, slipping through the entryway and into the kitchen. She filled the kettle with water and turned it on, got down a china teapot and a couple of matching cups from the cupboard. The tin of tea sat on the back of the stove. Mal pulled that onto the counter, too.

Then she started coffee, just in case someone preferred that. She found cookies in the pantry and put them on a plate in a pretty semicircle while the water for the tea boiled and the coffee perked. When she finished, she felt a little calmer, a little more in control.

She could get through this. For Travis.

He and his mother were sitting in the living room on the flowered peach couch when Mal carried in the tray with two pots, cups and cookies. They both smiled, their matching gray eyes watching her in the same easy way. Mal felt her heart thump.

She put the tray down on the old, scarred table. The top of the sugar bowl rattled until she reached out to lay a hand on it.

"Shane and Dad are at the funeral home with..." Travis's voice trailed off. Mal stopped pouring tea and pressed a comforting hand to his arm while he took a deep breath. "Handling the paperwork," he finished.

"I couldn't bring myself to go." Donna reached out to grip Mal's other hand. "I should have. She's my mother. But I just couldn't..." Mal saw her throat bob as she swallowed, searching for strength. "Thank you for coming. I couldn't do this alone."

"You're not alone." Mal patted her hand, waiting until Donna let go before she finished with the tea and handed Donna a cup.

Mal looked at Travis, but he shook his head and pulled her down beside him. "We're here now, Mom. So what can we do?"

Donna's hand fluttered to her hair. It was perfectly groomed, as befit her position as Duthie River's best hairdresser. "I don't even know. There's so much to do." Her eyes welled up and she swallowed. "They took her to Doose's."

Mal assumed Doose's was the funeral home. She glanced at Travis. "Why don't I call them?"

The Kincaids would need to make some decisions as a family. Donna might not have wanted to go to the funeral home originally, but she'd want to be part of making final arrangements for her mother.

Travis nodded. Mal's heart felt as heavy as her feet as she rose and walked back to the kitchen.

The funeral home was polite and efficient, and Mal was able to speak with Shane who guessed he and his father would be another hour. They decided to schedule another meeting at the funeral home later today, so the family could spend some time together before they had to make any decisions on the service.

But when Mal hung up the phone, she didn't return to the living room. She sat on a wooden ladder-back chair and looked out the window.

This could have been her dad. Instead of seeing him get better, she could have been making arrangements and determining who to call, how to organize the service, trying to hold herself and everything else together.

Mal pressed the heels of her hands to her eyes.

It wasn't her turn to fall apart. She knew that. Her dad was alive and well, making jokes and growing vegetables in his garden. But it had been close. So close. Too close.

And when she inhaled, it wasn't the firm and calming breath she needed but one that shuddered and wheezed. One that feared what might have been.

Mal could hear the low murmur of Travis and his mom in the other room. She knew she couldn't stay at the kitchen table forever. They'd come looking for her, wondering if she'd spoken to the funeral home, wanting to know what was next. And Mal knew she needed to be the guiding hand that allowed them to go through the steps when they felt overwhelmed by it all. But she needed a minute.

Travis found her in there. "Babe? You okay?"

Mal's head shot up. There were stars in her eyes from the press of her hands. She blinked but they remained. She pasted on a smile anyway. "I'm fine. Just thinking." She saw his brow furrow, felt guilty that she was adding to his worries. "I'm fine." She rose and put her arms around him. "Just fine."

He held her close. She could hear the thump of his heart when she rested her head on his chest. A slow, rhythmic drumming. She let herself be pulled into it, taking strength from the steady beat.

"I'm glad you're here." He whispered the words into her ear.

Mal hugged him tighter. She was glad she was there, too, even though the circumstances were less than ideal. But then, what had been ideal the last year? Not a lot. Not work. Not home. Not anything. She looked up at him. This was the closest she'd been to ideal since Aruba. Her heart swelled. "I'm glad, too."

His arms tightened so much that it hurt, but it was a good kind of hurt. One born from the need for closeness and support, as though the idea of even air coming between them was too much to bear. He kissed her then. A hard, possessive kiss that lifted her off her feet and into his arms. She couldn't breathe, but she didn't care. This was what she needed. What he needed.

"What about your mom?" Mal finally said when she came up for air. She already knew his father and brother would be a while.

Travis worked his way down her neck, biting lightly the way she liked. "She's gone to the salon to make sure everything's running. I think she just needed something to do besides wait."

He licked his way down to the little hollow in her throat and sucked. Mal shivered and pressed closer. His belt buckle bit into her stomach, but she didn't care. Her hands clutched his shoulders, pulling tighter, wanting more. They had the house to themselves, and the desire for human connection, to feel alive, was so great that she felt weak with it. "I need you." Her voice came out as a rasp.

Travis's only response was a low rumbling in

his throat as he gripped her thighs, wound them around his waist and headed for the stairs. They bumped walls as they went, hands yanking at hems and zippers, collars getting in the way, always pushing for more of each other.

Mal got one arm out of her jacket before she stopped trying and set her attention back on Travis. Her spine hit the doorjamb as he hurried into his old bedroom. Mal had been in here many times over the course of their relationship, but never quite with this urgency.

The bed was small, a twin that probably hadn't fit Travis even when he'd been a boy, but that suited her today. Nowhere to go but to each other. Travis kicked the door shut with a bang and Mal twined her arms around his neck. Her jacket flapped around her, half off, half on.

They fell onto the bed, limbs still entangled, mouths kissing and licking. Mal could feel the light sting of Travis's stubble since he hadn't shaved, reveled in the rasp of it across her skin, marking her as his in a way she hadn't been for so long.

"I need to touch you." His fingers were clumsy, wrenching at the arm of her jacket that was already off, fumbling at the hem of her shirt before skimming along her exposed stomach. She sucked in a sharp breath and tried to help, but her hands were just as clumsy. Shaking with emotion, her movements were thick and sloppy with the need to rush. To get as close as possible to Travis in the shortest time permitted.

Mal heard the rip of a seam and then her jacket was off, her white T-shirt close behind. Travis tugged down the cups of her bra and sucked on her nipples. Her eyes closed as the sharp sensation of pleasure swept over her.

But it wasn't enough. Not today. She yanked his shirt up, exposing the length of his long torso and the dark tattoos that decorated it. Oh, she loved his ink. The fierceness of it, the way it shifted and moved as though it had life. More than simple body art.

She dug her nails into his shoulders while he sucked harder, pulling the nipple deep into his mouth and then letting go with a pop. Her body grew loose, opened, welcoming him. She lifted her hips and helped wriggle her jeans down her legs. Like the jacket, she only managed to get it partway off, but it was enough.

Travis dragged his own jeans to his knees, rolled on a condom he produced from somewhere and sank into her with a moan.

Mal moaned back. She wanted to feel the connection every time their bodies met. The arch of her back as she took him deeper inside, the way her body wrapped around his. He ran his hands up her arms, pushing them over her head and linking his fingers through hers, holding her there so she was stretched out, exposed.

She rocked harder, setting a fast pace that left no question of whether she wanted to be here with him. This was all she wanted. Their eyes met, the speed of their motions increased. Heat started low in her belly, rippled out in waves until she was warm all over.

"Kiss me." She needed more, needed every part of their bodies to touch, to feel. Travis bent his head, his mouth hot on hers, his tongue following the same rhythmic pattern as his body.

Mal felt the pressure build, the heavy weight pressing and pushing against her until she could stand it no more. She broke the hold of their hands and clutched at him, clasping him toward her as she wrapped her legs back around his waist just as the pressure erupted through her.

Travis groaned again. She could feel her nipples rubbing against his chest, felt the tension as it took hold of him and then swept through in sweet release a second later. They lay there for a moment, panting. Sweat beaded on his stomach and dripped onto her. Mal didn't move. Except to hold Travis close when he moved to rise.

"No." It was all she said. All she needed to say. He sank back down to her, his body pressing hers farther into the bed. She could hear his pulse, no longer that slow steady pump, but hard

and strong. The kind of pulse that could be relied on. She stroked her hands up and down his
back, wanting the contact, the feel of his skin
gliding beneath her touch. The ripe roundness
of his butt, the ridges of his spine, the hairless
patch of skin on his lower back. Mal wanted to
touch it all. And did.

Slowly the heat began to fade, dissipating away
in the day, though Mal's desire to stay right where
they were didn't. She shivered.

Travis lifted his head. His gray eyes were
warm and heavy, but happy, that pinched look
around the edges gone. "Cold?"

Mal shook her head. She didn't want to break
the moment, afraid of what might happen if she
did.

Travis smiled. "Well, I am." He pulled down
the covers of the bed, still keeping their bodies tight together and maneuvered her under the
sheets. Then he stripped off his clothing and hers.

Mal burrowed against him, sucking up his heat
as much as the contact. She remembered this.
How on cold nights she'd curl against him or,
when she was being silly, cling to him like a koala
bear. How he'd sigh and agree when she asked
if she could press her cold feet against him. The
way she'd wake up the next morning, never quite
in the same position but some part of them always
touching. Maybe just a hand in the summer when

it was hot and even open windows and a light breeze did little to bring down the temperature. Arm against arm in spring or fall, and the full tangle of winter, hands tucked into the folds and hollows of each other's bodies.

Travis put his arm around her, hauling her closer against him, and pulled the covers up. They barely fit on the bed side by side. Mal was more sprawled across him than beside him.

She closed her eyes, cocooned in Travis's warmth, his arms looped around her, ensuring full body contact. He kissed the back of her neck, then the side before settling in with a sigh. She felt like sighing, too. Releasing the little tension that remained after sex. But suddenly it seemed like so much effort, drawing in the breath, forcing it back out, when she could just close her eyes instead.

She heard the smooth cadence of Travis's breath mirroring her own and smiled to herself about how in sync they were, and then she drifted off.

A knock at the door woke her up.

"Travis?" Mal recognized his mother's voice. Donna cleared her throat. "Are you up?"

When Travis didn't answer, Mal nudged him in the ribs. He snorted as he jerked to alertness. "Your mom," Mal whispered and pointed at the door.

God, she was nearly thirty and she still felt as

if she'd been caught doing something bad. As though Donna wouldn't realize their relationship included sex. Of course, it was one thing to know it theoretically and another to find them naked in his childhood bed. Mal yanked the covers more firmly up to her chin.

"Just a sec, Mom." Travis climbed out of bed, fumbling for his jeans and running a hand through his hair, which was messy from sleep and Mal's fingers. He started toward the door.

"No," Mal hissed. "You look like…" Well, he looked like he'd been having sex, which he had, but she didn't think he should be announcing it to his mother. "Put a shirt on and your socks and do something with your hair." She smoothed her own hair and then realized she did not want to be seen at all in her current state and gathered the covers around her and rolled off the bed to sit on the side that didn't face the door.

Donna would probably notice the messy bed, but at least Mal wouldn't be in it. Maybe she'd think Travis had taken a solo nap.

Travis opened the door and Mal slunk down a little lower, making sure her head didn't poke up over the tiny bed.

"Your dad and Shane are on their way," Donna said. "I finally got ahold of them."

"I'll be right down." Mal peeked under the bed and saw that Travis hadn't put on his socks.

"And Mal? Is she…"

"She's hiding behind the bed."

Mal gathered the covers more tightly around her, as if that would change anything. "I'm not hiding, I dropped something."

"Okay, she dropped something." Travis sounded as though he was laughing, but she couldn't tell from staring at his toes.

There was quiet for a moment and then a surprised laugh. "Well, make sure you're both covered before you come down. I don't want your dad to have a heart attack. And put on some socks."

Mal waited until she heard the click of the door closing before moving, and even then she only poked her head out. Just in case. Travis leaned against the door, grinning at her with his arms crossed so his Celtic cross peeked out beneath the sleeve of his T-shirt.

"You are not as funny as you think," she told him as she rose to her feet, trying to look dignified, which didn't really work when her only cover was a rumpled bedspread.

"I am so." He grinned wider. "And it made my mom smile. Are you going to deny her the solace of humor?"

"That's not fair." Mal scooped her underwear off the floor and her bra. "How can I defend against the sympathy card?"

"You can't, which is why I brought it out."

He thought he was so smart. Actually, she had to hand it to him, it was pretty good. But she couldn't let that slide. He might start thinking he could use it to get anything he wanted, abusing his power. It was the principle of the thing. "Well, then. In return, you don't get to watch me dress." She sat on the bed, keeping her back to him and pulled the cover up high enough that she could get her underwear on.

"Now who's not playing fair?"

"You reap what you sow," she told him, and slipped into her bra without dropping the cover. Her jeans went on next, but her shirt was across the room. No longer on the floor, it dangled from Travis's finger.

"Looking for something?"

"Actually, I thought I'd go down shirtless."

Travis lifted his eyebrows. "Well, don't let me stop you." He motioned to the covers she still clutched to her chest. "Or I can hand it over for a kiss."

"Are you bargaining? With my clothes?"

His eyes flicked down to the shirt then back to her face. "It looks that way."

"And if I say no?" She lifted her chin in challenge.

"Then I'll be sad. Very sad." He handed over the shirt when she reached for it.

Mal tugged it over her head, only releasing

the cover once it was on. Again, the principle of the thing. She looked up at him. He put on his best sad face. "Well, I guess I'll have to kiss you all better." She curled her arms around his neck.

He was still warm with sleep as he lowered his head. "Just one of the things I love about you," he said just before his lips brushed hers.

Her eyes fluttered shut. "My amazing kissing ability?"

"That too." Another kiss. "But I meant your big heart."

Mal felt the organ in question grow, swelling so it felt as if it filled her entire chest. It was really getting a workout these days. For so long she'd walled it off, kept it hidden so it didn't hurt. But she'd cut off so much, too—so much that she'd missed out on. She pressed closer to him.

"Thank you for coming with me."

She brushed her lips across his instead of answering.

TRAVIS DIDN'T WANT to let go of Mal. He either kept an arm around her shoulder or her hand wrapped in his the entire time they were at the funeral home. It helped, knowing she was there, knowing how happy it would have made his grandma to see them together.

He was glad he'd kept their breakup to himself. It would have disappointed his grandma and somehow it helped knowing that she hadn't been let down. That she'd continued to consider them a couple and imagine the great-grandkids they might give her. Even if she would never see them.

His fingers, currently entwined in Mal's, tightened.

Doose, the funeral director, was going on about their options. Burial or cremation, casket type, service, music, until it all became a whirl of noise and choice.

Travis tried to listen. The list Gram left had specified certain requests, but she hadn't updated it since the late sixties when she'd buried her own husband, so most things she'd wanted then were no longer available. He knew his mother would only be overwhelmed. And his dad wasn't much of a talker, while Shane would go with whatever the majority wanted. Which meant he needed to pay attention and make recommendations.

"So, as you can see, if you go with an open casket, you'll want something with a nicer interior." Travis stared at the picture. "This one goes especially well with the pink lilies you said she wanted."

Travis was sure it did, but then so did the other ones. He looked at Mal. She glanced back and gave his hand a squeeze. It helped settle him, or at least let him gather enough focus to listen to what Doose was saying.

It took another hour to finalize decisions and the service. Travis held onto Mal's hand the entire time. He continued holding it when they stepped out of the funeral home into the still-warm evening.

The group was quiet as they walked to the parking lot. Of course, his father was always quiet but it was weird not to hear his mother and brother chatting. He couldn't blame them. Travis didn't feel much like chatting either.

His mom was leaning against his dad as they walked. She looked delicate, her usual good cheer having worn out over the course of the day.

"Let's go out for dinner," Travis suggested. He knew he didn't feel like cooking and he doubted anyone else did.

His mom turned her head to share a tired smile. "I'm not really hungry."

"You need to eat," he paused. "And now I sound like the parent. Clean your room!" Which garnered a small laugh and made him feel a little better.

"Why don't you kids go out?" his mom suggested. "Your dad and I will have something at home." His dad just nodded, which was closer to normal behavior.

Travis looked at Shane. "You hungry?"

"I am." He jangled the keys in his hand. "Joe's?"

"Done." Travis boosted Mal into the cab of

Shane's truck and climbed in beside her. It was cozy, the space limited to begin with and made more so by a hooded sweatshirt and some empty juice bottles Shane had left behind. Travis tossed the bottles onto the floor and placed the sweatshirt along the back of the seat, then he took advantage of the tight space and slung his arm over Mal's shoulder.

It was a short ride to Joe's and they were seated right away. "I'm so sorry to hear about your gram," said Loretta Joe as she showed them to a booth. Loretta was the hostess for the bar and grill she owned with her husband and had gone to school with Travis's mom. "She was a good lady."

"She was," he agreed. "Thanks, Loretta."

Loretta nodded and doled out menus. "You tell your mother I'll be by tomorrow to see her."

"She'll appreciate that."

Another nod and Loretta was off.

"I can't believe this place looks exactly the same." Mal gazed around the room. "It's nice. It feels like a homecoming."

"It hasn't been that long since you were here," Shane pointed out. "What? A couple of years, max? Did you think you'd never see it again?"

Mal glanced at Travis. "I wasn't sure."

"I'm glad you came," Shane said, oblivious to the silent conversation happening in front of him. He flipped open his menu, perusing the selections, yet those also hadn't changed in years. "Next time don't stay away so long. We all missed you."

A small V appeared between Mal's brows, though she merely said, "I missed you, too."

"Good. Then you'll be back sooner next time. I think I'm gonna have a burger." He put down the menu, picked it back up and put it down again. "I need a drink. You guys want a drink?"

"I'm sure a server will be by in a minute." Joe's would never be mistaken for fine dining with its claim-to-fame buffet, its plated selections that consisted of burgers with or without cheese and nachos for appies, but the service was good.

"Well, I need to do something, you know?" Shane was already out of the booth. "Beer?"

"Please," Mal answered.

"Water." As good as a cold one would taste, now was not the time to start drinking. Not even in moderation. Because nothing about the current swirl of emotions inside him felt moderate.

Shane nodded and headed over to the bar to place their order.

Travis glanced down to find Mal was still watching him, the little V now a frown. He leaned down so his lips were beside her ear. "If you keep frowning, your face will freeze that way."

"Why did Shane assume I'd be coming back?"

Damn. Travis had foolishly hoped this might

not come up on the trip—and especially not with his brother along for the ride. Shane's attention was currently on the TV hanging behind the bar while he waited for their drinks, but even Shane would notice a serious discussion happening right in front of him.

"Can we talk about it later?" He brushed a thumb across the line between her brows.

She looked at him closely, studying, then nodded slowly. "Yes."

Travis wasn't sure if it was a promise or a threat.

THE FUNERAL SERVICE remembering Mildred Dawes took place on Friday evening, but Mal and Travis stayed in Duthie River until Sunday. He was quiet during the flight back and Mal was, too. She knew they needed to talk, but she thought it best to wait until they were back on solid land, back in their daily lives before broaching it.

He was still upset about losing his grandma and, to be fair, Mal was, too. Mildred had left her a pair of sapphire earrings, the set matching the ring Travis had given her for their engagement.

Donna had asked about the ring and Mal had had to lie and say it was being cleaned, which was why she wasn't wearing it, when in reality it sat in her jewelry box at home. But now she had to question if it should stay there. What were she and Travis?

She hadn't needed a degree in astrophysics to figure out that Travis had kept their breakup a secret. The question was, why? She hadn't broached the subject yet, feeling as if it was a conversation that should wait. But as their plane neared Vancouver, she had to ask herself how much longer she could put it off.

The roar of the plane's engine made it hard to talk unless you pressed your mouth practically against the other person's ear. Mal shivered when Travis did just that.

"Can I come to your place tonight?" He pressed a kiss just below her ear when he did. He'd done that a lot this trip. Kissing, holding, touching, always making sure some part of them was in contact.

"I have to get up early for work." She had a lot to do, having been away for nearly a week. And she needed time alone to figure out how she felt about everything. The secrets…and her own participation in them as she'd allowed his family to continue thinking they were still together. And how she felt about the realization that she'd liked them thinking it, liked pretending that the breakup hadn't happened and she and Travis were as strong as ever.

He kissed her neck again. "Please."

Mal's eyes slipped shut. Maybe the conversation and her feelings about it could wait one more night. Just until they were both in a strong enough headspace to talk rationally and reasonably. Just until she could figure out what she wanted. "Okay."

CHAPTER TEN

TRAVIS SPENT THE night at Mal's apartment. And the one after. And the one after that. He was grateful that she didn't raise the subject of why his family had no knowledge of their breakup, but he knew it would come up eventually. It was just a matter of *when* and where they were in their new relationship. He hoped to forestall it as long as possible, feeling as though the longer they waited, the less power it would have to crack the foundation of this new love they were building.

Not that she'd said she loved him. Not yet. But he hoped it was only a matter of time.

He knew that he loved her, that he wanted to be with her, and he was willing to do whatever it took to ensure she understood that. He'd screwed up before. But this was a new start. One free of mistakes.

Mal had left early for work, so Travis had returned to his own place for a shower and coffee. He'd been looking over plans for The Blue Mermaid and considering new names for the space. He wanted to maintain something of the original, but didn't want to confuse anyone into thinking it would be the same kind of establishment.

He would like Mal's opinion on the name and on other things to do with the business, as well. She was incredibly good at what she did. And if it meant they needed to spend more time together, that was all good with him.

A quick glance at the clock told him she'd been at the office for a couple of hours. Certainly long enough to deal with her email and any questions that might have come up overnight. She probably needed a break, and he was just the man to provide one. He scooped up his phone and called.

Her voice mail answered. "Hello. You've reached Mallory Ford, director of marketing for the Ford Group. If you'll leave your name and number and reason for your call, I'll get back to you as soon as possible. Thank you."

"It's me." He was confident that she'd recognize his voice even if she didn't check her missed call list before listening to her voice mail. "I was thinking you might like to join me on a tour of my new place." He doubted she'd be able to turn down the offer. The opportunity to shape the future of the restaurant she'd loved so much would be irresistible. Or so he hoped. And if not, he had a backup plan. "I was thinking of ripping out the bar and replacing it with something glass. Call me later. Or I'll call you."

He hung up and sat down with his fresh coffee. He had no intention of ripping out the bar or replacing anything wood with glass, but he knew it would light a fire under Mal who'd once waxed poetic about the long wooden bar for twenty minutes.

When his phone rang two minutes later and her number came up on call display, he practically rubbed his hands together. "Hello?"

"If you rip out that glorious bar, I want to buy it."

"Oh?" He took a casual sip of his coffee. "Not kill me?" The bar was a masterpiece, as Mal pointed out multiple times during her twenty-minute tribute.

"Oh, I'll do that, too. Once I have the bar away from you so you can't do any further damage. Seriously, Travis, I'll do it even though I look terrible in orange."

"You don't look terrible in anything." Mal looked great in everything. And *out* of everything.

"I didn't call to be flattered by you." But he could tell she was smiling.

"No?" He was enjoying himself and leaned forward onto the counter. "Then why did you call? To set up a date?"

She snorted. "I didn't call to listen to you flatter yourself, either."

"Well, somebody has to. So, do you want to

come and see it? I've been going over plans today for the renovations."

He heard the excited intake of breath. "When can I come?"

Travis grinned. He'd known she wouldn't be able to turn down the chance to help shape the space. "This afternoon, and then I'll thank you by taking you out for dinner."

"I'm busy tonight."

"Oh?" His tone was light, but the disappointment settling over him was not. She hadn't mentioned anything about having plans tonight. He'd assumed they'd do something together. "What's happening tonight?"

"I have a business meeting."

"With your brothers?" Some of his disappointment eased. Maybe he could take her out for a late dinner. She had to eat sometime, didn't she?

"No, for an event I'm organizing. I can meet you at four."

What event? Why hadn't she mentioned it to him? The questions rose on his lips, but he swallowed them. Mal was allowed to make her own plans, have her own interests. He'd just like it if she chose to share them with him. "I'll see you at four then."

MAL'S STOMACH TIGHTENED the moment she hung up the phone—as it had been doing lately whenever she thought about Travis. They needed to talk. Not just about why he'd chosen not to tell his family the truth about them, but about what was happening between them. Both now and before.

She took a long, deep breath until her stomach no longer felt as if it was twisting in on itself. But it was only a temporary fix. The time to ask the tough questions and to deal with the answers was drawing near.

Ten minutes before she was due to leave, Mal headed out of the office and hailed a cab. She could have walked the twenty blocks from her office to meet Travis, but she was wearing a pair of stilettos that were more for show than use. Her statement shoes. Ones that said she was strong and powerful—the kind of woman who didn't dance around questions and feelings, but one who handled them.

Still, she took more than a few calming breaths during the short cab ride, and when the door to The Blue Mermaid flew open at her knock to reveal Travis looking handsomer than ever, she felt her mouth go dry.

"You made it." Travis smiled and the joy in his voice and on his face, tinged with a hint of surprise, made her step hitch. He looked good. Why did he always look so good? Even with his tan long faded, there was a glow about him that made her want to bask in his light.

At least his tattoos were covered. Though knowing they were just out of sight, all badass and rebellious, somehow made them more appealing. And she was in on the secret. On the outside, Travis Kincaid was a smart, well-put-together businessman. But on the inside he was a renegade. Mal shivered.

"Are you cold?" Travis was instantly solicitous, attentive to her every need whether she wanted him to be or not.

"I'm fine." But she tucked her hands into her coat pockets to hide the sudden shaking and forced a smile. "So, let's see the place." Hopefully the shaking wouldn't migrate to her legs. If it did, she'd have to try and distract him with her shoes.

"Sure." But he didn't move right away, just looked at her, as though he was drinking her in. Mal stopped shivering and started feeling too warm. Being around Travis was bad for her internal temperature. "Where should we start?"

"Wherever you want." She should break eye contact. She needed to break eye contact. She was falling into that silvery gaze, forgetting the issues that lingered between them, prevented them from truly moving forward.

She saw the edges of his eyes soften, the confident upturn to his lips and the way he leaned forward into her space, taking up all her oxygen.

"You know what I want, Mal." He bent his head to kiss her.

Mal knew she should keep it short, keep her focus. Instead, she wrapped her arms around him, drank him in. He felt so good, so right.

He murmured something against her lips and tightened his hold.

"Travis?" His name popped out of her mouth. He pulled back to look at her. Mal felt the shaking start up again, placed her hands on his chest for balance. She swallowed. Now or never. Or that's what she was going to tell herself for fear she'd chicken out again. "What's going on?"

"Well, I'm going to show you around, ask you what you think and maybe kiss you again." He lifted one of her hands from his chest and pressed a kiss to her palm.

Mal's knees wobbled. But she needed to do this. "Why didn't you tell your family that we broke up?"

He stilled, her hand caught in his. Then he pressed his cheek against it, rubbing and closed his eyes. "For one thing, I felt like an idiot."

"Why? Because we broke up?"

"Partly." His eyes opened, centered on hers. "Because I didn't fight for you. Because our breakup let them down, too." He exhaled softly. Mal felt the brush of breath across her forearm.

"People break up, Travis."

"But not us."

His touch was distracting her. She pulled her hand back. "Yes, us."

He reached out to cup her face. "I wish it had never happened."

Mal would be lying if she said she didn't feel the same. "But it did happen. And you kept it a secret." She took hold of his hand, slid it down her cheek so that it rested between them.

"You didn't tell your family everything," he pointed out.

"I didn't, but keeping the details private is pretty different than letting them think we were still together." She felt his fingers tighten over hers.

"I know. I didn't plan to keep it a secret. At first, I just didn't want to talk about it. So I didn't call them for a while. Then when I did, I tried to avoid the subject. That worked for a couple of months."

"And then?"

"Then it reached this awkward stage where I didn't know how to tell them. I kept thinking that something would happen. I'd meet someone else or—"

"So you were dating." The thought was a smack in the face. She should have considered the possibility before, but she hadn't. This time, it was her fingers that tightened, squeezing his hand until his fingertips turned white.

Travis met her eyes. "I tried." His voice was quiet. "I didn't want to be this pathetic guy hung up on a woman he could never have."

Mal's lungs burned. She drew in a quick breath, but even that hurt.

"But no one was you."

"Did you sleep with them?" It wasn't her business, but she asked anyway.

"No." His denial was swift, the truth of it clear in both his tone and expression. "I never even got close."

Some of the tension in her body loosened. "Good."

Travis pulled her hand into his chest. She could feel the steady thump of his heart. "Do you want me to tell my family the truth?"

She thought about it. Part of her did—she wanted to know that he was being honest with those he counted as important in his life. But she wasn't sure what purpose it would serve. To assuage her own feelings? She flattened her palm to cover more of his chest.

"I'll call them right now. While you're standing here, so you know I did it."

Mal shook her head. She didn't need to oversee anything. She knew Travis well enough to be sure that if he said he'd do something, he would. "You don't need to call them." Maybe too much time had passed anyway. "I just wanted to know why." To know that his reason hadn't been because she was unimportant—that she'd held such a small place in his life that he hadn't even bothered to tell his family they'd broken up—was enough.

"So." He laid his palm over hers. "Does this mean we're back together?"

Mal swallowed. She could say no, but it wouldn't make it true. Plus, did she really want to say no? The time spent with Travis and his family had shown her just how much she still loved them and, she thought, how much they still loved her. Was she willing to give that up? Or did she want to take a chance that this time things would work out differently?

"Too soon?" he asked.

"No." She took a step toward him…and her future. "Not too soon."

His body pressed against hers. He felt so big and warm, a rock to hang onto when her emotions stormed inside her. Travis slid a hand beneath the curtain of her hair and cupped the back of her head. When he lowered his mouth to hers, Mal felt all his pent-up emotions, too—relief, gratitude and deep, deep pleasure.

She wrapped her arms around his broad back and held on as he slowly and methodically kissed the breath out of her. He lifted her up, holding her tight to him as he walked farther into the bar. Mal simply held on. She opened her eyes when he set her down on the bar. The now polished wood ran nearly the width of the bar itself—it was the one thing in the place that looked ready for the opening.

Travis settled himself between her thighs and kissed her again, his fingers tangling in her hair, flicking open the top buttons on her shirt, stroking her collarbone. Mal shivered under his ministrations. He'd always known how to touch her, known how to make her moan. She sighed when his fingers strayed lower, tugging on the hem of her skirt as he began working it up her legs.

Mal clutched at his shoulders as her eyes slid shut. It was just them—the two of them in the quiet space. She felt her body warm, her temperature rise with her skirt, the slow pull of the silk blend against her skin, the touch of Travis's hands, his breath as he lowered his head to trail kisses from her knee up. Her breath caught, held, as the skirt nudged higher, up to the tops of her thighs.

She heard the thump of her heels as first one slipped free, then the other, until she was left with nothing between her and Travis but her thin layer of underwear. He cupped her soft center and rose to his feet, his body leaning into hers as he kissed her hard.

Mal felt as though she was drowning, she was falling so far, so fast. But Travis was with her, a buoy in the ocean, and she held on tight. She fumbled with the tails of his shirt, pulling them out of his pants so she could stroke the soft skin on his back, feel the bunch of his muscles when he shifted and moved.

And then he was sliding her skirt over her hips, lifting her with one hand while he worked on the fabric with the other. He ran a finger over her silky underwear, and she felt her entire body leap to attention. She burned, became an inferno, when he dipped a finger inside and found her ready and waiting. Her body responded to his touch like a flower to the sun.

"You are so beautiful," he murmured against her lips, his thumb beginning a slow, intense circle that sent sparks racing over her skin.

"Travis." It was all she could manage as the blood rushed from her head to the center of her body.

"So beautiful. Here." He kissed the spot on her neck just below her ear. Mal felt a tingle race from the spot. "And here." He slipped her shirt down her left arm and pressed a kiss to her shoulder. Goose bumps rose when he tongued the spot and blew. "Here." He ran a thumb over the silk covering her nipple before he sucked it into his mouth. The ivory material of her bra grew wet, transparent, the strawberry color of her nipples showing through when he finally moved again, dropping further down her body. "And here."

He pushed aside the thin strip of fabric between her legs. Mal felt a rush of hot and cold as she was exposed. No longer anything between them. Oh, yes. She wanted this, she so wanted this, but when he lowered his head and placed that first kiss, she froze.

Images of another woman, another workplace, another time tumbled through her mind.

Travis's hands stroked the insides of her thighs, bringing them to rest on his shoulders before he twisted her underwear out of his way. Mal's muscles tensed. "Travis." She tugged on the shoulders of his shirt.

He stopped, his mouth less than an inch from her body and looked up. "Babe?"

She shivered. And though the images faded, they didn't dissipate entirely. She couldn't bear the thought of him doing to her what he'd done to that other woman. "I want you inside me," she told him.

His fingers spasmed on her legs and she knew he wanted to be inside her, too. Good, then maybe he wouldn't question why she still couldn't let him go down on her. He rose to his full height and kissed her. Mal finished opening the buttons on his shirt while his kisses washed away the ugly memories.

She stripped him of his shirt and belt, and slid her hands beneath his waistband to find him hard and wanting. He fumbled for a condom and she took it from his hands, sliding his pants and boxers down his legs before rolling it on. He jerked under her touch.

She soothed him with a long kiss, spreading her legs and shifting to the edge of the bar, so her hips were barely hanging on. Then he slid inside her, filling her, chasing away the last vestiges of other women, anyone who might have come between them before. And as they found their rhythm, bodies meeting in slow, pulsating pleasure, Mal felt something close to peace.

They clung to each other afterward, finding comfort and support in each other's arms. Then Mal lifted her head. "Now show me around your place."

Travis was happy to oblige, and he chatted animatedly about his plans, how he was going to make the gorgeous long bar the centerpiece of the whole space, drawing people in with its glossy top and comfortable stools. How he envisioned it as a high-end pub, bringing back drinks that had gone out of style, making them fresh again. She got caught up in his vision, too.

Or maybe she was just caught up in him. It was

hard to be sure, since she couldn't tell where one ended and the other began. Maybe it didn't matter. So long as he was happy and doing the space proud, she was content.

The restaurant didn't look all that different from how she remembered. A little shabbier, a little dustier since it had been boarded up for so long, but it was still the space she'd known and loved. And although his vision didn't run to the little girl fantasies that came with pink cakes and birthday tiaras, Mal realized she didn't feel sad. It was time for the space to change. And maybe it would be better than ever.

Travis's hand caressed the bar when he talked about it, his other hand running along her arm, her hips, whichever part of her he happened to be touching at the moment in the exact same fashion. "So, what do you think?"

Mal felt a tug in her chest. "I think this will be great." She could picture it, could see it becoming one of the city's hot spots.

"Just the space?"

She paused and didn't answer.

"Too soon?" he asked again.

Mal started to breathe again. "Maybe a little."

"Then we'll pretend I never asked. Now, how about dinner?"

"I still have my meeting at Elephants."

"You never did tell me what that's about."

Since that felt a lot easier to talk about than the swirl of emotions running through her, she gave him the rundown of the upcoming event she was helping plan. The single night when participating bars and restaurants would give all their profits to local homeless shelters and the food bank. "It's a lot of work, but it's so satisfying."

He brushed a lock of hair from her face. "You're amazing."

Mal ducked her head, feeling embarrassed. "I'm getting something out of it too."

"Amazing."

She swallowed. She could get lost in the silvery color of his eyes, lost in the moment, lost in him. But she'd done that before and when she'd lost him, she'd lost some of herself, as well. She felt as though she'd gotten some of that back lately, in part because of Travis, but she refused to let herself go so completely again. Not without some sort of safety net, something that could catch her if she fell. "I really do need to go."

Travis pulled her into a warm hug, burying his face in her hair. "I just need a minute." He inhaled again. "I've missed you so much."

She opened her mouth to say his name, but the words got tangled. Just like her arms around Travis. And she decided to let herself revel in their embrace for the minute that Travis had requested.

A minute that felt as if it ended too soon. "I should go." She took a step back.

"Okay." But Travis's eyes didn't leave hers. She could feel the heat as if he were still wrapped around her.

Mal reveled in that, too. Then realized what she was doing and shook it off. He overwhelmed her. They overwhelmed her. She couldn't let that happen. Not so easily. "I'll call you later."

"After your meeting?"

"It'll run late." They were restaurateurs and bar owners. Evenings didn't end until well after midnight, and they were friends as much as colleagues. Meetings alone tended to run until at least ten.

"I can wait."

Her heart rose into her throat. He meant it, and she didn't think he was just talking about the meeting. He'd wait for her, too. Her cheeks grew warm. "I'll let you know." She gave him a brief kiss and then exited the bar before she did something foolish, like ask if he wanted to come to the meeting, if he wanted to participate in her project.

They were barely back together. She didn't know where things were headed. Involving him in all parts of her life was not a good idea. Yet even the breeze off the ocean didn't cool her desires.

TRAVIS FORCED HIMSELF not to follow Mal, not to chase her down the street and extend their afternoon together. But, no, he had to take it one step at a time.

It seemed they were back together. And she definitely wanted him. And yet, the fact that she'd stopped him when he'd started to pleasure her orally bothered him. That had always been one of Mal's favorites, but twice now she'd insisted on skipping it. He knew why, too—and that didn't make him feel any better. It was a wedge, a reminder of how things had gone wrong before.

Travis knew they couldn't go back and erase the past, but he feared that they might not be able to move beyond it, either. Of course, they were only just back together. Travis didn't expect things to revert to the way they'd been before. And maybe he didn't want them to.

He felt as though he'd done some changing, some growing up in the time they'd been apart. Come to recognize what was important in life and how he maybe hadn't treated those things with the respect they deserved.

So he stayed at The Blue Mermaid, made some notes on the space—where he'd like to start the renovations and what could be salvaged. Things he'd bring up when he met with a few of the contractors this week. He planned to hire one of them before the weekend so they could get started. The idea energized him. Soon enough, the pub would fit his image and would be open to the public.

He hoped Mal would be by his side on opening night.

Travis made a few more notes, then exited The Blue Mermaid, locking the door behind him. The wind kicked up as he walked, reminding him yet again that he wasn't in Aruba anymore. He ducked his chin into the collar of his coat, though the temperature bothered him less than it had even a couple of weeks ago. He was growing used to being back, to being home. It filled him with a sense of completeness. No matter how much he'd enjoyed Aruba—and he'd certainly loved walking the three minutes from his apartment along the beach to his bistro—it hadn't been home.

The idea that he was home now, that this was where he was supposed to be, felt good. He nearly whistled aloud, and realized as he neared the turn to his apartment that he didn't feel like going inside.

Owen's apartment had everything a bachelor could want—flat screen TV, comfortable seats to lounge in, bottles of water, salty snacks—but with no one to share it with, it felt empty. Lonely. And he didn't want to be lonely today.

It was a feeling he hadn't realized had permeated his life until he'd come back to Vancouver. In Aruba, his days and nights had been filled with work. But here, without a staff who needed him and customers who demanded attention, his lack of personal connections was more obvious. It was something he didn't plan to repeat. He pulled his phone out of his pocket and called Owen.

"Owen Ford, at your service."

"Pepperoni pizza and the hockey game tonight. You in?"

"I'm sorry. Who is this?"

"Hilarious." Although Owen's cheerful snort was kind of hilarious. "So, you busy?"

"I'm working."

"Right." Travis was still getting used to the fact that Owen worked six nights a week and actually seemed to enjoy it. Even more surprising was how well it suited him. Travis had never seen Owen happier, and he didn't think it was solely because of his new marriage. He seemed more fulfilled and more sure of himself. Owen had always had confidence, but it was different now. Less surface and more internalized. It was a good look on him. "Maybe we could hang later this week, then?"

"I didn't say you couldn't come hang out with me. Elephants has TVs and I can assure you top-of-the-line service. I have some pull with the owners."

Travis paused. He'd love to see Mal, but he wasn't so sure she'd be thrilled to see him show up while she was working. On the other hand, he wanted to support her event. Maybe even participate if he could pull off the renovations in time. "Mal mentioned something about a meeting there tonight."

"Are you using me to get to my sister? I am hurt, deeply hurt."

Now it was Travis's turn to snort. "Yes, I can tell you're crushed."

"I am. I may require my own pizza. With anchovies."

Travis made a retching sound.

"Fine. No anchovies. And no ordering off the menu. The chef will kill me."

"Oh, is Julia working?"

Owen laughed, "No, but she's trained me well. So, you want to come watch the game here or not?"

He debated internally. Mal shouldn't mind him being in the same area. It wasn't as if he was going to crash her meeting and try to make out with her. He might think about it, but he wouldn't actually follow through. And maybe they could have that late dinner once she was finished with business. He was always up for a second dinner. "See you around six, buddy."

He showed up at five. Travis didn't see any reason to continue walking the familiar downtown neighborhoods. If Owen was busy, Travis was certainly capable of entertaining himself until his friend was free. And maybe Mal would show up early for her meeting and he could steal a few moments.

"Travis." Owen greeted him as soon as he walked through the door and welcomed him with a hearty handshake. "You're early."

"Don't let me interrupt. I'll grab a seat."

"That's the best spot." Owen indicated a booth off to the side that had a good view of the TVs without being in the heart of the lounge. "What can I bring you?"

"Just water." His stomach growled. "Is there pizza on your menu?"

Owen laughed and clapped him on the shoulder. "Yes. Julia and the chef tried to fight me, said it wasn't high class enough. So I told them to make it fancy. You've got your choice of pears and Camembert, sweet potato and goat cheese, or pancetta, figs and Brie."

"Pancetta," Travis answered immediately. "It's almost like bacon."

"Fancy bacon, but don't let Julia hear you say that." Owen grinned. "She gets a little heated up about food."

"Noted." Travis grabbed a seat in the booth Owen had indicated, his eyes scanning the half-full room for Mal. He didn't actually expect she'd be here yet, but he figured it didn't hurt to look.

"She's not here," Owen said when he plopped down beside Travis and shoved a bottle of water in front of him.

"Who?" Travis played dumb, which didn't fool anyone. "When will she be here?"

Owen shrugged. "Seven? You can go upstairs and ask her if you really want to know."

Travis considered it. "You don't think that would be pushing?"

"Yes."

"Feel free to think about it before answering." Travis cracked open the water bottle and took a sip.

Owen took a slug from his own bottle, then said, "You chased her into the kitchen during dinner at my parents' place. I rest my case."

"That was one time."

"And you're scanning the bar like a hunter searching for prey."

Travis realized that wasn't far from the truth and stopped. "I can be cool."

"Not around my sister, you can't." Owen clapped him on the shoulder. "Hey, I was sorry to hear about your gram. I know how close you were."

Travis swallowed another glug from his bottle. "Thanks. It helped having Mal there."

"I know." Owen clapped his shoulder again. "I'm glad she was."

"Me, too."

"Do you want to talk about it?"

Travis looked at him. "Are we having a moment?"

Owen didn't laugh. "If you want."

It touched him, the sincerity that Owen offered. "Thanks. But I'm okay. I think I'd like to just feel normal for a night."

"Understood." Owen's finger squeezed Travis's shoulder in a show of support before letting go. "But if you ever want to bond over ice cream and a chick flick…I am so in."

Travis punched him in the arm. "I see marriage hasn't helped your sense of humor."

"Grace likes it." Owen grinned. "You should try it."

The idea of sharing a life with Mal appealed to him. "It's not the worst idea you've ever had." He sent Owen a look. "That would be those frosted tips."

"I was young."

"You were twenty-five and old enough to know better."

"You were blond, too," Owen pointed out as they'd both gone through an unfortunate bleaching period in their youth.

"Yes, but I pulled it off."

"You keep telling yourself that."

"I will if you will."

Owen lifted his water bottle and tapped it against Travis's. "Deal. Now let's eat some pizza and pretend you actually came here to see me and not my sister."

"I came to see you," Travis defended himself.

"So, if I tell you she just walked in you won't—"

"Where?"

"—ditch me?" Owen chuckled. "You are so busted. Also, I lied. She's not here yet."

"Evil."

"Sneaky. There's a difference. But maybe you should consider it."

Travis looked at him. "What? Ditching you? Where do I sign up?"

"Well, there is that…" Owen faked a cough. "Meeting about the charity event tonight. Cough, cough."

"You think I should sit in?"

"That's brilliant, Travis." Owen opened his eyes wide. "How did you think of that all on your own?"

"I seriously wonder why we're friends."

"Because you'd be lost without me." Owen pulled out his phone and began tapping on the screen. A moment later, Travis's phone vibrated in his pocket. "Get informed. Impress her."

"You act like you think I need help."

"I'm going to choose not to answer that."

"But we're gonna watch the game." He didn't want to be the kind of person who ignored their friends for a new—or not-so-new—relationship.

"There will be plenty more games, buddy." Owen grinned. "Anyway, aside from getting to hang out with my sister, the event might be a good test or a soft opening for your new place, if you can get ready in time."

Travis blinked. "That's actually a really good idea."

"You don't have to sound so surprised. Bad enough I still get it from Donovan, though he's shown marked improvement lately."

"Not what I meant." Travis shook his head. "I just hadn't thought past the renovations." But he'd need a test run before a grand opening and something controlled, like a charity event, could be just the right fit. And any kinks would be more easily forgiven since it was for a good cause. Excitement buzzed through him. "You think Mal would go for it?"

"I don't see why not. Doesn't hurt to ask."

CHAPTER ELEVEN

MAL SPENT TWO hours in her office preparing for that night's meeting and handling the few issues that had arisen while she'd been with Travis at The Blue Mermaid. Although the charity event was still a couple of months away, organization was ramping up. There were media to contact, promotional materials to distribute, tickets to sell and the actual day's set of requirements to arrange. So Mal had scheduled weekly meetings, which would probably become more frequent as the event neared.

Not everyone participating needed to attend every meeting, but as the head of the organization, Mal did. Which was good. It gave her something to do. Something more than sitting at home alone, begging her new sister-in-law to meet her for a late session of Pilates or going to a late session of Pilates on her own. Although she supposed she had Travis to fill some of that time now.

The thought sent a warm curl of pleasure through her even as she reminded herself that she wasn't going to shape her whole life around another person. She would carve out some space for him, but she would have her own things too. Like Pilates and dinner with Grace, and the charity event. Maybe that had been part of their earlier problems. They'd been so wrapped up in each other that when outside life intruded they hadn't been able to handle it. Definitely a thought that bore consideration, though not tonight.

She should go down to Elephants and make sure Owen had set aside the table she'd requested. The one in the corner so the group could work without upsetting the after-work vibe of the rest of the patrons. She'd already pre-ordered some appies and other nibbles so they could eat while they worked. She'd discovered during an earlier meeting that ideas seemed to flourish and efficiency improved when there was food available. Plus, it was conducive to discussing menu trends they were considering for their own places.

Mal spent another twenty minutes in her office and then went down to Elephants. The place was already full of patrons eager to watch the hockey game. Mal was only a casual fan, but even she knew that tonight's game was important and could determine whether the team made the playoffs or not. She hoped the other attendees wouldn't be too distracted.

She took a seat at the table and unloaded her

laptop and tablet, getting everything set up before the committee or the food arrived. One of the servers swung by and dropped off her usual, a glass of soda water with a twist of lime. Mal hadn't even taken a sip when someone picked it up and took it from her.

No, not someone. Travis.

"Delicious."

Her face flushed as she was reminded of their afternoon together. How she probably still smelled of him and sex. "What are you doing here? Besides drinking my water." She reached out, waiting for him to return it to her. Instead, he took her hand and kissed her palm. Heat sizzled through her.

"I missed you."

"It's been two hours." She pulled her hand back.

"So you've been counting." Travis took a seat beside her.

Mal was grateful that she'd chosen to push together a group of hightops to make one large table where her guests would each have their own chair, rather than using one of the oversized booths. She had no doubt that Travis would have pushed right up next to her in a booth. He was practically doing that in the chairs. "It hardly requires counting. What are you doing here, Travis? I told you I have a meeting."

"I know." He smiled at her.

"Well?" she asked when that seemed to be his only response.

"I thought I might join the committee."

"Oh." She hadn't considered that. "I'm not sure you're the right fit." His place wasn't even ready. While she appreciated the thought, they were trying to raise money and awareness with this event.

"Do you still have a lot of work to do before the big day?"

"Yes." Too much, though Mal knew she'd find a way to get it done; she always did.

"Then I'm the right fit." He leaned forward and Mal felt her temperature go up another notch. Whether it was the heat his body was kicking off like a furnace or those arousing fragments of this afternoon coming back to her, Mal wasn't sure. Didn't matter. She was warm, she needed water and Travis had drunk most of hers. "I'm here to do whatever you need."

"Then stop flirting."

"Why? Is it working?" The corner of his mouth turned up and laughter flashed in his eyes. Mal swallowed and told herself he didn't look appealing. Not at all. And she was sticking to that story. At least until her meeting was over.

"This isn't a joke. The event is something I and the committee take very seriously."

"I'm taking it seriously. Very seriously." He

leaned forward so his lips were barely an inch from hers.

Mal felt a hitch in her chest and leaned back. She wanted to kiss him. She wanted to do more than kiss him, but not now. Not when the rest of her committee was due to walk in any second and would see him sitting with her, leaning into her, sexing her up with his eyes.

"So, do you want to give me a proper welcome to the committee?" Travis reached out and stroked the back of her hand. Her skin tingled. "We make a good team."

They did. They always had. His finger lay across her hand, the tanned skin a direct contrast to her working-indoors-all-winter paleness. "You can stay for the meeting," she told him and moved her hand.

Travis moved it back and left it there even when the rest of the committee started to arrive.

TRAVIS SPENT THE rest of the week dealing with contractors during the day and Mal at night. He definitely preferred the nights.

Though, on this fine Sunday morning, he was flying solo at his own place. Mal had needed to do some work at the office this morning and he needed to do laundry. Not glamorous, but necessary.

Of course, when his phone rang he practically leaped to answer it. "Hello?"

"Finally." Sara's cheerful voice came over the line. "I've been trying to reach you for days. We need to celebrate the purchase of your new space. Brunch today?"

Travis didn't hesitate in responding to his real estate agent. "Yes, please." And not just because he didn't feel like doing laundry. He'd just drop off the clothing at a dry cleaners and buy some new underwear.

"Wonderful. And we can talk about getting you an apartment at the same time."

Right, they had briefly discussed that when looking at spaces for his business. But that had been before Mal. "I might need to hold off on that."

"Oh?" Sara's voice rose at the end, her interest clear even over the phone. "I expect you to fill me in over brunch. I was thinking of Sophie's."

"How about Elephants?" If Travis was going to spend his money at a local establishment, he'd prefer it go to the Fords' place.

"Eleven?"

"See you then." He hung up, his morning looking a whole lot brighter. Skipping out on laundry could do that to a person.

He headed for Elephants, wondering if he might be able to convince Mal to join him and Sara. She'd already be on site at her office, and she needed to eat anyway. But when he called, it went to her voice mail. So he left what he thought was an awfully charming message inviting her to come down.

The sun beat down, actually feeling warm as he walked the last block to Elephants. He was finally acclimating to the new, nontropical weather. But when he pulled open the huge wooden door, the coolness of the interior swept over him. And it was full, as he'd suspected.

Plenty of people were recovering from the previous night, which was obvious from their hunched shoulders and bleary eyes. But there were plenty of other brunchers who'd obviously been up for hours and had probably already completed the trek up and down The Grouse Grind, a hiking trail that basically went straight up the side of a mountain.

Travis looked for Owen, but didn't see him or any of the Fords. He did, however, spot a pair of chairs at the bar and snagged them before someone else did as there were no tables currently available. He didn't mind sitting there. In fact, he enjoyed it as it offered the chance to people watch and talk to the bartender about the industry.

Conversation was at a low hum, the industry's version of being out for a Sunday drive, but servers were hopping as they doled out omelets, breakfast wraps, hamburgers, water and coffee—and Caesars for those choosing a little hair of the dog. Travis saw people in what looked like last night's clothing—tight jeans and T-shirts that mimicked tattoos, heels and low-cut tops—as well as those who'd probably gotten a good night's rest. They wore yoga pants with matching hoodies, sneakers and casual sweaters and their eyes were bright instead of tired. It was a good mix of people.

He kept an eye on the door, flagging Sara down when she entered wearing yoga gear, her blond hair tied back in a ponytail. They chatted about his plans for the bar as they ate their food—a veggie omelet with home fries and a giant coffee for him. Yogurt with granola and fresh fruit, and herbal tea for her.

"Now, what about an apartment," Sara said, dabbing her mouth with a napkin as their plates were cleared. "You mentioned you wanted to be close to your bar?"

"Yeah, about that." Travis swirled the coffee in his mug. "I think I might need to wait before pulling the trigger."

"Oh?" Sara raised an eyebrow at him.

"My previous needs have altered."

She continued to watch him with that raised eyebrow. "Are you looking to work with someone else? Because I can recommend another agent."

"No." Travis was quick to answer. "Not at all. I want to work with you." Her blond eyebrow lowered. "I'm just not sure that a one bedroom will be sufficient."

The confusion on Sara's face cleared. "You met someone."

"Re-met," Travis clarified. It felt good saying it.

"Well, fill me in."

Travis looked at her. "You sure you want to hear all this?" He felt close to Sara, as she'd helped him reach the dream of ownership in Vancouver, but he didn't expect she would feel the same about him. She must have lots of clients, and while it was good business to keep a positive relationship, Travis didn't think that extended to him rhapsodizing over the awesomeness that was Mal—even if Sara was being polite by sounding interested.

"Are you kidding? I live for this. It's been years since I felt the butterflies of a new relationship. Or a reestablished one," she amended.

"Married?"

"Five years." She flashed the elegant silver band on her left hand. "So let me live vicariously through you. If you don't mind me prying."

They talked until Travis's coffee was gone and there was no water left in the small teapot for Sara to freshen up her cup. She gave him a big hug when she rose to leave. "You promise you'll stay in touch, even if you aren't buying a home?"

"Of course." Travis figured he would have liked Sara even if she wasn't a barracuda when it came to negotiations. "And you can expect an invitation when the bar opens."

"With free drinks." Sara grinned, ever the negotiator.

"Until you're under the table or wearing a lampshade."

She threw back her head and laughed. "Sold."

Travis ordered another coffee after she left. He didn't have anything to rush home to and maybe Mal would be answering her phone by now. But when he called, it went to voice mail again.

He turned his attention to the early season baseball game on TV and chatted to the bartender who was finally able to catch her breath after the morning rush. "You're friends with Owen," she said as she wiped the bar, her eyes scanning to make sure no one required her services.

"Guilty as charged. I'm Travis."

"Stef." She held out her hand.

"Nice to meet you, Stef." She was good at what she did, smooth and friendly, but Travis noted she was ready to respond to a customer's need almost instantly. "I'm actually going to be opening my own place soon."

"Whereabouts?" She wiped the bar down.

"Gastown. In a couple of months. If you know anyone looking, I'll be hiring soon."

"I'll pass the word along."

"I'll also be looking for a bar manager. If you're interested."

Stef paused in her wipe-down to look at him. Her eyes flicked past him. "I appreciate the offer, but I have a job."

Travis had a sudden prickling sensation along the back of his neck. "Owen's standing behind me, isn't he?"

"Yep."

Owen cleared his throat. "I cannot believe you're trying to poach my employees."

Julia joined them and poked Owen in the shoulder. "You mean how you poached Stef from me." She turned to Stef. "I still haven't decided if I've forgiven you." She poked Owen again. "You either."

Travis caught Stef's eye and said, "You could leave all this behind…"

"She's not leaving." Owen bellied up to the bar and flashed Stef his best smile. "You'd never leave me in the lurch, would you, Stef?"

She lifted one shoulder and looked at Travis. "What's the pay? I have student loans to think about."

Owen slapped a palm on the bar. "Fine. You get a raise." He slapped the same palm on Travis's shoulder. "And you're coming with us. Before I end up with no staff."

Travis checked over his shoulder and saw Donovan and Grace settling into a booth, but his eyes barely skimmed across them before stopping on Mal. She was slipping into the curved bench seat beside the pair, her skirt sliding up her legs and exposing all that smooth pink skin. He swallowed and allowed Owen to steer him over to the large booth. It would be rude to refuse to join the Fords.

"Look who I found." Owen proudly announced their arrival and then ducked down to give his wife a kiss.

"Travis. What a lovely surprise." Grace was effortlessly, eternally polite, always overlaying it with a warmth that added sincerity. She rose to give him a quick hug. Donovan shook his hand while everyone sorted out their seats until the only person he hadn't officially greeted was Mal. Not that he was standing on ceremony.

He slid in beside her, her scent filling his head. "Hi."

"Hello." The word was careful, as was her gaze, which met his only briefly before returning to her lap. She clasped her hands together.

He leaned down so his lips were nearly on her ear. "I thought you were working this morning."

"I was." She smiled up at him. He felt the butterflies Sara had mentioned flutter through him and he wanted to kiss her. Who cared that her family was here, not to mention half the city? "I still am."

"This is work?" Travis looked around to find four interested gazes turned his way. Great. Now they were entertainment, and apparently rather humorous as the four of them were smiling. He smiled back. "Are Evelyn and Gus coming?"

"No, they don't know we're meeting." Donovan's head swiveled to the door as though, just by mentioning it, he might have summoned them. "We'd appreciate it if you didn't mention it, either."

Julia snorted. "Yes, Donovan. Because the first thing he's going to do is call them and report that he saw us." Donovan grinned and kissed his wife hard.

Owen groaned. "Stop. We're in public."

"Like that's ever stopped you?" Julia tugged Donovan's arm around her shoulder.

"No, but I can pull it off. I'm charming." Owen jerked a thumb at Donovan. "This guy? Not so much."

"He has charm you don't appreciate." Julia was grinning.

"That's right." Donovan looked plenty pleased with himself and not at all annoyed by Owen's teasing. It surprised Travis. "You're no longer the only charming Ford, Owen."

"Yeah, but I'm still the *most* charming."

"I think that might be up for discussion," Grace murmured, which caused Owen to laugh.

Travis looked at Mal, delighted to be included in the family gathering and even more delighted to find her watching him with a slightly puzzled expression. He leaned closer. "Everything okay?" He spoke quietly while the good-natured joking continued at the table.

"Fine." She flashed a smile that didn't quite reach her eyes. "Why wouldn't it be?"

"I don't know." He studied her. She looked good, her dark hair loose around her shoulders. He wanted to run his hands through it, rub the slippery strands between his fingers. She loved it when he stroked her hair. Maybe he could do it casually so no one would notice. He stretched his arm around the back of the booth, hovering just above Mal's shoulders. "So why are you all out for brunch this morning?"

The Fords were a close family, but their get-togethers generally happened later in the day, over dinner, since for so many years one or another of them was involved in the day-to-day operations of the family holdings, which meant they'd been up late working the night before.

"Anniversary." Mal leaned back so his hand brushed against her shoulder. "My parents have been married forty years this June."

"And still in love." Travis curled a finger,

catching a tress of Mal's hair, feeling the silky strands slip against his skin.

"They are. Which is something to celebrate."

They looked at each other for a moment, and for Travis the moment was fraught with meaning. He'd once been so certain that he and Mal would celebrate many happy years of marriage, that their kids might one day plan and hold an anniversary party for them.

Then she looked away, a light flush on her cheeks, which caused Travis to wonder if her thoughts had been at all dissimilar from his own. "We're planning."

"And doling out jobs," Owen announced.

Mal nodded. "So no one would be offended if you made an excuse and skipped out."

Like hell. Travis reached over with his other hand to touch her arm. "I'd like to stay."

He saw the bob of her throat. She didn't pull her hand away. "Okay. But if you don't like the task you get assigned, remember that you had your opportunity to bolt."

Travis lowered his arm so that it no longer hovered over her shoulders but rested on them. He waited until she looked at him, those huge dark eyes focused on him as though he was the only person in the world. Then he bent his head so no one else could hear. "I'm not going anywhere, Mal. I'm here to stay. Forever."

Her eyes flicked down at his last word, but only for a moment. She looked back. "I'm beginning to think you mean that."

He leaned forward and put his lips right up to her ear. He heard her short inhalation of breath, felt the curve of her body against his. "I do mean it."

She turned her head. Their lips were mere millimeters from meeting, her hand still clasped his and the moment was right.

"All right." Owen slapped his hands on the table. "I officially call this meeting to order and name myself president."

And suddenly the moment wasn't so right. But Travis didn't mind. He would find another moment. Or make one. Whatever it took. "I call vice president," he said, knowing job titles would go fast and he didn't want to be left with last pick.

And suddenly everyone was calling for positions, each one more grandiose than the last until they were all satisfied.

"As president of festivities, I now declare this meeting is in session." Owen tapped his finger against the side of his glass.

The rest of them—CEO of planning, global director of dessert and beverages, executive financier, prom committee head and vice president of scouting—all straightened to attention. Or pretended to.

"Our first order of business, location. Who's got ideas? Go."

"I think Elephants is an obvious choice," Donovan said.

"And that's why you're executive financier. Next?"

Julia laughed while Donovan shook his head.

"What about my place?" Travis offered.

"That apartment is still mine," Owen pointed out. "At best, you'd be deemed a squatter."

"He means his bar," Mal explained.

"Oh, I like that idea." Grace, aka CEO of planning, jumped in. Travis assumed that everyone else then turned to listen to her. But he couldn't be sure, as he was still looking at Mal and she was looking back.

She was giving him the secret smile that said they'd joke about this later, that for the next couple of months, whenever the opportunity arose, she'd call him a squatter and he'd have some witty response that would make them both laugh. And a year from now, when the joke had passed its best-before date, something would happen and they'd both make the joke and then appreciate how nice it was to be with someone who got you.

Travis reached for her hand with the one that wasn't currently playing with her hair, wrapped his fingers around hers and just enjoyed the connection while the hum of conversation went on around them. The dynamic rise and fall of voices as ideas were suggested and thrown out or expanded on, the burst of laughter when something was particularly humorous. He only had eyes for Mal, and their eyes never left each other, their bodies shifted to fit against each other until there was no space left between them.

Travis declined the invite to attend the family dinner that night at Gus and Evelyn's, even though he wanted to say yes. Mal had promised to call him later and he really did need to work on his plans for the bar if he was going to have it finished in time for both the charity event and the anniversary party.

He told himself not to get too excited about his inclusion on the anniversary party planning. But it was hard not to. Hard not to feel that things were falling into place.

His thoughts on the bar were coming together nicely, too. After reviewing the proposals from three contractors, he placed them in order and made a call to the one at the top of his list. He didn't expect anyone to answer, but after looking things over, he knew this was the one he wanted to work with and he didn't want to wait another minute to offer him the job. He was thrilled when not only did the contractor answer, but he happily accepted the job and suggested he could have a crew in place to begin work on Wednesday.

Deal in place, Travis suddenly felt edgy. Maybe *eager* was a better word. He wanted to share the news, to celebrate. But the only person he wanted to celebrate with was at a family dinner and he wasn't about to crash that. He glanced at the clock, then out the window at the darkening sky.

The Fords would be finished eating, probably still sitting around the table, laughing, sharing and bonding. They'd be leaving soon, the children and their spouses returning to their own little nests of shared living. All except Mal—she'd be going home alone.

Travis saw no reason why she shouldn't have her own partner to come home to. He scooped up his keys, not bothering with a coat. He was too warm, too primed, for another layer. And it was just one more layer between him and Mal—layers he was doing his best to peel away. No point in adding to the mix unnecessarily.

The cool evening air slid around him. He barely felt it. Or maybe he didn't want to feel it. He didn't want anything to talk him out of his idea or his mission of winning back Mallory Ford.

He was out of breath by the time he reached her building, but that was less about the cold and the fact that he'd pretty much run the entire way there, and more that this felt big. Bigger than the other times he'd visited. Bigger than signing up to help with the charity event or lend a hand with her parents' anniversary party.

Travis punched in the code for her apartment. If she didn't answer, he'd just wait. There was the coffee place down the block that was open until midnight. He didn't need to worry.

"Travis." She'd clearly checked the closed-circuit camera before answering. Her voice curled around him.

Before he even got a chance to say anything he heard the click of the building's door, the buzz announcing that she was granting him access. He hoped it was to more than just her building.

It took less than a minute to ride the elevator to her floor. She was waiting for him, standing in the door frame of her apartment. He could see every breath she took, the steady rise and fall of her chest and the slow blink of her eyes. The way she looked at him through her lashes. Adrenaline flooded his system. This was how it was supposed be. Them. Together.

Travis walked faster. He didn't say anything. And when he reached the door, he reached for Mal, cupping her face in his hands. Her eyes fluttered shut, the black lashes a sharp contrast to her pale skin. But he didn't kiss her, not even when her lips seemed to instinctively pout at him, begging him for his touch.

"Mal?" His voice was a whisper. A barely there question that shimmered between them.

She opened her eyes and looked at him. He felt their connection like a jolt. "You came." As if she hadn't been sure.

"Always." He'd always come back for her.

"I want to believe that."

"Then believe it." He walked her backward into the apartment, still holding her face. "I'm here now. I'm not going anywhere."

She lifted her hands to rest on top of his. "I know."

Travis heard the "but," even though she didn't say it, and he didn't fill it in for her. "I love you." He heard her breath catch, felt the hitch in her step. "You know that, too, don't you?"

Mal just stared at him, and for a second Travis feared she was going to say no. That he'd pushed a little too soon. That he'd scared her. Then she nodded. Slowly. "I do."

Sweet relief spilled through him. "I love you." Because he had to say it again. He pushed the door shut with his foot. The click seemed to be a final point, a sign that they were moving forward and putting the past behind them, behind that closed door where it would no longer peek out at them, sticking its fingers where they didn't belong.

He kissed her, lifting her to her toes so she was

pressed against him. She slipped her hands along his, down his arms, exploring their length before looping her arms close behind his neck.

Travis flicked the lock closed on her front door and then carried her into the bedroom. It was a long time before he finally caught his breath enough to tell her the good news about hiring a contractor.

MAL FOUND HERSELF smiling at the oddest moments. When she was reviewing the details for the charity event. When her mom asked if she preferred chicken or pork for Sunday dinner. When the Pilates instructor took them into Side Twist on the Mat, which was no Open Leg Rocker. But mostly when she thought of Travis, which was always, hence the random smiling.

"You seem happy," Grace said as they left the gym together, entering the sunshiny morning.

Mal blinked, surprised. She was happy, but she didn't think—random smiling aside—that she was behaving all that differently in general. "I am happy. Things are good."

Grace looked at her as they paused on the street corner, waiting for the light to change. The traffic rushed by, cars, trucks, cyclists and pedestrians. "Things with Travis?"

"That's part of it." She wouldn't lie and say that their newly realized relationship wasn't part of her cheerful attitude, but it was more than her relationship with him. She felt like a complete person, a full package.

"Sparrow would say you seem self-actualized. Growing into your full potential. It looks good on you."

A light blush of pleasure warmed Mal's cheeks. "It *feels* good." But then everything did these day. The way her rain shower head beat down, massaging her shoulders, the way food tasted, how both the charity event and her parents' anniversary party were coming together so easily. Maybe she was just in a better place to appreciate things these days. She supposed it didn't matter why, just that it was.

It was also the way she was trying to treat this newfound connection with Travis. It wasn't the same as before. It could never be the same, but that didn't mean it was better or worse. Simply different. As they were both different.

"I'm glad you gave him a chance."

"Me, too." They stepped off the curb together, crossing to the opposite side of the street and entering the small, cheerful café that catered to the gym crowd. Along with coffee of every size, flavor and calorie, they offered eggs, quinoa salads, kefir smoothies and other meal choices designed specifically to thank your body after a hard workout.

The café smelled of roast coffee and fresh pastries, which filled a glass case at the front. Mal eyed them as they passed, promising herself a raspberry tart for completing the Side Twist on the Mat without even complaining in her head.

"So, you worked out what happened before?" Grace asked as they settled at a table in the corner. Neither of them bothered picking up the menus since they always ordered the same things.

Mal felt a little hiccup in the region of her chest, but she breathed through it. "We did." Which wasn't entirely true—they just hadn't talked about it. But he'd said he loved her and although she hadn't replied aloud, she knew her actions told him she felt the same. And they'd talked about why he'd hidden their breakup from his family, which was a start. But they didn't need to talk about the reasons behind their breakup or why she still wouldn't let him pleasure her orally, right? She was okay and he was okay, so they were okay.

"I'm glad." Grace folded her hands in front of her. "I think it'll make your relationship stronger, going through this."

Mal swallowed and stuffed down the hurt that tried to rise up just from talking about it. *It was over.* Travis had come back to her. That was enough. But her lungs felt tight and she focused on the Pilates breathing that had seemed so easy only thirty minutes earlier.

"Are you okay?"

"Fine." Mal practically choked on the word. "We're back together and everything is fine."

Grace nodded slowly.

"As for the other stuff," she waved a hand, "I just feel like it's all better left in the past. It'll just bring up hurt feelings." The fact that Travis hadn't been there for her—that he'd had another woman in his arms an hour after their official breakup—well, that wasn't worth talking about. Her brothers would be angry. So would her parents. And it would confuse her own feelings. So, really, sweeping it all to the side was the best way to move forward. Best for everyone.

Grace didn't speak, just cocked her head to the side and studied her. Mal tried not to shift under her insightful gaze. Grace had seen plenty of relationships, often at their most stressful times, as couples orchestrated their wedding day, and she well knew the ones that could handle the strain and the ones that snapped. Maybe not immediately, but at some point. When there just wasn't enough something there. Love, respect, compromise. Maybe all of those and more.

Mal ignored the shiver that ran a cold finger along the back of her neck. She and Travis had had all of that. They'd walked through trouble and still come out together. Okay, so it had taken a long time and more than a year of living apart, but they'd gotten there in their own time.

She wasn't sure she wanted to think any deeper than that.

"It's not stuff, Mal." Grace's voice was gentle, but her eyes were insistent. "It's important. You didn't just break up for no reason."

No, they'd broken up because she'd needed to come back to Vancouver permanently. Because when she'd needed him, he'd chosen business. But that was then. Things were different now, right?

"Have you and Travis talked about what happened?"

Mal swallowed, trying to down the stone that had suddenly lodged itself in her throat. It didn't move. "I don't see the need to dwell in the past."

Was her voice croaky? Or did it just sound that way in her head? She gave a small cough in an attempt to clear it.

"I don't either." Grace's face was composed, but then she wasn't the one reliving an incredibly painful scene from her past. "Just so long as you're not ignoring it."

"Why? Do you think we'll be doomed to repeat it?" She tried to play it off as a laugh, but the stone dropped into her stomach. She was awash in heavy materials that threatened to weigh her down, to tug her head under.

"I think doomed is a little dramatic." And Grace's easy smile went a long way toward appeasing Mal's concerns. "I'll support whatever you choose, but I wouldn't be a good friend if I didn't mention it. I do think that what happened was powerful. Powerful enough that it split you apart for over a year."

"Because we were living on opposite sides of the continent." They hadn't even shared the same landmass. And she knew just how much Travis had longed for a place of his own, how proud he'd been of achieving it. She hadn't been able to take that away from him, couldn't ask that of him.

"That's not why you weren't together." Grace reached over and patted her hand. "I'm glad to see you happy and I want you to stay that way. But these types of things have a tendency to come up if they're never really dealt with."

Mal was sure that Grace had actual empirical evidence. She'd seen couples who, in the midst of planning what should have been a celebration to start their lives together, imploded, spewing hurt and fear all over each other, against each other, instead of standing with each other. "So you don't think I've dealt with it."

"I don't know. I do know that you've kept it all a secret from your family when you generally share everything."

"I didn't want to ruin the friendship between

Travis and Owen." It was her standard line—
the one she'd been repeating to herself since the
breakup.

"I don't think that's the only reason."

Mal didn't think so, either, but it was an un-
comfortable thought and one she didn't feel like
analyzing in a café. Or maybe anywhere.

"We don't need to talk about it." Grace gave
her hand another comforting pat. "But I'm always
around to listen."

Always. It seemed as though Mal was hearing
that word a lot these days. She nodded. "I appreciate your concern, but it's unfounded." She put
in a little effort to ensure her voice sounded firm
and confident, more so than her quivering insides
might indicate. "I'm fine. Everything with Travis
is fine." She even managed a smile, though unlike
the ones earlier, this one felt weak and forced, as
though it would slip off her lips if she dropped
her guard for even a moment.

And Mal wondered if she'd traded one type of
hurt for another. She looked at the table for a moment, her eyes following the grain of the wood,
the corners that had been rounded slightly to prevent scraping or injury. She was feeling a little
scraped herself.

Had she been right in the first place? To block
Travis out of her life completely? Because it
felt as if it was all or nothing. Either they were

together or they could never be in the same room at the same time again. The cold finger traced down her spine this time, followed by the fearful thump of her heart.

Did Grace think she was making a mistake? Would everyone agree? Was she?

Mal looked at Grace and she could feel the little furrow between her eyes. "You didn't say anything to Owen, did you?" She had this sudden image of her brother storming over to see Travis. Demanding redress as though her honor was at stake and her marriageable status ruined.

"No." Grace's voice didn't waver. "I've kept that between us and I'll continue to do so."

Mal eased out a breath. At least she wouldn't have to worry about Owen going to battle on her behalf. She knew her brother well enough to know he wouldn't back down even though Travis could hold him off with one hand and pummel him with the other.

"But, Mal." Mal looked up into Grace's clear blue eyes. There was worry there and a shade of disappointment that didn't sit well. "I think you need to consider why you're keeping it a secret. Why you're hiding it if you are truly past it. And who are you hiding it from?"

The fact that Grace's tone never rose, never filled with an impassioned plea, only made her words all the more powerful. And Mal wondered if the person she'd really been hiding from was herself.

CHAPTER TWELVE

TRAVIS WAS HAVING a good week, a good month. In fact, it was shaping up to be a good year. He'd been invited back to dinner with the Ford family twice by Mal. And he'd spent most nights in her bed as well as her arms.

He hadn't dared to dream when he'd decided to come back to Vancouver that things would end up this way, but he wasn't one to question his good fortune. No, he was a man to appreciate what had come to him and enjoy it to its full advantage. Which meant back massages and new coffeemakers, pancakes in bed and whispered words under the cover of night.

Mal hadn't said the words yet, but Travis sensed they were coming, that they were working their way toward him, and after all that had passed, he was content to wait. They'd only been back together a few short weeks, there was no need to rush. They had an entire lifetime ahead of them.

Travis rode up the elevator to Mal's apartment after work. She still hadn't given him his own key or fob swipe to enter the building, but he sensed it would be soon, too. Everything was heading that way.

He was dusty from being on site all day and there was a hole in the hem of his jeans where it had gotten caught on a nail. But he had clothes stored at Mal's, and after a quick shower he'd be ready to go.

"Hello, babe." He pulled her into his arms and gave her a long and thorough kiss.

She squirmed for a moment. "Travis. You're getting me all dirty." Then she wrapped her arms around him and kissed him back.

"You dry clean all your suits, anyway," he pointed out and then kissed her again.

"Not after one wearing." But she didn't look upset and she didn't let go, either. "And you got it on my hands and face, too."

"Oh, no." Travis pretended concern. "Guess you'll have to join me in the shower to wash off."

"All part of your evil plan?" she asked as he steered them down the hall toward the clean white tile of her master bathroom.

"I wouldn't say evil. More like inspired." He kissed her once more and then proceeded to strip both of them out of their clothes.

He washed her thoroughly. It was only right, considering he was the reason she had to take a shower in the first place. And as the warm water ran down his body and Mal melted against him, sated and satisfied, he felt his heart expand. There was so much joy, so much love, he sometimes felt as if he couldn't contain it. But every time he wondered if there was too much to handle, more space seemed to open up. It wasn't a finite chamber, but one that swelled and grew to admit all the love he gave and received.

And as he lay in bed that night, his belly full of Chinese takeout, his arms full of Mal and his heart full of happiness, he wondered if it really was possible for one man to be so lucky. If it wasn't, he didn't want to think about it, didn't want to tarnish this great gift he'd been given.

"Babe?" His lips barely moved, pressed against the crown of her head.

"Hmm?" Mal shifted. Her body was heavy against his, weighted with sleep, as was her voice.

"I love you."

She didn't answer, but he felt her smile and she snuggled more closely against him. For now, that was enough. Travis felt his heart grow a little larger. "I think we should get married."

Clearly, this was what they had been moving toward and Travis saw no point in waiting. He loved her. He knew she loved him, even if she'd yet to verbally confirm it.

He felt her jerk beside him, her whole body growing stiff. "Pardon?"

"I love you." He looked into her eyes, loving what he saw there. Loving her. "I want to spend the rest of my life with you, starting now."

She blinked at him in the dim light. "Are you serious?"

"Yes. I'm not joking." Though he supposed he should have actually bought a ring before popping the question. He *had* a ring. One he'd purchased back before they'd ever broken up. But he didn't want to use that ring. It was the old them and they were starting fresh. He hoped. "I told you that I wanted to start our lives together."

"I didn't think you meant tonight." He noticed that she still hadn't said yes. Of course, she hadn't said no, either...

"Why not?" He ignored the ache circling his chest, pressing down and preventing him from drawing a full breath.

"Because." She ran a hand through her hair. "Just because."

"Why wait?" His gram's death had taught him that life could be short. Okay, fine. His gram had lived to a ripe old age, but there were things he still hadn't done with her. Things he'd missed out on. He wouldn't let that happen with Mal. A sentiment his gram would have loved.

"Travis." She was trying to look strong, but he saw the quiver of her lower lip. He wanted to kiss it away, but he was still waiting on that yes. "You can't just spring this on me."

"I'm not." Because while he might not have put together the list of details, ensuring a trail of flower petals or whatever it was that Mal thought should be part of a proposal, he felt as though they'd been working toward this moment ever since Owen's wedding. "Can you honestly say this comes as a surprise? Did you really think I didn't mean marriage when I said I loved you?"

Her eyes darted to the side. "No, but we've only been back together a little while."

"It's long enough."

She looked back at him. He could see the uncertainty in her gaze. She wanted to say yes, he could see the hope flashing out, but it was marred by something else, something that made his insides cold and he reached for her hands.

"I'm all in, Mal."

"I know."

"Are *you*?" The words nearly stuck in his throat, but he forced them out. He needed to know, needed her to admit that this was more than just dating, more than just seeing if they could work things out. This was all or nothing.

She tilted her head. "Are you sure this isn't just because of your grandma's death?"

"It's not." He gave her hands a tug for emphasis. "This is about us."

Mal slipped her hands free and clasped them in front of her. Travis could see the knuckles turning white. "I wasn't expecting this, Travis."

"Give me an answer."

Her mouth turned down. So did her eyes. "I'm not ready. I need to think."

He closed his eyes. He'd been so sure that this was what she needed. That once he asked, she'd be ready to admit that she loved him, too, that this was what she wanted. He wished he could shrug it off, pretend that his heart wasn't breaking. Again. "It's okay, Mal. I just want you to be happy."

It nearly killed him to say it, knowing that this was the last goodbye. That his hopes were now truly shattered.

He untangled himself from her, from the sheets. His clothes were scattered around the room. He didn't care, as long as he found enough to cover up so he wouldn't be wandering down the street naked.

"Travis." She sat up in bed, holding the sheets to her chest. "Wait. It's…just that…three months ago we weren't even talking. I don't think this is the time."

"I laid my heart out for you. I can't possibly think of a better time."

There was a set to her mouth, a firm line that he knew and loved even when it was directed at him. "Your grandma just died, Travis. You aren't thinking straight."

No, he'd never been thinking straighter. There was no point in waiting. No point in holding back or holding off. "She didn't *just* die. It's been a month, Mal, and, yes, I still miss her. I'm sure I'm still grieving. But that isn't why I'm asking. I love you. I want to be with you."

She blinked. "We're not ready."

"I'm ready."

She shook her head as though to clear it. "You can't just decide we're together without discussing it with me."

That irked him, though he did his best not to let it show. Getting heated wouldn't help the situation and it certainly wouldn't get him the answer he wanted. "We're discussing it now, aren't we?"

She scowled. "I'm saying you can't just spring it on me."

Spring it on her? As though they hadn't been working toward just this moment since they got back together? His hands fisted. "I can't believe you're surprised."

"Well, I am." She lifted her chin. "I did not expect we'd be having this conversation tonight."

"No? Then when did you think we'd be having it?" He wanted to know. Had she expected it would never come up at all? Or was there some secret code he was supposed to know that he'd yet to decipher?

"I hadn't thought about it at all."

His insides went cold. "I don't believe you."

"Contrary to what you might think, Travis, I haven't spent the last year and a half thinking about you." He took the shot without responding. "I've been busy living my own life."

"I didn't expect you not to." He scooped up his jeans, stepped into them without looking away from her. He couldn't believe this was happening—again. That he'd so badly misread the signs. "But I thought you were making room for me in this new life."

"That isn't what I meant."

"No, but it's what you said." He zipped up. "Apparently, you've already made the decision for us. Sort of like how you decided you were returning to Vancouver and we were breaking up." This time he couldn't prevent the bitterness from creeping into his voice.

Her lips thinned. "That's not fair." Maybe not, but he wasn't feeling fair. "I didn't want to break up." Her voice broke as her eyes flicked up to meet his. Travis saw the naked emotion in their depths. "You didn't give me a choice."

Was that really what she thought? That he'd been the one to force the choice? Had she forgotten that she was the one who'd walked into the bar and informed him that she was leaving for good? "You had a choice, Mal. You just didn't choose me."

And she wasn't choosing him again.

It hurt more than the last time. Hurt so much that he struggled to draw breath without wincing.

"Travis." Her voice softened.

He swallowed. The lump in his throat didn't budge. "I want to spend the rest of my life with you. But if you feel differently, I can't force you to love me."

He found his shirt and slipped it over his head. Socks, underwear, anything else could remain scattered on the floor. He didn't need them. Mal watched him without saying a word.

"So, this is it." His lips felt numb. They weren't alone. He couldn't feel the tips of his fingers, his feet, his heart. He closed his eyes for just a moment, long enough to take one deep breath, and then started toward the bedroom door.

He heard the rustle of material, glanced back to see her getting to her feet, sheet still clutched to her body, and his heart stopped. Was she going to explain this had all been a misunderstanding? Would they work out what had come between them and move forward together, stronger than ever?

But she didn't say anything until he put his hand on the doorknob. "Travis?"

He stopped, waited for her to say the words he longed to hear. That this fight was all a mistake, that she wanted to start their life together, too, that she wanted him to stay. And he realized his hopes were written on his face, when an answering expression of sympathy flashed across hers. When the words she spoke were most definitely not the ones he wanted to hear.

"I'm sorry."

He swallowed and forced the hurt down. "I'm sorry, too." Then he opened the door and walked out of her life.

MAL WATCHED TRAVIS GO. The slump to his shoulders almost undid her. She even reached for him, opened her mouth with the words halfway out before she stopped herself. She couldn't change things—not her own feelings, not the past, not anything.

If he wasn't even willing to discuss the fact that he was the issue here—his lack of follow-through with regard to sharing with his family, his desire to still keep their breakup under wraps. Well, she didn't know what she was supposed to do.

But she didn't feel good about it, and as she shut the door behind him, turning the lock with what sounded like a final click, her stomach rolled. A long, sickening roll.

Mal swallowed the panic. She wasn't wrong.

Not this time. And not last time, either. But her eyes felt prickly and she could feel the tears. No. She shook her head as though it might dry them. She didn't want to cry. She wouldn't.

Her throat grew tight, her lungs ached with the effort to maintain breath control. And when she called Grace, her voice shook. "Hey. Do you think you could come over?"

Mal was grateful that Grace and Owen lived so close. She put on a comfy pair of yoga pants and a T-shirt and hung on to her self-imposed calm until they arrived, and only then did she finally let it out. In one loud sob, as soon as she opened the door to the pair. "Travis and I are done."

"Done?" Owen asked the question while Grace hugged her and made soothing murmurs.

"Yes." She struggled for some of that much-vaunted control she had once prized so highly. Sadly, it seemed to have left the building. Along with Travis.

"How? When? I thought things were good." Her brother spoke quickly.

"Owen." Mal could feel Grace's glare over her shoulder.

"What? I'm not supposed to ask?"

Grace rubbed Mal's back. "Give her a chance."

"She called us," Owen said. "But fine. I can see I'm outnumbered." He walked into Mal's kitchen, as at home there as he was everywhere. "Do you have ice cream?"

Mal sniffed and looked at Grace who only shrugged. "I don't know. Are you hungry?"

Owen stuck his head back into the entry. "Isn't that what you do when you cry? Eat ice cream?"

Mal rolled her eyes, which had thankfully stopped leaking. "Have you been watching Lifetime movies again?"

"Of course. I'm what you call an evolved male."

Mal blinked. She could think of many things to call her brother. Had called him many of them in the past. But, until tonight, *evolved* had never made the list. Of course, he'd never offered ice cream before. She smiled. And it wasn't even faked.

"So?" Owen wiggled his eyebrows. "Ice cream?"

"I think there's some in the freezer."

Owen grinned and disappeared into the kitchen. The rumble of the freezer door opening was followed by his outraged shout. "Mal! How long has this been in here?"

She had no idea. "A month…maybe two?"

"It has ice hair."

"I'm sure it's fine," Grace called. She patted Mal's shoulder. "Have a taste and make sure."

Owen reappeared. "I am not eating that. I wouldn't feed it to anyone. Well, maybe Donovan, but only because he vetoed my idea to serve brunch at Elephants all day." He eyeballed Mal. "He said it would take sales away from more traditional lunch and dinner items that had a better profit margin. But I said it meant people would spend more on alcohol because they hadn't spent their money on food. And we all know the profits are in alcohol sales. Could have used you on my side, Mal."

"Owen. Really?" Grace gave Mal another hug.

But Mal was actually okay with the random conversation. It distracted her, which was the reason she'd called Grace, even if she hadn't expected the bonus addition of Owen. She stared back at him. "Maybe I'd have sided with Donovan."

He snorted. "You probably would have. You also probably think this ice cream is edible."

It was true. Mal wouldn't think twice about digging into it. Which was why she marched into the kitchen past Owen, grabbed a spoon from the drawer and scooped up a mouthful. "Mmmmm."

Owen shook his head. "Don't blame me if that makes you sick. Hey." He looked at his wife who walked by and grabbed her own spoon. "I kiss that mouth, you know."

Grace grinned around her spoon. "And you will again."

Another head shake. "I do not understand you. Either of you."

"And you call yourself evolved." Mal tossed

her hair and scooped up some more ice cream. It was vanilla and had probably been in the freezer closer to six months, but it was delicious.

"Fine, fine. I can tell when I'm outnumbered, but I'm not eating any of that ice cream." But he grinned when he said it, and he walked over to sit on the nearby couch.

Grace looked at her. "Got any wine?"

Mal pointed to the fridge.

Grace opened the door and perused the selection, choosing one. "Excellent." She poured them both a glass and handed one to Mal. "Now, tell me what happened."

Mal took a sip of the white wine to fortify herself. It didn't really go with the sweetness of the ice cream, but she took another sip anyway. Another way to distract herself, she supposed. "He asked me to marry him."

Grace's glass thumped down onto the granite countertop. "Oh."

Mal appreciated that she didn't come after her, asking why or wondering how that had caused a breakup. But Grace was good that way—an excellent advisor, but an even better listener. "I didn't expect it. Obviously. And I just..." She swallowed, no longer tasting the clash of flavors between vanilla ice cream and crisp wine. All she could focus on was the memory of Travis's face, the hopeful look that had appeared just before she'd told him she couldn't.

The ice cream settled like a lump and she put the spoon down in the sink, no longer hungry. The very idea of downing another mouthful made her ill.

"But I thought you guys were getting along." Owen's brow wrinkled in confusion.

Grace quieted him with a look. "Mal, did something happen?"

Mal exhaled and stared at the spoon in the sink. Yes, something had happened. Or not happened. "We didn't talk about it." She knew she didn't need to explain to Grace.

"Talk about what?" Owen wanted to know.

Mal kept talking, ignoring her brother's question. "I didn't think we needed to. I thought I was okay with it. All of it." Even though oral sex was still off the menu. "But then he popped the question and I realized I wasn't."

Grace hugged her again.

Mal shut her eyes, felt tears slide down her face once more. "Everything was great and then suddenly he was asking me to marry him and I panicked, and then he thought it meant I didn't love him and he left."

There was silence for a moment, broken only by Mal's loud sniffle. "Do you?" Grace finally asked. "Love him?"

Mal swallowed and lifted her head from Grace's shoulder. "I don't know."

"Then you did the right thing," Owen said.

"If only it were that simple." Why couldn't life be that simple? Why did it have to be so complicated? So confusing? Why was her heart breaking when she was the one who'd refused the proposal? Shouldn't she be feeling some sort of relief or at least acceptance?

She picked up her wine glass, but put it back down without taking a sip. Suddenly it wasn't sitting well with the ice cream.

"And then we did talk about it. Well, argued about it." She raised her face to look at them. "He said *I* was the one who broke up with him. Sure I chose to move back here, but *he*'s the one who said we had to break up." She rolled the stem of the wineglass between her thumb and finger. "I guess it doesn't matter now. Because this breakup isn't something we're coming back from."

They were all silent.

Mal exhaled slowly and looked at Grace. Her sister-in-law's sympathetic smile almost undid her. "I know, you said we should talk about it before. And you were right." Maybe if they had, they'd have been able to hold a reasonable conversation. One that wouldn't have ended in tears and closed doors and hearts that felt as if they could never be put back together again.

"I'm so sorry, Mal."

"I know." Mal felt her shoulders droop. That

awful wetness returned to her eyes. She hugged herself, but it didn't help. "I just felt so unimportant. I needed to come back and he just let me. Waved me off without a fight and then consoled himself with another woman before I'd even caught my flight home."

"What?" Owen slapped a hand on the counter. "You didn't tell me this."

Mal sniffled. "It wasn't exactly something I was proud of. I was hurt and I didn't think anybody else needed to know."

"I'm going to kick his ass." Owen pushed away from the counter where he'd been leaning.

"Owen." Mal's hand shot out. "Don't."

"Why not? He cheated on you."

"Technically, we weren't together."

"Then I'll give him a technical knockout."

Owen's quick and unquestioned support made Mal realize how much she'd needed it. Maybe they all would have been better off if she'd spilled the whole story way back when. Of course, it was too late to do that now. She wiped at the tears trickling down her cheeks. "Thank you."

"Don't thank me yet. I still have some ass to kick."

TRAVIS WAS MOPING or wallowing, or whatever you called it when what you really wanted to do was beat up something but had just enough self-control to settle for grinding your teeth and punching the couch. He was pretty sure he'd ground off enough to make his dentist wince when someone knocked at the front door.

He didn't move from the couch. He was in no state to speak to anyone right now, especially not whoever was at the door. The TV was quiet and a punch to the couch cushion made no sound, so there was no reason for a neighbor to be knocking. And if it wasn't a neighbor, then it was someone who shouldn't be in the building at all.

Actually, maybe he should tell them that, give them a personal escort out. For the safety of the other residents. He shoved off the couch.

Another knock was followed by the click of the lock being opened and Owen's angry voice. "Where are you, you asshat?"

A pump of adrenaline flooded his system with no place to go. He wanted to punch something, but not Owen, even if he was calling Travis an asshat. He punched the couch instead. "What do you want?"

"Did you cheat on my sister?" Owen stormed into the living room, hands fisted and cocked.

Travis blinked and scowled. "No, I asked her to marry me."

"Not tonight." Owen twitched. "Before. In Aruba. Did you cheat on her?"

Travis ground his teeth again, so as not to unload his fury on Owen—he wasn't mad at Owen. "A court of law would say no, but yeah. I did."

Owen drew back his fist. Then slowly lowered it. "I should punch you."

"Probably."

"But it'll hurt and Grace will be mad. For the record, I still think you're an asshat."

"I know." Travis punched his own thigh. It did about as much to ease his emotions as punching the couch had, which is to say he might as well not have bothered. He looked at Owen. "Is she okay?" He hated the thought that she was hurt and upset, that he couldn't be there to ease her pain.

"No." Owen's eyes warmed a fraction. They were still as hard as frozen tundra but they were practically tropical compared to how they'd looked when he first walked in. "But I appreciate you asking."

"I still love her."

"And I still think you're an asshat."

"Gee, thanks."

"You're welcome."

They were both quiet for a moment. Travis finally cleared his throat. "Are we okay?"

Owen exhaled. "No, but we will be. One day."

Travis nodded slowly. He hadn't just lost Mal tonight. But somehow the pain of that realization didn't mean much. Or maybe there was just so much pain a person could handle at once and Travis was full up. "You want me to move out?" He wouldn't blame Owen for saying yes.

Owen thought about it. "No." He ran an eye around the apartment. "But I don't think I want to see you for a while."

"Understood."

When Owen stood to go, Travis didn't stop him. There didn't really seem to be anything else to say.

CHAPTER THIRTEEN

MAL DIDN'T GO in to work for three days. On the fourth, she gathered her strength, took a much-needed shower and stood in front of her bathroom mirror, focusing on her breathing instead of the anxious thoughts flowing through her head.

She might have stayed home today, too, but she had a charity meeting, and as the event was only weeks away, it wasn't something she could cancel. Not even knowing that Travis would be there.

The thought made her chest tighten. She gripped the bathroom counter and inhaled slowly, then released until she no longer felt as though she might pass out. In and out. Slow and steady. She wouldn't think about anything else. Not the breakup, the look on Travis's face, or the uncertainty that rolled through her stomach every hour on the hour. She would get through the meeting and only then would she worry about what came next.

Her fingers curled into the granite counter again, hanging on for support, trying to absorb some of its cool strength. She couldn't go on like this, not indefinitely. Okay, so it had only been three days since the breakup. Three days and ten hours, if she was counting, which she was. Oh, God. She wasn't ready. She wasn't ready to have him walk into her space and sit through the meeting, the two of them acting like professional colleagues, as if their personal relationship hadn't fallen apart only days ago.

Her eyes felt sore and puffy, which was to be expected when she'd spent pretty much the preceding eighty-two hours in a state of tears. She'd have thought there would come a point when they'd dry up, when she'd finally be so dehydrated that there would be nothing left to cry. But even as she thought it, she blinked before more tears tracked down her cheeks, taking her newly applied mascara with them.

They were over. But things between them weren't. They still had the charity event and they still worked in the same industry in the same city. Owen and Travis were still friends, though Owen had made an offhand comment that things weren't so peachy there.

Regardless, there were any number of as-yet-to-be-determined situations where they'd run into each other. Where they'd have to smile and make nice and pretend that they hadn't once loved each other so hard that their hearts had been permanently imprinted.

Mal sucked in a shaky breath. She felt as though she couldn't do this, but she had to. She would have to do her best to remain above it all, even while she wept inside. She finished putting on her makeup, only needing to reapply her mascara twice.

She'd dressed for success. Or for protection. Selecting a dress in the shade of gunmetal gray and pairing it with a sharp blazer. In high black heels, her hair tied back into a tidy knot, she didn't look like the kind of person anyone should mess with.

Her eyes swept over the bedroom as she walked in. The space was clean, pristine. She'd spent the time she hadn't been sleeping in cleaning. Clearing out any remaining signs of Travis. New sheets and duvet cover for the bed, the old ones bagged up and stuffed in the back of the closet in a rarely used clothes bag to donate to the homeless once she could look at it without crying. She'd made Grace take home the bottled water Travis had favored. And then she'd cleaned and cleaned, erasing every trace of his scent. Her nose twitched as the smell of the lavender cleaning product hit her in the face. She might have gone a little overboard, but it had given her something to do besides mope.

Mal flipped open the jewelry box on her dresser. She wouldn't think about it—about what returning the earrings and ring to Travis meant. She never should have kept the ring in the first place, but maybe she hadn't been ready to let go back then. Now she was. Even though it crushed the breath from her lungs and made her legs feel heavy to think that she'd never see him again. That all ties between them would be cut. Forever.

She choked on her next inhale. Mal had never been one to imagine her wedding, the dress, the shoes, the cake and flowers. But she'd always pictured herself married, sharing her life with someone. With Travis.

She swallowed the sob, blinked away the wetness blurring her vision and looked inside the box. The sapphires gleamed back at her. They weren't particularly expensive, but their value was sentimental. She reached down to pluck them off the velvet cushion. This would truly be it. The final moment between them, those awkward future encounters excluded. This would be saying goodbye.

Her hand hovered over the gems, fingers twitching. Then she gritted her teeth and took them out. She still had the velvet boxes for them tucked in the top drawer of her dresser. She pulled them out, one box in blue, one in gray, and carefully placed the pieces inside. She might be angry and upset, but there was no reason to take it out on the jewelry. Then she slipped the boxes into her purse, double checking to make sure they wouldn't bounce around on her trip to the office, all the while ignoring the wailing voice in the back of her head. The one that wanted to know if she was sure, if she really wanted to go through with this, if she'd given it enough thought.

She was and she had.

"Ms. Ford." Bailey greeted her from behind the reception desk when she breezed into the office. "Are you feeling better?"

Since Mal hadn't wanted to tell anyone why she was out, she'd simply lied and said she was ill. She supposed heartbreak was a type of illness. She forced a smile she didn't feel. "I'm fine, Bailey. Thank you for asking. Is the boardroom ready for my meeting?" She needed to focus on something else, anything else.

"Yes. But please let me know if you need anything."

"That will be fine, Bailey. Thank you." Mal wasn't usually so abrupt with the staff, but she just wasn't up for small talk today. She still had some time before the meeting, which allowed her a moment to go into her office and take a few more of those necessary deep breaths. She also needed a few minutes to visit the washroom and touch up her lipstick, brush her hair and pretend that not only did she look okay, she felt okay.

When she returned to her desk, she pulled

up some files on her computer, reviewing the agenda for the meeting, but she jumped when Bailey buzzed her to let her know the first meeting guest had arrived. And her heart didn't leave her throat, even when she saw it wasn't Travis. Really, it just would have required too much luck for Travis to arrive first so she could hand him the jewelry in private.

No matter. Mal would just request that he stay an extra minute and do it after the meeting. The timing wasn't important. All that mattered was that she return the pieces to him. After that, he could do whatever he wanted with them.

The rest of the group trickled in, helping themselves to the coffee, tea and pastries Bailey had ordered. No Travis, though. Mal kept a sharp eye on the door, waiting to see his shadow a moment before he stepped through, all strong shoulders and dark ink.

But he never turned up and she couldn't bring herself to ask the group if they'd heard from him, afraid that everything she was trying to keep deep inside, safely contained in the walls she'd put back up, would show on her face. So she waited until the last people left, walking the three stragglers out to the lobby and personally seeing them onto the elevator before she allowed herself to inquire about Travis's absence.

"Bailey? Did anyone call while I was in the

meeting?" Mal didn't say his name. She wanted to, but her tongue twisted and all she managed was, "We were short one attendee."

"No." Bailey shook her head. "No one called the main line. Do you need me to call anyone for you?" Her hand was poised, ready to take down the number or make the call.

"That's fine, thank you. I'll follow up." And a fresh, clean anger burbled inside her. After all the angst, the emotional drain on her life, and he didn't even show up? She stormed down the hall to her office, grabbed her purse from her desk and retraced her steps to the lobby.

No, she had not gone through all of this to be foiled so easily. She was returning his gram's jewelry. And she was doing it today. And while she was at it, she planned to remind him that the charity event wasn't some feel-good celebration for dilettantes, where the money earned was used to pay for the cost of putting it on. This was about raising money for the homeless in the community, and she expected him to honor his commitment, no matter what had happened between them.

Bailey blinked when she saw her reappear. "Ms. Ford? Is everything all right?"

"No, but it will be soon. I just need to step out," Mal said. "If anyone calls, I should be back before noon."

"Of course." Ever the professional, Bailey took

the change in routine in stride. "Should I order lunch in for you?"

"No." Mal nearly ground her teeth with the effort to keep her tone mild. "I don't think I'll be hungry."

Her stomach was hard, full of knots and tension, as though she'd swallowed a stone of discontent. She huffed out a breath as she climbed into her car and accelerated out of the parking lot onto the busy city streets. But she'd grown up here and knew the streets well. Which ones were filled with tourists. Which ones curved and changed direction before you realized you were now heading away from your destination. Which ones turned into routes for buses only. And which one was the fastest way to Travis's new pub.

Her car growled as she punched the gas, darting through an intersection, past a minivan with tinted windows and a hatchback that had an empty ski rack on its roof. This wouldn't take long.

Mal saw the construction trucks parked by the curb and squeezed in behind one. It was marked as a loading zone, but she didn't intend to be any longer than five minutes. The sound of saws buzzing through wood and the scent of sawdust greeted her as she stepped out of the car and slammed the door.

She ignored the sign that said she was entering a construction site, banging on the door with a flat palm. The sawing didn't stop, but a grizzled man whose jeans had seen better days pulled open the door. "Yeah?"

"I'm here to see Travis." She tapped one high-heeled toe. Her footwear was wholly inappropriate, as was her expensive silk dress, but then she hadn't chosen her clothing with the idea that she'd be crashing a construction zone. She glared at the man when he didn't move. "Now."

"Just a minute." He wasn't happy. She could hear him grumbling behind the door after he shut it in her face. Mal didn't care. He could grumble all he wanted about people showing up without proper footwear and how he was supposed to be told about visitors in advance, but she was still getting inside.

It took longer than a minute, but eventually Mal heard the clomp of returning footsteps. The same man opened the door, a battered orange hard hat in one hand, a reflective vest in the other. He thrust them at her. "Here."

Mal put them on without complaint and told herself not to think of where either item might have been. She didn't have to wear them long. And maybe the five second rule applied, although in this case it would need to be a five minute rule. She followed the grumbler inside.

The interior was in mid renovation. Mal found

herself checking things out as they walked. Bright
spotlights had been set up to give extra light as
various people worked on the walls and the posts.
The ceiling had undergone a renaissance and now
gleamed, well oiled to a golden glow. She wanted
to pause and drink it in. It looked so similar to
how she remembered, but better. But she wasn't
here to see what Travis was doing with the place.
It was of no importance to her.

But as she crossed the floor, scarred and half
torn up, seeing the posts, which had also been re-
furbished, her eyes straying to the long bar, which
was covered in a thick drop cloth weighted down
by rocks, she couldn't help but imagine the finished product. The place was going to be beautiful, with elements of all the many things she'd
loved about the original brought forth and highlighted in a new, modern style. The one place she
didn't look was the bar. That long, beautiful bar
where such a short time ago she'd been intimate
with Travis.

"Hey." The grumbler waved at her from across
the room. "This way."

Mal shook off her thoughts of that day and her
imaginings of what the space would look like
when finished. If she wanted to see it, she could
visit once it was open for business. No need to
use any brain power to fantasize about it now. She
picked her way across the floor, avoiding loose

nails, boards and the occasional tool, catching up with the grumbler who was now mumbling about people not watching where they were going and how he had better things to do with his day than play tour guide.

"There." The grumbler was a man of few words when it came to actual conversation, simply pointing down a short hall with three doorways. Only one had an actual door installed.

Mal paused in front of it, her nerves suddenly jumping. The back of her neck prickled and she felt a roll of jitters run through her. But she wasn't about to be done in by some jitters and a prickle. Not even one that made her knees wobble. She lifted her hand and knocked, sucking in a deep breath for courage.

"Yes?"

Mal knew she could have bolted then, gone back the way she'd come, tossing her hard hat and vest at the grumbler, or anywhere, really, and escaped out the front door as though she'd never been there at all. She'd be lying if she said she didn't consider it. But she refused to leave without getting closure. She'd done that the last time and thus had begun the longest year and a half of her life. She wouldn't do that again. Couldn't.

Instead, she gathered her poise, clutched her purse more tightly against her side and pushed open the door.

Travis sat behind a plain wood desk that had seen better days. A battered file cabinet sat in the corner, a pair of work boots beside it. There was a long table with blueprints and other papers spread out on it and a metal folding chair for guests. Mal remained standing in the doorway.

"Mal." Travis blinked when he looked up, emotions running across his face. Surprise and wonder, before he shuttered his eyes and sent her a tight smile. "What are you doing here?"

She felt the anger rise anew. He hadn't even remembered. Her event had been so unimportant that in only three days apart, he'd managed to wipe it completely from his mind. "You missed the meeting." Her tone was frosty, as she'd intended it to be.

"Ah." He sat back in his chair. "About that, I thought it was best that I skip this one."

That was it. No apology. No excuse. Not that she wanted his apology. "You should have left me a message. We waited for you."

"I did leave you a message." The whine of the buzz saw filled the room, drowning out the rest of his words. Mal stayed where she was while Travis's mouth stopped moving. He pushed himself out of his battered-looking desk chair. He was dressed for the site—a pair of old jeans, and a plain white T-shirt that had seen better days, worn so thin from washing that she could see the outline of his tattoos through it.

Mal couldn't take her eyes off them as he walked toward her. Her mouth felt dry, and not from inhaling sawdust. Her fingers flexed and she curled them against her palms. They weren't her tattoos to touch. Not anymore.

He reached toward her. Mal's heart thumped. She didn't know what to do. Run? Tell him to keep his hands to himself? Let herself be held for just a minute? But he simply reached past her to shut the door.

She could smell his scent. That particular mix of wood and oranges. She let her eyes drift shut and took a deep breath. But just one. And then he was back on the other side of the desk.

"I called and left a message on your phone this morning."

Right. She was supposed to be angry, not absorbing his essence. "You should have come." Travis merely shrugged, which triggered her aggravation. "The charity event is important. More important than whatever's happened between us."

"No." His voice was firm. "It's not. Nothing is more important than us."

Mal ignored that. She hadn't come here to talk about them. There was no them. "You made a commitment to the event."

"And I'll honor it. I'm sorry I didn't come to

this morning's meeting. I thought I was being prudent. Now I know better."

His easy acceptance tamped down some of her fire. "Well, good. Because there are a lot of people counting on us."

"I won't miss another meeting."

Mal swallowed and nodded, tried not to think of the actual logistics of seeing Travis across the table and having to act as though there was nothing wrong. She slipped her hand into her purse. "I want you to have these."

She pulled one box free and placed it on the desk. His eyes tracked the motion of the blue box and then looked back at her. Mal then produced the gray box. She nudged both boxes toward him when he didn't reach for them. She saw his fingers flex, noted the ripple of his biceps highlighted by the edge of the Scottish Cross tattoo peeking out beneath his shirtsleeve.

But Travis still didn't touch them. "What are those?" His voice was tight, the outline of his jaw suddenly sharp.

"They belong to you. To your family." It was the right thing to return the jewelry, so Travis or his brother could give them to someone else, someone who would be a permanent part of their future.

His hand flashed out, grabbed the gray box, which held the earrings. He flipped the lid open and stared at them. Then he looked at her. "Are you kidding me?"

"No." Mal was taken aback. "They belong to your family."

His fingers curled around the box and she was pretty sure his gaze could melt steel. "My grandmother willed these to you. My grandmother, who loved you, left you something personal to remember her and you're throwing them back in my face?"

CHAPTER FOURTEEN

TRAVIS NEARLY CRUSHED the box in his hand he was so angry. So hurt. That she could just hand his gram's jewelry over as if it meant nothing to her. Held no place in her heart. The box flipped open under the pressure from his hand, but Travis didn't look away from the woman in front of him.

Mal shook her head. "No, you misunderstand."

"Oh, I think you've been clear." It was a rejection. Another damn rejection. Or perhaps a final exclamation point on the original one. Only this time it was more than a rejection of him. "She was a good woman, Mal."

"This isn't about your grandma."

"No?" He snapped the box shut so he didn't have to look at the gleaming jewels anymore. He didn't even reach for the other box. He already knew what was inside. "Then what is it about?"

"The jewelry should stay in your family." Her throat bobbed, her hands twisted around each other. "Maybe Shane will want to give them to his future wife." There was a long pause. "Maybe you will."

He could have exploded then, let out all the pent-up disappointment and regret and frustration in one volcanic eruption. He gripped the edge of the desk instead, feeling it bite into his palms. "She willed them to *you*."

"She thought we were still together. Don't you think that influenced her decision?"

He couldn't definitively say no, which only highlighted the fact that his grandma wasn't here. The thought was a punch to the gut. Yet another one. He felt as though he'd been taking a lot of them lately. He ran his thumb along the edge of the desk, striving for control. "My point stands. It was your name she put down."

"Only because you didn't tell her we weren't together. She didn't know."

"That wouldn't have mattered to her. She loved you. She'd have wanted to give you something to remember her."

"Sure, something." Mal put her hands on her hips. "Not heirloom jewelry."

"You don't know that."

"Neither do you."

They glared at each other for a moment. "Fine. Neither of us know. Satisfied?"

"No." She crossed her arms over her chest. "I didn't come here to get satisfaction, Travis."

"Then why did you come?" He put the box down on the desk, his eyes never leaving hers.

"You could have called about the meeting, used a messenger to drop off the jewelry."

"Don't go twisting this into something it's not," she told him. "I don't have any secret agenda."

"No?" Because it occurred to him that, even now, she could just walk back out the door, seeing as she'd completed what she'd come for. And so hope, that vicious little beast, dug its claws into his heart.

"No." She straightened her shoulders. "And tell your family I'm sorry."

"For what?"

She frowned and looked at him as though he was missing the point, which he obviously was. "That I won't see them again. It's a normal thing to say after a breakup." She paused. "You did tell them, didn't you?"

Travis ground his teeth together. "No." He'd been sort of busy the last three days, focusing on not punching something or someone, finding a new place to live, because as generous as Owen was allowing him to stay in the apartment, Travis no longer felt comfortable there.

"See?" Mal threw her hands into the air. "This is what I'm talking about. You just keep everything important hidden. Secreting it away."

"It's my business to tell them—my choice to share or not." So sue him. He didn't want to call his family, who were still in mourning, and tell

them that he and Mal were over. He didn't want
to answer the questions that would arise. Like
what had happened, since they'd seemed so happy
together. His jaw ached from clenching. They
had been happy. At least, he'd thought they were
happy.

Mal shook her head. "You can do whatever you
want with your life, Travis. It's not my place to
say, but I will tell you that you create distance.
You make people think you don't care."

"What are you talking about? How many times
do I have to tell you that I love you? That you're
the only person in the world for me."

"But you don't mean it." He saw her face crum-
ple, sensed the tears before he saw them make
her eyes shiny with grief. "You let me go when I
needed you most."

"What do you mean when you needed me
most?"

"My dad was sick, the family was in turmoil. I
had to come back and you let me. You didn't offer
to come with me, you didn't even want to try and
make it work. You just washed your hands of me."

"Mal." His voice grew quiet. "It wasn't like
that."

The tears were running freely down her cheeks
now. "Yes, Travis. It was like that. We'd been
separated for what? An hour when you took that
woman into your office and—" Her voice broke.

Travis was grateful she didn't finish her sentence. "I've told you that was a mistake. It didn't mean anything. She didn't mean anything. I was hurt, too, Mal. And I just wanted to forget the hurt, bury my head."

"In another woman's lap." She wiped at her eyes. "I have to go."

"Mal." He stood, started around the desk after her. This couldn't be it. They couldn't end it like this.

She looked back over her shoulder, one hand on the door. "Just let me go, Travis. Please."

He looked at her, deep into the dark eyes, searching for something, anything that might hint she was feeling torn. That she didn't mean it.

She dropped her gaze to the ground. "Please."

He studied her, the brief shudder of her shoulders before she wrapped her arms around herself, protecting, comforting. He wanted to be the one providing those comforts to her. Irritation grated across his nerves that he couldn't. That she'd step away from him, avoid all contact if he tried.

"Mal?" He waited until she lifted her eyes to him. "I meant it when I said that I want you to be happy."

She didn't say anything, but tears spilled down her cheeks. She turned and wrenched open the door, hurrying down the hall. He watched her go, keeping enough distance that it wouldn't seem as if he was chasing her while also making sure she didn't hurt herself.

Then he went back to his office, shut the door with a firm click and punched the wall.

It didn't punch back, though he would have welcomed the response. Mal was wrong. He hadn't created distance. Not intentionally or otherwise. He'd simply been protecting his family. Keeping information from them that he knew would upset them. And, if he were honest, he hadn't told them because he was embarrassed.

He'd been wrong to take that woman into his office, wrong to think it would help and wrong to think it wasn't dishonoring what he'd had with Mal. He'd been an idiot.

His knuckles throbbed. He glanced down and saw he'd scraped them raw. Still, it didn't ease the throb of his heart. The painful saw of breath that pushed in and out of his lungs.

Because, although Mal had been wrong in some respects, in others she was right. At least, she was right about how he'd hidden parts of himself from his family. And so far he'd done nothing to fix it. Taken no steps to make things right. To be the man he wanted to be.

Maybe it was too late for him and Mal. His eye flicked over to the pair of velvet boxes now sitting on his desk and another round of pain washed over him. He hadn't realized how much hope he'd gotten from the knowledge that she'd held onto his gram's ring until now—until she didn't.

Travis picked up the blue box, the one with the ring inside. He ran a thumb along the hinged seam but didn't flip it open. He knew what was inside, so there was no need to verify it. Instead, he shoved it into his front pocket. Shoved the gray box in, too. Then he strode through the work-space and out the front door.

There might not be much of a chance with Mal, but if he wanted any sort of chance at all, he had to start making things right. With her, with her family, with his own family. There was no point in waiting. He couldn't wait. Been there, done that. Had the scars to remind him of it.

He called Shane and asked if he could pick him up at the terminal, then he caught the next flight home.

IT WAS A quiet trip back, the plane carrying only one other passenger, which left plenty of privacy for thinking. Travis would have preferred some sort of distraction, anything that might keep him from reliving the scene with Mal in his office or thinking of the scene to come with his family. But it was just him and his thoughts.

And the jewelry.

He hadn't bothered to go home and change. Hadn't bothered to pack a suitcase or even a toothbrush. He didn't plan on staying long and he could buy whatever he needed or get by without it. What he couldn't do was wait any longer to tell them the truth.

He was practically vibrating with it when he stepped off the plane and made his way to the pick-up area where Shane waited in his big red truck.

"Did you miss me?" Shane asked when Travis opened the door.

"Yes, and this sty you call a vehicle." Travis shoved a batch of burger wrappers, empty plastic bottles and a paper bag from the seat onto the floor before climbing in. "Seriously, Shane. This is an embarrassment to garbage."

Shane merely shrugged. "I clean it up for dates."

"Wow. I bet that impresses the ladies."

"It does." Shane gunned the engine and pulled out of the parking lot. He grinned at Travis. "Speaking of ladies, where's Mal? Couldn't come with you this time?"

"Something like that." Just the mention of her name was enough to punch Travis in the gut. But he curled his fingers into his palms and pretended it didn't. He wasn't about to get into it here, on the short drive home. Not just because it wasn't the kind of thing you told your brother in a moving vehicle, but because Travis couldn't stand the thought of telling the story more than once. He figured it would be tough enough getting through it the first time and he wasn't about to set himself up for failure or for his brother to blurt something out to their family first. This needed to come from his own lips, his own heart.

He leaned his forehead against the cool glass of the window and stared at the scenery as it flashed by. But he didn't really see it, and when they pulled up in front of his childhood home Travis was surprised they'd already arrived.

The scent of his mom's potato chip casserole greeted him when he pushed open the front door. "We're here," Shane called, giving Travis a light shove as he walked past.

Travis gave him a slightly harder shove, as was his right as the older and therefore wiser brother. Shane turned and punched him in the shoulder. Travis punched back.

It was typical behavior they'd engaged in as teens. One time, in a particularly memorable scuffle, Shane had climbed on top of the portable dishwasher for better positioning and Travis had simply shoved the dishwasher and Shane through the door. Their mother had not been amused.

But they were older now. And tougher. And the dishwasher was a permanent installation with no wheels for rolling. Their mother, however, was still not amused.

"No." She came into the hallway where they

were circling each other, half crouched, looking for an opening. "Absolutely not." She flicked the lights on and off. "No fighting."

"Fine." Travis rose to his full height and Shane tackled him—which signaled fair game. He wrestled Shane into submission, pinning his younger brother's shoulders with his knees. It took a lot longer than it had when they were kids and Travis outweighed him by thirty pounds and had an extra inch in reach.

"You're getting slow," Shane said, trying to unpin himself.

"Still fast enough to take you down." Travis grinned.

"I let you win."

"Sure you did."

Their mother flicked the lights again. "Enough. Quit acting like animals or you aren't getting dinner." It was the same threat she'd used when they were kids. It worked then and it worked now. She returned to the kitchen and both boys followed, though Shane did give him one more shove.

Travis let this one go. He'd bested Shane once. They both knew he could do it again. "Dinner smells good." He realized he hadn't put anything in his stomach since this morning, and that had been nothing more than coffee. His stomach had been too tight for food, but now, with the familiar scent of childhood swirling around him, it growled.

His mother was peering into the oven, checking on the meal. "Did Mal have to work?"

"She did." Travis couldn't be sure, but it seemed a reasonable assumption. One he'd let her believe until he got the whole family together. "Is Dad here?"

"He's in the basement." She stood up and began pulling plates out of the cupboard, handing them to Travis. He laid them out on the table, just as he had as a kid. And just as when they were kids and work was involved, Shane made himself scarce. Travis heard the thud of his footsteps as his brother headed down to the basement to join their father.

"How long are you staying?"

"Just for tonight." He pulled forks out of the drawer and placed them beside the plates.

His mother nodded and checked on the meal again. "Did something happen?"

"No. I just wanted to be near family and you're my family." He answered too quickly and with too much information. A stranger would guess he was lying. His mother was sure of it.

"You want to talk about it?"

No. "Yes, but I think it should wait until after dinner." No reason to ruin his own appetite and possibly everyone else's. Travis wasn't self-centered enough to think that his breakup would affect their lives to the same extent it affected his, but they did care for Mal and would be disappointed to hear about it. That it came so soon after his gram's passing would be an added blow.

He fiddled with the forks, straightening them when they were already straight. Maybe he shouldn't be telling them now. They were still in mourning. Maybe he should wait until things were more settled and the pain of losing his gram wasn't quite so fresh.

But even as he considered the idea, Travis rejected it. They needed to know. Or he needed to tell them. And what other reason would he give for showing up so suddenly mere days after he'd just been there? He missed them? No, it was better to tell them. Like ripping off a bandage, fast and without too much thought.

He waited until after dinner then asked them to gather in the living room.

"What's this about?" his mother asked, her eyes darting to the kitchen where there were still dishes in the sink and on the counter.

"I'll clean up, Mom. Sit." Travis remained standing.

His father sat down, stoic, the only hint that he found any of this unusual was the small line between his eyes. Shane lounged back on the couch. "I'm prepared to be entertained."

"It's not that entertaining." And something in his tone must have clued Shane in because he sat up and the same line between their father's eyes showed up on his face, too.

"Travis?" his mother asked, concern wrinkling her brow and turning her mouth down at the corners. She sat on the edge of the couch, perched as though ready to leap to her feet at the slightest provocation.

"I have something to tell you." He swallowed and reminded himself not to think about the details. Just get through the facts. "Mal and I aren't together anymore."

"Oh." His mother sat back and some of the tension on her face smoothed out. "Well, that's a relief."

He blinked. "I thought you liked Mal."

"I do." She smiled. "But the way you were acting, I thought you were going to tell us you had three weeks to live."

"I was hardly being that dramatic."

All three of them stared back at him with the same "Sure, you go on thinking that" expression.

He stared back, feeling sullen and a little put out. Had he really dropped his life for the day and hurried all the way here for this? "I wasn't." And if he spoke the words a little too loudly, it was only because he was trying to put a point on it. He wasn't being dramatic.

"You could have just called." Shane raised an eyebrow.

Travis shook his head. "Not the point." Although, really that had been part of the point. But he needed to get back on track with why he'd actually come to talk about the information and not his delivery of it. "Mal and I broke up."

He waited for the reaction. A hand raised to her mouth from his mother, a loud question from his brother, a slow shake of the head from his father. But they merely continued to look at him.

"She dumped me." A small pause for emphasis. "It wasn't the first time." Again, he waited for a reaction that didn't come.

"Do you want a beer?" Shane offered.

Travis shook his head. "I'm fine. Is this not news to any of you?" His father maintained a stoic demeanor while Shane and his mother glanced at each other and then back.

"We thought something had happened, but when she came back with you last month, it was clear that you'd sorted things out," his mother said.

"We had."

Shane frowned. "I thought you said she dumped you."

Travis's molars were getting quite the workout, sawing back and forth against each other. "She did, and thanks for being so concerned about my feelings."

"I offered to get you a beer." Shane pushed himself off the couch. "You want one, Dad?"

Travis looked at his mom. She would understand. But she was looking at Shane. "Actually, I could use a beer, too."

Seriously? "I'm glad you're all taking this so well."

"Are we supposed to sit in a drum circle and talk about our feelings?" Shane returned with the beers, handing them out like candy. Travis accepted his with a nod, but didn't open it. "Because I'm down with the sharing, but I'm not taking off my clothes."

"What are you talking about? No one wants to see you naked, Shane."

"Wrong. Melissa Jones asked me out just last week and she was totally undressing me with her eyes."

"I give up." Travis felt as though he was having a completely different conversation from everyone else. "Clearly, this didn't matter and I should have stayed in the city."

"Now who's *not* being dramatic?" Shane grinned as he twisted off the bottle cap and took a swig.

"Well, apparently I need to be since my life is so uninteresting."

"It's not uninteresting. I'm interested," his mom said, but she looked tired.

"It's fine, Mom. I don't need to talk. I just wanted to tell you and I felt it was something I needed to share in person."

There was quiet for a moment, then Shane asked. "All right, drum circle or not, I want to hear what happened."

"Only if you promise to stay fully clothed."

"Agreed. Unless Melissa Jones shows up, then all promises are null and void."

The telling went far better than Travis had expected. He didn't know why he'd thought it would be such a huge deal. Even after he'd shared everything, including the general details of their first breakup, no one pointed a finger at him and called him a damn, dirty cheater. No one lectured him about upholding a moral code. And no one told him he needed to move the sun and stars to win Mal back.

They simply listened and offered their support. Okay, so his mom said she hoped he'd learned from his mistakes and his dad nodded his agreement. And Shane had asked if it would be wrong for him to ask Mal out, which had earned him a solid punch to the shoulder, but other than that his family just offered listening and support.

Despite the fact that he spent yet another night in his childhood bed, and this time without the comfort of Mal tucked in beside him, he felt okay. Maybe not great, but okay.

The jewelry boxes remained in the pocket of his jeans. Travis had asked his mother to take them, but she'd declined and explained that his gram would have wanted Travis to decide what to do with them. He wasn't as convinced, but didn't want to argue. He could put them somewhere safe and revisit the situation at a later date.

He stayed at his parents' a little longer than he'd anticipated, hanging around through the weekend and mowing the backyard, wrestling with Shane and eating his mom's home cooking. When he boarded the flight home Sunday night, he felt almost okay. Or better than he had on the flight out. And it was a good thing, because there'd been an email from Mal the previous night, inviting him to the next charity meeting. Tomorrow.

He didn't intend to miss it.

MAL READ OVER the agenda for the Monday morning charity meeting on her computer screen. She'd have said she was experiencing déjà vu, but it was really more like *Groundhog Day*. Reliving the same time over and over. But she had no intention of getting into it with Travis.

Unless he didn't show up. Then all bets were off.

"Knock, knock." Owen walked into her office

without actually knocking and grinned when Mal frowned. "Having an excellent morning, I see."

"I have a meeting in ten minutes." She glanced at her wrist, even though she didn't wear a watch. She still felt it helped drive home her point. "What do you need, Owen?"

"Can't a brother just have a visit with his little sister without there being some ulterior motive?"

"He can." She clasped her hands on the desk in front of her. "But *you* can't. You're never in this early. What's up?"

"I am occasionally in this early, but I'm not here to defend my work ethic. We need to talk about Travis."

Mal felt her face grow cold, then numb. "There's nothing to talk about." She heard the words and knew her lips moved though she couldn't actually feel them. The numbness was a marginal improvement over the dull ache that generally colored her daily experiences. But only a marginal one. "Besides, I didn't think you were talking to him."

"I'm not." Owen's genial expression dimmed. "I'm here to talk about the anniversary party."

Mal blinked. As far as she knew, the party planning was still on schedule. Had something happened and they'd all decided to keep it from her? Fearing she was too sensitive to handle the situation? "Is there a problem? Did you accidentally blab to Mom and Dad and ruin the surprise?"

"I can keep a secret," Owen told her. "But in case you've forgotten, we'd talked about holding it at Travis's place."

Mal's heart dropped. She had forgotten. How could she have been so shortsighted? "Oh." It was the only word she could get out through the sudden sinking feeling in her stomach. The charity event would not be the last scheduled time she'd see Travis. She'd still have to get through the anniversary party, an event designed to celebrate love and togetherness when she had just lost both.

"I think we should move it to Elephants."

For her. It was the subtext of Owen's statement. She looked into his sympathetic gaze. "We don't need to change the location on my account. Travis and I are fine." Or doing a darn fine imitation of it.

"Are you sure?" Owen's dark eyes pinned her. "It's not a problem to change locations. Now." But it would be if they got much farther in the planning.

Mal pinned him back with a stare of her own. "Give me some credit. I'm not an infant."

"No, but you're upset. Understandably."

She wanted to wave a hand, show that he was wrong and she wasn't upset, or at least not so much that it affected her every action. But her arm remained glued to her side, incapable of the smallest jerk let alone a full wave. "It will be fine. I won't bail on the party and I won't even leave early." Or no earlier than was appropriate. She wasn't going to promise to stick around until the bitter end.

Owen nodded. "If it makes you feel better, I'll probably be avoiding him, too."

It didn't, but she knew he was trying to be supportive. "Then we'll get through it together." She pasted on a smile, wishing she could paste her heart back together as easily. "I need to get ready for my meeting."

"Mal."

But she looked away, unable to stare at his sad, sympathetic face any longer. "I'm fine, Owen. Really." Or she would be just as soon as he stopped talking about her failed relationship and left.

"Okay. If you need me, I'm right down the hall."

She forced another smile and reminded herself that she could get through this. That she'd been the one to insist that Travis put the charity before himself, before *them*selves. She could do this.

And she truly believed that. Right up until Travis walked into her boardroom and smiled at her.

Mal managed to make it through the meeting without any major issues, but only because she didn't ever meet Travis's eyes. Instead, she looked slightly past him or at the people on either side of him. It did the trick. She was even feeling a little proud of herself when the meeting adjourned.

The charity event was well in hand and she was certain it would raise lots of money. At this point, the only major concern left to handle was media coverage and she had a call in to a friend at a local paper as well as other media outlets. The coverage was nearly as important as the event itself, encouraging people to donate after the fact.

The committee milled around for a few minutes, finishing the last sips of their coffee or bites of their muffins, chatting about the industry and life in general. Mal hovered around the edges, making polite conversation when required, always keeping one eye on Travis, who hadn't yet left.

Why was he hanging around? Yes, she'd asked —okay, guilt-tripped—him into staying on the committee and helping with the charity event. But that didn't mean he had to loiter, watching her whenever he thought she wasn't looking.

Her pulse sped up when he headed her way. Mal turned, looking for something or someone to use as a shield. But the rest of the committee members had finally headed for the exit. And, aside from a few coffee cups, there wasn't much in the way of protection.

"Hey." His voice curled around her.

Mal forced herself to meet his eyes, tightening her muscles to keep from visibly shaking. "What can I do for you?" Maybe he simply had a question about the event and his role. She mentally crossed her fingers.

"How are you?"

"I'm fine." But sadness swept through her as she spoke the lie. She didn't ask how he was, afraid of his answer. She didn't know which response would be worse. That he was hurting or moving on.

"I wanted to tell you that I went to see my family. I told them."

He'd told them? She raised an eyebrow, but was careful to keep anything else from showing. "I see."

"About us, I mean." He took a small step forward. She could smell the bright and woodsy scent of his cologne. Her muscles loosened a fraction. He smelled so good and it was so unfair. "About everything that happened."

She felt like crying again, but finally, it seemed her tears had evaporated. She looked at him with dry eyes.

"You were right, you know, about telling them. I shouldn't have hidden that. I think I was actually hiding from myself."

"Were you?" She feigned politeness. "Good."

Travis took another step forward. The rest of the committee had gone, leaving the two of them alone in the boardroom. But the size of the room didn't feel nearly big enough. She had the sideboard filled with coffee paraphernalia behind her, the table to her left, a wall of windows to the right and Travis in front of her. Mal put a hand down on the table for balance.

He peered into her eyes. Mal wanted to shut them tight and click her heels while chanting about home. Maybe, like Dorothy, she could be whisked away by a tornado. But she couldn't look away, couldn't pull herself out. She could only look back at him. Searching for what, she didn't know.

"Mal, I—"

"Is there something you need Travis? I have a busy day ahead of me and I should really get started."

"No. I guess that was all I needed to say." But he was still peering at her. As though looking for an answer to a question he hadn't asked.

Travis remained standing in front of her, close enough to touch, for another moment. Then his shoulders dipped. She knew because she was looking right at them. As it turned out, they were almost as dangerous as his eyes. She had memories of those shoulders. Laying her head on them, curling her fingers into them, watching them flex and bunch as they heaved around furniture or suitcases, making the weight look minimal. But they weren't hers to enjoy. Not anymore.

"I guess I'll see you at the next meeting," he offered.

"You will." Mal indulged in one last look as he turned away from her, walking himself, his shoulders and his tattoos out of the boardroom. Out of her life. And only once the door closed behind him did she risk taking a breath.

The air still smelled like him.

CHAPTER FIFTEEN

MAL MANAGED TO keep a reasonable distance from Travis right up until the night of the actual charity event. But now it was showtime. And despite her suggestion to the reporter that they should do their interview at Elephants, the woman had been more interested in filming at the new, not-yet-open-to-the-public bar owned by Travis. Apparently buzz for The Blue Mill was already strong.

Mal might have stood her ground, but when the reporter had offered live coverage on the six o'clock news, she'd known she couldn't pass it up. What kind of hypocrite would she be, shaming Travis for missing a meeting and then turning around and insisting on having the interview anywhere but at his place?

Despite the fact that she had a zillion other little things to attend to besides prepping for the interview, her brain continued to focus on just one.

Seeing Travis Kincaid.

She fiddled with one of the glass candle holders that dotted the tables at Elephants and tried not to think about the fact that she would be on his turf. And he'd certainly be there. That, at exactly six-thirty, she'd be on site, on camera, smiling brightly as she talked about the event and tried to pretend that it didn't bother her even a little bit to be in her ex's space, no doubt with him hovering nearby.

Mal swallowed and shifted another of the glass candle holders on the table so it was precisely centered. Or maybe Travis wouldn't hover or hang around. Maybe he'd continue to give her the space she so desperately needed.

She wished she didn't feel this way, wished she could brush off her feelings and fears and forge ahead, excited to tackle new situations and opportunities. She rolled her shoulders. Maybe after tonight, when she no longer had to deal with seeing Travis every week. When her schedule would return to normal and she could focus on other things, on non-Travis things. And maybe tonight would be easier than she expected.

It was a mantra she chanted on the drive over, while she chatted with the reporter, at the close of the interview and when she saw Travis in the center of his restaurant, looking like a tattooed god. But she could chant her mantra until the sun set and rose again, it didn't make it true. Especially when a very pretty, very tall, very blonde woman appeared at Travis's side and greeted him with a warm hug that he returned more enthusiastically than necessary.

And suddenly Mal couldn't deal. She wished she felt numb. A lovely icy numbness could protect her from the knowledge that maybe he'd accepted her decision, moved on and was leaving her behind.

Mal snagged her purse from behind the bar where she'd placed it for the interview. Didn't he know that *she* was supposed to move on first? He was supposed to pine over her and then graciously let her go when he saw that she was happy with someone else. He wasn't supposed to find someone first.

She was halfway to the door when she heard her name. She considered ignoring it, acting as though the voice had gotten lost in the buzz of cheerful conversation, but it came again. Louder and considerably closer.

She stopped and turned, a practiced smile in place, fingers wrapped tightly around the handle of her bag. She wished she hadn't stopped. Not only was Travis bearing down on her, but the attractive blonde was by his side. Mal drew in a shaky breath and reminded herself that she could do this. That she had to because turning and running was not an option.

"Travis." At least her voice was clear. "Good to see you." Polite banalities were always good.

She tried not to notice how he filled out his suit. It wasn't her business to notice that any longer.

"Mal." His smile was warm, reaching all the way to the edges of his eyes. She drew in another breath. "You were great in the interview."

She nodded and tried to maintain her decorum, tried not to glare at the blonde beside him. Tried not to notice that she looked very much like the woman Mal had found him with in Aruba. Maybe that was Travis's type. Maybe he preferred them nearly Amazonian in stature and with hair that rivaled the brightness of the sun. And really, it was of no matter to her. Even if her heart was trying to beat its way out of her chest.

Mal smiled at the woman and held out her hand. She could be mature and polite. She could pretend her spirit wasn't being crushed by the fact that he'd chosen someone other than her. Again. "Hello. I'm Mallory Ford."

"Nice to meet you. I'm Sara Thompson."

Mal studied her, while trying to hide the fact that she was checking her out. Her smile was bright. Good teeth. Gorgeous skin. Firm hand-shake.

"Sara is my real estate agent. She helped me buy this place."

Some of the tension in Mal's chest loosened. Maybe Sara was simply a friend who had come out in support of the event. Mal knew she'd sent out invites to all her business associates, too. Why would she expect Travis to do anything different?

"He makes it sound so professional. Like all I can talk about are property values and commission rates, which—" Sara's blue eyes sparkled with good humor "—I am willing to negotiate on if you're looking to enter the market."

Mal faked a laugh that sounded sad even to her own ears. "I'll keep that in mind." She noticed the easy smile that passed between Sara and Travis and felt sick. She could manage polite for an introduction, but she wasn't about to stand here and watch the two of them make googly eyes at each other. "Well, it was very nice to meet you."

She swallowed the bile burning the back of her throat. She would not throw up. She would not embarrass herself by running out. And she would not reveal how much her insides felt as though someone had shredded them. "I should let you get back to your customers."

"Can you stay for a drink?"

Mal noticed that Sara, for all her pleasantries, didn't jump in to encourage that notion. Mal couldn't blame her. She wouldn't want the intrusion of another person on her date, either. Especially not an ex. Though she doubted Travis had told Sara about that little fact. Probably just said she was an old pal from his university days.

"I appreciate the offer, but I need to get back to Elephants."

She didn't. Elephants practically ran itself these days, and if it needed any overseeing, Owen took care of it. But it made for a viable excuse.

"You sure?" Travis's eyes bored into hers. Mal's knees wobbled. He shouldn't be looking at her like that. Not anymore and certainly not with another woman standing beside him. It wasn't fair to anyone.

"I'm sure." She forced a smile. "Nice to meet you, Sara." Then she turned and left.

She was almost at the door, nearly within touching distance when she felt a hand on her arm. A warm, strong hand. And the scent of cedar and oranges. "Mal?"

She closed her eyes, an extended blink, and she prayed for control and a cool head as she spun around to find Travis behind her again. But this time he was alone. "Forget something?" She went for light but feared it came out a bit flat.

"I wanted to say thank you." His hand was still on her arm, and she was still enjoying it far more than was suitable. She should not appreciate his touch let alone crave it. "For coming here tonight."

Mal shifted her purse, which dislodged his hand. "It was for a good cause. The charity."

"You could have insisted the interview be held somewhere else. I appreciate that you didn't."

Her throat tightened. It sounded like farewell— a fond farewell, but a farewell all the same. She tried to hang on to the knowledge that this was her choice, what she wanted.

"Right. So…" So she just wanted to go. Why had he followed her and insisted on this little tête-à-tête? Hadn't they done enough tête-ing? A flicker of movement caught her eye. Okay, a flicker of a very pretty blonde woman moving caught her eye. Sara laughing at the bar, her hair rippling under the lights.

Mal's hands fisted more tightly around the handle of her bag. And just what was up with that, anyway? Shouldn't Travis be hanging out with his new girlfriend instead of bothering her? And wasn't it rude to be throwing this new relationship in her face anyway?

There was moving on, and then there was trying to make her feel bad. And this definitely fell into the latter category. As though he couldn't wait to show her just how okay he was with everything. Well, fine. She was fine too.

Mal lifted her chin. "I want the earrings back." Okay, maybe *fine* was pushing it.

His brow furrowed. "You want the earrings back?" He sounded as confused as he looked, which made her feel embarrassed. Nothing to do but brazen it out.

"Yes." She raised her chin another notch. "Your grandma left them to me and I've decided I'd like them back. She'd have wanted that." Mildred certainly wouldn't have wanted to see them on the lobes of some woman she didn't know. Even if that woman was very blonde, very pretty and very personable. Just what was Sara saying to make the bartender and everyone else within a foot of her laugh so hard?

"All right."

Mal's attention snapped back to Travis. A whip of longing followed. She stamped it out. It was okay to feel sorrow about the breakup and it was okay to experience moments of discontent. It was not okay to let them take root. "Good." She probably sounded petulant, but then she felt a little petulant.

Travis looked surprised. Okay, so maybe dial back the petulance a tad. "I'll have to get them out of the safe."

"Okay." She stood, waiting.

"At the hotel." Owen had mentioned that Travis had vacated his place and moved into a hotel.

"Right." Because of course he wouldn't have them here. "That'll be fine." There was that word again. As though it was following her, taunting her by pointing out that she was not fine. "I should go."

And she wasn't waiting around to see what he might or might not say, might or might not do. She just spun on her heel, pulled the door open and walked into the warm evening.

TRAVIS WATCHED THE door swing shut behind Mal and frowned. He'd hoped she might stay for a few minutes, hoped they might grab a couple of moments of privacy and talk. But she'd beetled out of here at the speed of light. And now he was left alone, with words he wanted to say and no one to say them to.

The door pushed open and Travis stepped out of the way as a group of three wandered in. Their tight jeans and thin mustaches marked them as hipsters, their pricey watches and expensive shoes marked them as spenders. Travis smiled as he watched them wander to the bar and proceed to order top-shelf drinks, those made with the most expensive and exclusive alcohol. They were definitely the clientele he was looking for.

He should be feeling happy and proud. But as he walked the floor of the bar, he felt more as though he was pacing. A jungle cat trapped in a cage of his own making. And the fact that the place was packed and everyone seemed to be having a great time didn't help.

He'd liked having Mal here, seeing her face as she looked over the place, her eyes lovingly grazing each surface, the way she stroked the bar when she walked over to ask if she could store her purse there during the interview. He'd wanted to go to her then, just to talk, to see her up close and wish her good luck, but he'd feared upsetting her before she went on camera. So he'd bided his time, knowing that this was an important night for her. He certainly wasn't going to ruin it for his own selfish needs.

"Travis." Sara's cheerful voice plucked him out of his morose thoughts. "Over here." She waved at him from a couple of feet away where she stood with a redhead who was just as tall and attractive as she was. "I want you to meet my wife, Jill."

They talked for a few minutes. Jill was as bright and friendly as Sara and worked as a lawyer for a nonprofit in the city. But Travis, as much as he tried not to, couldn't help checking over his shoulder every so often, watching the door, just in case Mal came back.

"Looking for someone?" Sara's tone was casual, almost a throwaway.

"Just keeping an eye on things. I am the owner, you know."

"Right. So this wouldn't have anything to do with Mal?" Sara turned to her spouse. "Remember how I told you what a pain in the ass he was being about finding a place to live? I think I just found out why. Or—" her eyes slid over to Travis "—should I say who?"

"I haven't been a pain in the ass." He and Sara had only viewed about twenty places. It wasn't his fault none of them were right.

"Yes, you have." But Sara didn't look mad, more amused. "And I notice he didn't deny my theory. What do you think?" She winked at Jill. "Proof?"

"Yes. Though it wouldn't actually hold up in a court of law."

Sara turned her attention back to him. "So, what happened?"

"Sara." Jill placed a hand on Sara's arm. "Maybe he doesn't want to talk about it."

"Well, I'm sorry, but he's going to have to. He needs to stop turning his nose up at every apartment we see. Is it because you keep looking at it and wondering if she'll like it?"

Travis didn't want to admit it, but that was the reason. Exactly. He was finding an issue with every single place because some small part of him still held out hope that he and Mal might get back together. That he pictured Mal in the kitchen, dishing out Chinese takeout because they were both too tired to cook, or curled up on the couch with her feet tucked under his thigh, or walking a baby up and down the hallway, a maternal glow making her smile even though she was exhausted. "I just don't want to jump into anything."

"No." Sara's face was full of faux concern. "Much like you waited months before finally deciding this place was right."

She had a point. "That was different." He felt obligated to defend himself. Sara and Jill simply looked back at him. "This place was perfect."

"And is Mal?"

"No one's perfect." Even though Travis could think of a million ways she was.

"Maybe not," Sara mused. "But is she perfect for you?"

Travis didn't answer. Not because he didn't know, but because he was afraid to say it out loud. Because what if that wasn't enough? What if his love wasn't enough?

CHAPTER SIXTEEN

MAL WAS SITTING in her office, staring blankly at her computer screen when Donovan walked in. She felt as though she was doing a lot of blank staring since the charity event last week. Seeing Travis had rocked her—seeing him with another woman had turned her upside down.

"Mal." Donovan took a seat without asking. "We need to talk."

She blinked and focused on him. He was frowning, an expression she hadn't seen on his face much of late. "Okay." She forced a smile she didn't feel. "Let's talk."

"I'm worried about you."

Mal felt her smile wobble and then fall. "I'm fine," she said, even though she knew it wasn't true. She hadn't been fine since she'd refused Travis's proposal. In truth, maybe it had been even longer than that—all the way back to the first breakup. She'd just been able to hide it better from herself and everyone else then.

"You're not fine," Donovan said, smashing any

hope she might have at least fooled him. "We all see it. We're all concerned."

"I'll be fine." She clasped her hands on her lap, holding tight as though, by virtue of sheer grip strength alone, she could make herself okay. "No one needs to worry."

"Too late." His dark eyes turned down at the corners. "I don't like seeing you this way."

Mal glanced away, busied herself with some papers on her desk. "Then maybe you should stop looking." Maybe he and everyone else should just let her deal with things in her own way, in her own time. Eventually, she'd get through it.

"Mal, come on."

"Come on nothing, Donovan." The paper crumpled in her hands. "What's done is done. It's over. It's not going to change."

"You can't live like this again."

"Like what?" Her head shot up along with her temper. Was there some problem with how she chose to run her life? "Do I need to remind you that I'm an adult and can make decisions about my own life without your input?"

"That isn't what I meant and you know it." He tilted his head, drummed his fingers on his knee. "You're really spoiling for a fight."

"I'm not spoiling for anything." But she heard the waspish tone of her voice. She cleared her throat. "I'm just tired, Donovan. It's been a busy month."

"Right." He didn't look as if he believed her. Since she didn't believe it herself, she didn't call him on it. "You can't shut down again."

"I'm not."

He sat forward. "You are. We watched once—thinking it was best to let you work through it on your own."

"It was," Mal tried to agree, but Donovan wasn't finished.

"That turned out to be a mistake. We won't let it happen again."

Mal tossed her head. "Since, as we just discussed, it's my life, I don't see that it's any problem of yours." She glared, waited for him to disagree, prepared for her own defense of her behavior.

So she was hurting and spending the little time she wasn't in the office alone at her apartment. So what? She was trying to keep busy so she didn't start thinking about what she'd let go, what she'd lost. And maybe it didn't always work, but she was trying, which really was half the battle. That she felt as if she was losing was something she chose not to think about.

"I've got a job for you," Donovan said.

Mal blinked. Where was the "brother knows best" attitude? The bossy, oldest child syndrome, as he tried to tell her how she should feel about Travis. As though he had any clue how it felt to fail in a relationship not once, but twice. As though he wasn't living the perfect life. "I have a job, Donovan. Or are you firing me?"

He didn't rise to the bait. Mal wasn't sure if she was happy or sad about that. "Remember those meetings we had last summer in Calgary?"

"Yes." She drew out the word. About a year ago, around the time Donovan was beginning to plan his own wedding, the two of them had met with some investors in Calgary to consider the idea of expansion. Calgary was a growing town with plenty of residents that had come from Vancouver, so the Ford Group name meant something. "And I remember that we decided not to pursue that avenue."

Neither side had been able to agree on who would hold what share, where the bars would be located or even timing of openings.

"Well, they've reached out with some concessions. I think you should go there and meet with them in person."

Mal narrowed her eyes. "Is this serious? Or just something to get me away from the office?"

"It's serious." He eyed her for a moment before a small grin spread across his face. "And to get you away from the office."

Mal considered it. She certainly wouldn't

mind getting out of the office. "I don't want to waste my time—time I could spend doing something else." Even though she'd been spinning her wheels a little since the charity event. She had a few more things to do regarding the anniversary party for her parents, but Grace was handling most of the organization and Julia was on top of the food. Even her brothers were active participants, leaving Mal with only minor duties.

"It's not wasting time. They've made an interesting offer, but I want someone to go and talk to them in person—you know what a difference that makes. We need to know if they're serious, and you're the one I trust."

"You don't want to go?" She was surprised. Donovan liked to be in control. In fact, he and Owen still butted heads over things on a semiregular basis, though not as much as they'd once done. Marriage had mellowed both of them.

Her heart hiccuped. Marriage. Something that now seemed so off the radar for her that she thought it might not ever happen. Maybe she wasn't the marrying kind.

"I think you need this," Donovan said.

"And if it's a good deal? Am I signing then and there?"

"Don't go crazy. We'd need to discuss it as a family, but it's a possibility, which brings me to another question. How would you feel about moving there if the deal is a go?"

Mal sat back in her chair, the paper she was still holding rustling when she pressed it into her stomach. "Moving?" She'd never considered that. It hadn't come up in their previous conversations. Moving away from her family? Her life? Leaving it all behind?

She had moved before, and to a much more distant location, but she hadn't been going it alone then. She'd had Travis. Or so she'd thought. But he definitely wouldn't be part of the conversation now. She swallowed.

"I think it's important to have a presence if we decide to move forward with this. Someone who can oversee things on a day-to-day basis. Someone we can trust."

Mal understood all of that and agreed. But moving? Calgary wasn't far, not like Aruba was far. But it wasn't exactly next door. If she needed to get home, if there was an emergency, she couldn't just hop in a car and be there in five minutes. The drive was long and through mountainous terrain. Flights were considerably faster, but even though flights were daily—many times a day, in fact—and of reasonable times, it would still take hours to get home. And she could forget about Sunday dinners—she wouldn't be attending many of those.

"It's a real opportunity for us." Donovan's voice broke into her personal thoughts. "And an opportunity for you. You can grow the brand and the company, guide us into the future."

Mal did like that idea. She had plenty of thoughts on what the company could be doing, but she'd always thought about doing them here. Nestled in the city where she'd been born and raised, the place her family still called home. She looked at her oldest brother. "Have you told anyone else about this?"

"Not yet. I wanted to run it by you first to see if you were interested." He paused. "So, are you?"

That was the million dollar question. Or, if things went well with the possible expansion, the multimillion dollar question. "I need to think about it. It wouldn't just be moving to a new city. It would be like starting over." Even as she said it aloud, a little part of her wondered if maybe that was what she needed. A fresh start. A new place where the baggage of her past wouldn't feel quite so heavy. But she'd miss everyone.

And part of her couldn't help but question why she'd moved back to Vancouver in the first place, upsetting not just her own life, but Travis's too, if she was going to pick up and leave again.

"Of course. There's no rush to decide. We don't even know if the deal will work out, but it's something to consider. And if you don't want to move, but we do want to expand there, we should think about other options."

Mal nodded. "Okay." But her mind was already shooting down options that might be suggested. It was too big a project for any of their current staff to manage. They just didn't have anyone who could slide into the duties the role would demand and flourish. Which meant it would need to be one of them: her, Owen or Donovan.

Which meant her. Because Julia was the chef at their lone fine dining restaurant and was part owner, which meant Donovan wouldn't move. And Grace had a thriving and growing wedding planning business, which meant Owen wouldn't move.

Did she want to move?

"You sure you're okay?" Donovan asked. He still hadn't shifted from the chair.

Mal tamped down the thoughts rolling through her head. She didn't have to make a decision this minute. She might not have to make a decision at all if the deal turned out to be a lemon. But it was hard not to analyze the potential and the pitfalls now that it had been put to her. "It's a lot to think about."

"I know." He did rise then. "And whatever you decide, we'll support you."

Support her. Whether she stayed or went. Whether she chose what was best for the company or what was best for her. They'd be on her side. Mal drew in a shuddery breath and managed to keep the tears from rising to her eyes until Donovan stepped out of her office.

She waited until she heard him walk out and down the hall before she rose, closed the door behind him with a firm click and indulged in a nice, private cry.

TRAVIS STOOD BEHIND the bar at The Blue Mill polishing the already gleaming wood. They weren't open for the day yet and the closing staff had done a great job last night, but he liked doing this job anyway. The slow, easy circular motion, the steady movement going from one end of the bar to the other. It allowed him to fall into the zone, the busywork for his hands allowing his mind to wander.

He found he often did his best thinking this way, or his best not-thinking—keeping focused on the task rather than facing the issues that kept him awake at night. This way he wouldn't have to think about anything but ensuring the bar acquired a perfect polish.

Travis was halfway through his second effort when the front doors rattled. He kept rubbing down the wood, the lemon scent of the polish tickling his nose. They didn't open for business for another couple of hours, which the door-rattler outside would figure out by looking at the sign posted beside the door. If that didn't work, the lack of response would help him figure it out.

The rattling came again, followed by a short, impatient knock. Travis ignored those, too. He knew from experience that if he answered, the customer would try to talk his way in. And even if it wasn't against his business license, Travis didn't feel like letting anyone in at the moment.

It was just him and his bar.

"I know you're in there, Travis." The knock was louder this time and more forceful. It put the previous rattling to shame.

What was Owen doing here?

Travis put down the rag to find out. He'd had limited contact with the Fords since Mal had turned down his proposal. In part because it had felt wrong to keep seeing them, as though the breakup had meant so little that it was business as usual. In part because it hurt to see them, to see the family he'd thought would join his. That future was all but shattered now.

He unlocked the door to find Owen standing on the sidewalk, arms crossed over his chest. "It's about time."

"Good to see you, too." Travis stepped back, allowing Owen entrance and then relocked the door. "What are you doing here?"

"Checking up on you." Owen took a seat at the

bar and turned, waiting until Travis joined him. "You look terrible."

"If this is your idea of checking up on me, your bedside manner leaves something to be desired."

Owen merely shrugged. "Doesn't change the fact that you look like ass."

Since Travis had seen the truth of that in the mirror himself, he simply ignored the comment. "Want a drink? Something to eat?"

The bar was fully stocked and he had a personal stash of potato chips in his office that he was willing to share, so long as Owen refrained from making any further comments on his appearance.

"I'm good." Owen rested his hand on the bar. Travis started polishing again.

They were both quiet for a full minute, one man leaving fingerprints, the other rubbing them away.

"So, this is what you do all day?" Owen rolled his thumb back and forth over the spot Travis had just cleaned. "Polish the bar and ignore your customers?"

"I'm not ignoring you and you're not a customer."

"Fair enough." Another minute of silence.

Travis glanced up as he polished, but Owen simply looked back and continued to make marks on the bar. Travis rubbed harder, as though that could erase all of his life's disappointments.

"She's thinking about moving."

Travis's fingers clenched the rag, the hard press sending out a waft of lemon. "Oh."

"To Calgary."

Travis didn't look up from the bar and kept polishing, even though Owen had moved his hands away from the wood surface. But while Travis's motions remained smooth and easy, his pulse was thundering—a storm of emotion looking for a place to unleash itself. Mal was moving. Away from him. He crumpled the rag into a little ball.

"What are you going to do about it?"

Travis looked up at his friend. "I'm not sure what you mean."

"Then let me be clear." Owen leaned forward and planted his hands on the bar top. "She's leaving. Maybe forever."

"Why are you telling me this?"

"Because—" Owen half rose from his seat "—she's miserable without you, and while I'm still mad about what happened, I know you love her."

"I do." Travis's heart flipped over when he said it.

"And I think she's happier with you than without you. Even though you aren't good enough for her."

"I can be." Travis straightened up.

"You'd better be. Else you'll be answering to the whole family."

Travis liked the sound of that. The whole family. All the Fords, big and small. And him, welcomed back to their warm embrace. With Mal.

"Well? Are you going to sit back and watch her go or are you going to fight for her?"

"I'm going to fight," Travis answered without thinking as adrenaline surged through his body. But this might be it. The last chance he'd have, because if she left before he talked to her, there really would be no going back. He eyed Owen. "You aren't planning to take another shot at me, are you?"

"If you'll recall, I didn't take that shot. Even though you deserved it. But I can rectify that." Owen grinned.

Travis held up his hands in mock surrender. "No, I'm good."

"And don't you forget it." Owen resettled on the bar stool. "Now, back to my sister. She's leaving tonight."

"You waited until now to tell me?" Maybe Owen wasn't really interested in helping them get back together at all.

"I had to figure out what was best for Mal," Owen said.

"Fair enough." In an odd way, Travis was glad

that Owen had given serious thought to the matter. It gave the information weight because Owen wouldn't be here telling him this if he thought there was no chance of reconciliation. "So you're saying I have a shot?"

"If you don't screw it up. What's that old saying? Third time's a charm."

"It will be." It had to be. At least he'd give it his best shot. He dropped the rag and started around the bar.

"Where are you going?" Owen asked.

"I have to see Mal."

"I didn't mean you should go now."

"She's leaving tonight," Travis called over his shoulder as he continued toward the door. "I don't have time to waste." He didn't yet know what he would say, but he'd figure it out.

"What about the bar?"

"Here." Travis stopped only long enough to toss him the keys. "Help yourself and lock up when you're done."

"Are you paying me for this?"

"Put it on my tab."

But when he reached the offices of the Ford Group and checked in with the receptionist, he discovered that meeting his destiny was going to take a little longer than expected.

"I'm sorry, Mr. Kincaid. Ms. Ford isn't in the office."

Travis swallowed his irritation. It wasn't the young woman's fault that Mal wasn't here. "When is she due back?" He'd wait. He'd already waited nearly two years, what was another few minutes—five, forty, sixty? He'd wait no matter how long.

"I don't believe she's coming back today. Would you like me to let her know you stopped by?"

"No." He answered quickly. He wasn't going to let a little thing like being at the wrong location stop him. "I'll give her a call. Thank you."

He was halfway out the door with his phone already in hand, dialing Mal before he even finished speaking to the receptionist.

"Hello, Travis."

"You can't move." It popped out before he had a chance to think about what to say. He bypassed the elevator for the stairs, feeling the need to keep in motion.

"Who told you…never mind. It doesn't matter. What I do isn't your concern, remember?"

"But what if I want it to be?"

"Don't make this harder." Her words gave him hope. If she really was over him, then she wouldn't care what he said.

"I need to see you before you leave."

"I'm busy, Travis. I have to pack. I have meetings to prepare for. It's not a good time."

"It's the only time we've got." He was out the door of the building and heading down the sidewalk now, dodging other pedestrians as he navigated his way toward Mal's apartment. "Will you see me?"

She took a breath, but didn't say anything. For a moment, Travis feared her answer would be no. That she would refuse to even give him a minute of her time. A chill ran through him.

"Fine. But you'll have to make it quick. I'm due at the airport in an hour."

"I'll be at your place in five."

He broke into a run as soon as he hung up and arrived at Mal's place in three minutes. He was breathing hard when he punched in her buzzer number, but he figured that was more from the adrenaline than the exercise.

When she answered, Travis wished he'd been faster.

"Maybe it's not such a good idea for you to come up."

"Then you come down."

"I have to pack."

"Then I'll come up." He sure wasn't going to leave without saying his piece, without making it clear that he wanted to be with her, was willing to compromise and make concessions. Until Mal understood without a doubt that she meant everything to him—or until he knew for certain that there was no chance for them to be together.

"Travis."

"Five minutes and then I'll go, if that's what you want."

Her sigh echoed through the intercom system. "Five minutes." Uncertainty came through in her voice, but at least it wasn't no.

Travis realized he probably should figure out what he was going to say in his allotted five minutes. Something more convincing than "You can't move." But nothing came to him as he rode the elevator.

Mal opened the door when he knocked, but she didn't look happy to see him. "Five minutes," she repeated.

Travis nodded and followed her inside the apartment. "You can't move." So much for thinking up a more convincing argument.

She didn't budge from the entryway. No doubt to ensure he knew she was serious about her five minute time allowance. "As I've already told you, that's not your concern."

"I want it to be." He wanted everything that affected her to be his concern. Her sorrow, her joy, even her annoyance.

"This isn't your decision to make, Travis."

The words reverberated through the small space, striking a chord in him with their familiarity. They were nearly identical to the ones she'd spoken in Aruba. Only that time she'd been coming to Vancouver, not leaving it.

A chill passed over the back of Travis's neck. He didn't want things to end the way they had then.

"Then let's talk. Tell me what's in Calgary." No recriminations or ultimatums this time.

"An opportunity to expand the business." Mal looked down and shrugged. "It would be good for the company."

Travis knew that was true, but would it be good for Mal? "So you'd live there."

"That is the plan." She shrugged again. "There's no reason not to go."

Travis could think of a few. "What about your life here? Your family?" His voice lowered. "What about us?"

"There is no us, Travis."

"But there could be. If you stay."

Her head popped up, her eyes lit with the fire of temper. "No." She shook her head, hair swinging back and forth in an angry wave. "You can't ask me that. Not again."

He knew the mental connection she'd made, the conclusions she'd jumped to, because she'd also felt the cold finger of similarity between now and then. "It's not the same this time," he said. Because they were different and so were the situations. She wasn't moving to be closer to her family who needed her, she was moving away from them.

But Mal wasn't listening. "They are. I have a reason to move and you're trying to keep me from doing so."

Her words stopped Travis cold. Maybe she was right. Maybe the situations were closer than he wanted to admit. "Then I'll move."

"What?" She blinked at him. "You can't move."

"Of course, I can. What's stopping me?" He was living in a hotel anyway.

"You just opened your bar, you can't move."

"I could sell it."

"I'm not letting you sell it." She crossed her arms over her chest.

"Then I'll find a way to run it from out of town." Maybe he could split his time until the bar was established or he found someone to handle the daily duties of managing. With technology, it wasn't as if he needed to be on site to do the paperwork.

"You're being ridiculous." But she sounded awed rather than annoyed. "You can't just pick up your life and move for me."

"Why not?"

"Because…" But she didn't finish her sentence.

Travis stepped forward and reached for her hand, slowly tugging it from the fold of her arms.

It was a risk. She might jerk away or shake him off. She might point at the door and tell him to leave. He rubbed a thumb along the back of her fingers. "I love you, Mal. I want to make this work."

She looked down at their joined hands, then back at him. But she didn't say anything.

"Do you?" He had to ask, had to know, even though the answer had the potential to devastate him.

Her eyes flicked back down to their hands. Travis felt a small tug, though she didn't let go.

"I think you love me," he said. It was true. If he didn't believe that, he wouldn't be here. He'd let her go and wish her the best. But so long as he had that last shred of hope, he'd fight. "But if I'm wrong, tell me." He gave her hand a small shake. "Look me in the eye and tell me you don't and I'll go." Even though he still hadn't used up his promised five minutes.

Mal continued looking at their entwined fingers. The little shred of hope stayed right where it was, lodged beneath his heart, equal parts pleasure and pain.

The silence stretched. Only the sound of their breathing filled the space until he couldn't stand it another second. "Mal?"

She swallowed. "Would you really move?"

Relief punched him harder than Owen ever

could, and he practically tripped over himself to answer. "I'll go with you tonight."

"I don't think that's necessary." She pulled her hand away then. "You've given me a lot to think about."

"I know." He waited a breath. "What we have is worth it, Mal. You know that." He knew *he* did.

She nodded slowly. "I'll only be gone a few days." She looked into his eyes. "I'll call you when I'm back."

"And then?" His breath felt trapped in his lungs.

"Then we'll talk."

MAL TRIED TO concentrate on her packing. Clothing for the office and the generally hotter summer days in the prairie region. Her toiletries and makeup. Jewelry. Her hand stilled on the top of her jewelry box, even though it no longer contained the ring and earrings.

He'd offered to move, to pack up his life and go with her. Eighteen months ago she'd have been overjoyed at the prospect. Would have helped him pack and insisted that he come sooner rather than later. But she was different. They were different.

Could they really go back to the way things had been? A return to the life they'd once shared? Maybe it was too late for that. Mal didn't know.

She glanced at the clock, saw that her cab

would be arriving in five minutes and started throwing things into her suitcase. It didn't matter if she'd need it or not—if it was close at hand and it fit, in it went. Everything except the jewelry, because she couldn't afford the distraction.

She needed to be focused. This was a good opportunity for the family business and she couldn't be sidetracked by her personal life. She had proposal notes to go over, budgets to review. She needed to be thinking big picture—location, cost, process. But her thoughts were filled with Travis. With his offer. With her own feelings about it and him.

Her phone rang, alerting her that the cab would be at her door in less than a minute. She wheeled her overstuffed suitcase out of her apartment. A few days away would be good for her. She could think, figure things out.

Except that when she got into the cab and the driver asked where she was going, she didn't say, "Airport." She gave him the address of Travis's bar.

"With a suitcase?" The cabbie looked at her in the rearview mirror.

"There's something I need to do." Something she needed to say. And then she would leave.

CHAPTER SEVENTEEN

TRAVIS WAS SITTING behind his desk when his office door banged open. He started and then froze when he saw Mal in her slim pale gray skirt and simple ivory top, shimmering like an angel or a harbinger of destiny. She stepped inside, closed the door behind her and turned the lock.

"Mal?" he asked when it seemed she wasn't going to say anything. "What are you doing here?"

It was too much to hope that she was here to tell him she'd considered his proposal and was going to accept. Way too much. Yet hope rose and fluttered in his chest anyway.

She didn't speak immediately, just leaned against the door, the pose showing off her long, sleek legs ending in sexy wine-colored heels. Well, if she didn't want to talk, he was happy to look for the moment. Although it made him want to touch and he didn't know if that would be permitted. He flexed his hands and then clasped them on his lap.

"You asked me if I loved you."

His tongue felt glued to the roof of his mouth. "And…"

And? Travis tried to swallow, but he was still frozen, paused in the moment, waiting for her to continue.

She took a deep breath. "I know we've made a mess of things. Me probably more than you, but—" her eyes flicked down and then back up "—something keeps pulling me back to you."

It was love, deep and true. But Travis didn't say that.

"I was hoping…no, I want to ask if we can start over." He heard the shake in her voice, the tremor of her lips before she pressed them together. "I want to start over."

"Mal." He heard the ache in his own voice. "That's all I've ever wanted."

When she straightened up and began to walk toward him, hips swaying in that tight skirt, Travis nearly broke his own knuckles to keep from reaching out for her. But he needed to let her come to him for a change. Needed her to admit that he wasn't alone here, that she felt the same way he did.

She didn't stop, coming around the desk so their knees bumped. She reached out and cupped his face, stroking his cheeks with her thumbs as she lifted his face to hers. "Me, too."

His pulse pounded and his ears rang, but there was no mistaking her words. His muscles kicked into action. "Say it, Mal." He caught her wrists in his hand, kept her hands on him.

She bent farther and brushed her lips against his. Travis swore he saw heaven. "I love you."

He swallowed, deciding the words, the conversation, everything could wait. Everything except him and Mal. He kissed her harder, and she sighed against his mouth, the sound like a homecoming, as she maneuvered herself between him and the desk, using it to brace herself so she could press closer to him.

Travis's fingers flexed again as he stroked down her arms and torso to settle on her hips, gripping harder, wanting to drag her against him, smother her with his love. It took all his strength, both mental and physical, to let her call the shots. To stay where he was while she set the pace, the intensity.

She stroked his cheeks, his eyebrows, sideburns, the sides of his neck, his shoulders. As though she was memorizing every inch of him or relearning him. He felt the flutter of her fingers, her lips, slowly driving him insane, to a place he might never come back from. And he was okay with that.

More than okay when she slid her fingers along

the neck of his shirt, tracing his skin before dipping to undo the buttons. Travis had to plant his feet on the floor to ground himself while Mal slid each button free, her fingers dancing across each strip of skin she exposed. She slowed to open his shirt, to lean back and see what her talented hands had wrought before kissing him again.

It was harder this time, hotter. Travis couldn't stay seated. He rose to his full height, feeling her body slide against his as he pushed them both against the desk. He wanted to feel everything, to lose himself inside her, with her. And it seemed she wanted the same.

Her hands roamed his chest, seemingly eager for more as she shoved at the shoulders, dislodging both his suit coat and dress shirt. Travis shrugged out of them, pleased when she looked at him long and slow before pulling him back against her.

He was fully involved now, no longer able to let her dictate the entire event. He slid her shirt up and over her head, exposing her lacy black bra. He knew she'd have matching panties on under the skirt. She always did. And when his hands strayed to the side zipper and tugged down, Mal answered by unbuckling his belt and following suit with his zipper.

Travis's breath came harder now, as did his

hope. Her skirt slithered to the floor and she stepped out of it to sit on his desk. He was pretty sure that he could die happy, right now, just like this. Was definitely sure when she smiled at him and leaned back on her hands, her beautiful body covered in the smallest scraps of pretty black lace that begged him to remove them.

But he halted. It nearly did him in, but he stopped. "Mal, are you—"

"I'm sure." She wrapped her legs around his waist and reeled him in. "I've never been more sure."

Her bra scraped against his chest until Travis stripped it off. Her underwear followed mere moments later, as did his boxers. Travis leaned her back against the desk, marking her body with his own. Hands, mouths, tongues—all mingled together in a slow, sweet promise of love. A promise of forever.

He lowered himself to his knees and felt her tense. He slowed, stroking the insides of her thighs as he spread them. "I love you, babe."

"I know."

"Can I...?" He didn't finish the question, looking up at her, instead. If she asked him to stop, he would. If it took time for her to learn to enjoy this part of intimacy again, he was up to the challenge.

But instead of gripping his shoulders and tugging him back up, or pressing her knees together in a silent request for time, Mal nodded. "Yes, I'd like that."

Her legs fell open, spread wider for him, not only granting access but begging him to take it. He ran his hands up the insides of her legs from her ankles to her inner thighs. "You are so beautiful," he said, and watched the pretty blush rise in her cheeks.

"Travis." But his name was lost in another moan as he pushed her legs farther apart and pressed forward to pay proper homage to her beauty.

The first taste nearly put Travis over the edge. His entire body swelled, grew hard for her. It sent her reeling, too, judging from her gasping breaths. He licked again, then slowed, taking his time, changing the pace. Driving out thoughts of anyone and anything but what was happening between them right now. He watched as she moaned, her head lolling back as the pleasure swept through her.

Her fingers gripped the edge of his desk. Travis wanted her to grip *him*, to hang onto him, to know that he wasn't going anywhere. He unfurled her hands, still slowly licking, his eyes never leaving hers and placed her hands on his shoulders.

Then he turned his attention back to the task at hand. Or at tongue.

He felt the first shudder, the small explosions as her legs began to shake and her back arched.

Travis placed a hand on her stomach, riding the waves out with her. When she opened her eyes, he smiled. "Thank you."

"I think I'm the one who should be thanking you." Her voice was breathy, her entire body now rosy with pleasure. He admired it for a moment.

"Are you done?" she teased.

His smile widened. "Not even close."

And when he rolled on protection and slid inside her, Travis felt as if he was home. For the first time in nearly two years, he was exactly where he should be, with exactly the right person.

Mal's eyes were huge as she looked up at him, her fingers digging into his biceps as their bodies rocked together. Desk sex might never catch on as the next big thing, but it felt right somehow. A return to what had once seemed insurmountable, proof that together they could handle anything as a team.

"I love you," she said. Travis felt a shudder of pleasure, one stronger and more powerful than any homecoming. "I never stopped."

"Don't." His hips moved faster. "Promise me you'll never stop."

"I promise." Their foreheads were pressed together, eyes locked. Her nails bit into his skin. He rejoiced in the connection, in the way she—unknowingly or not—was announcing that he was her choice, that this time, they'd chosen each other.

He saw the widening of her gaze, the flare of pleasure as he hit just the right spot and he stroked again, keeping up a steady motion until she jerked, arched her back and began to shudder all around him. He came then, too, the initial tidal wave of release followed by slow steady ripples.

Travis didn't move, didn't even make a motion to shift, to uncouple or straighten, though his left thigh was beginning to cramp. Small price to pay for the pleasuring of one's love. He could hear the thump of Mal's heart, the brush of her breath across his own and her low hum of satisfaction.

"I could get used to that," she murmured.

"You'd better." He grinned, plans to make this particular meeting a regular occurrence already thrumming through his brain. And then another thought joined it. One that made desk sex a distant memory, which was a pretty impressive feat considering they were both still naked on top of it.

Travis, being careful to maintain as much body contact as possible, reached down to pull open the top drawer of his desk. His fingers scrabbled

among the pens, paper clips and other office sup-
plies that were deemed necessary but rarely used,
until he felt what he was looking for.

He pulled out the small blue box and flipped
open the lid. The time was now and right.

"Mallory Ford, will you marry me?"

She stilled and then struggled to sit up. "I'm
not dressed." She sounded scandalized, as though
clothing was a requirement. Maybe it was for
most people, but they weren't most people.

"The only thing your outfit needs is a ring."
He shifted to a standing position and plucked the
ring from the box. Her eyes tracked the movement. "Well?"

She looked at him. "Travis, I…" Her lips pursed
and she studied the ring again. "That wasn't why
I came."

"No, you came for the sex, you stayed for the
ring." He picked up her left hand. "If we're going
to start over, then let's start over. All the way
over."

He saw her swallow, the nervous flick of her
head as she tossed her hair and looked from the
ring to him and back again. But she didn't pull
her hand away and didn't tense when he slipped
the ring onto her left finger.

"Mal?"

She looked up from the ring. "Yes." And she

smiled, a sudden brightening of everything. "Yes. I'll marry you."

And this time, Travis felt sure it would be forever.

EPILOGUE

M AL'S FINGERS STRAYED to her hip, gently stroking the skin beneath her party dress. The Blue Mill looked amazing. All done up and dressed up for her parents' surprise anniversary party.

"I still can't believe you pulled this off without anyone slipping up and telling us," her mother said, as she hugged Mal with one arm. "It's just wonderful."

It was. But then, recently wed in a small ceremony that included just her own immediate family and Travis's, Mal was inclined to think everything was wonderful. Rose-colored glasses, through the eyes of love or just sheer contentment, she didn't know. Really, it didn't matter as long as she and Travis were together. "Well, Grace did most of the planning."

"I can tell that you all put your own touches on it," Evelyn Ford said. "Julia's food, Donovan organizing the limo, Owen's slide show."

Owen had dug up family photos from the past thirty-some years and put them together in a slide show that played against one of the walls. Mal had seen the initial iteration, but true to his personality, Owen had added a few extras, including one of her at twelve, with scabby knees and braces, and one of Donovan with the mullet he'd sported at age six. She'd noted there were no such embarrassing photos of Owen in the show.

"Travis's restaurant, which is lovely. But the idea, the spirit?" Evelyn hugged her a little harder this time. "I know that was all you."

"It was all of us. Everyone had been excited by the idea, not just me." Mal was happy to share credit, except for the slide show.

"I know my kids." Evelyn smoothed Mal's hair away from her face. "Thank you."

"You're welcome." Mal led the hugging this time, her heart so full of joy and love that if it were possible, she was sure it would burst.

"Can anyone join in on the fun or is this a private moment?" Travis's low voice curled around her like a balm, and disengaged her from one family member to be enveloped by another, his arm slipping around her waist, forearm resting on her hip.

"Travis, I was just saying what an amazing job you all did." Her mother chattered for a minute, full of gratitude and attitude. "I promise to come back and talk more, but I see Gus." She started off, calling his name in a tone that Mal knew very well. And when Mal turned to look, her dad was guiltily putting down an extremely large piece of cheesecake.

"Poor guy can't even eat his own party food."

Mal leaned her head against her husband's shoulder. "Poor guy is on his third piece of cheesecake."

Travis laughed and settled his arm a little more securely around her waist. The side of her hip warmed, lit up as though she'd been spotlighted. She pressed it more firmly against him.

He lifted some of the weight. "Is it still bothering you?" His tone was solicitous.

"No. It's fine. I'm fine." She took his arm, flipping it over to display the latest tattoo, inked into the underside of his forearm.

The luckenbooth, two hearts intertwined, an old Scottish symbol of love. She sported a matching one on her hip. Both placements were carefully selected so that when his arm was around her, the tattoos met, a perfect match.

Mal pressed his arm back around her hip, the tattoos touching each other, and smiled. Maybe later she'd let him check it over personally. Perhaps he'd need to give it and her a thorough going-over. Just to be sure that it had healed properly.

Travis had wanted to tell everyone about their shared pieces of body art after the tattoos were inked—a permanent representation of their future together. He'd been so pleased when Mal had suggested getting them, but as much as she wanted to shout their reunion to anyone and everyone, she'd deferred from sharing her tattoo and had ensured that, as well as lining up with Travis's, it was placed in such a way that even in a swimsuit—so long as she stayed away from string bikinis—it would remain a secret.

While it was true Mal didn't want secrets, not from her family, not from her friends, there were still some things that were meant to be kept untold.

Known only by a husband and wife.

* * * * *

LARGER-PRINT BOOKS!
GET 2 FREE LARGER-PRINT NOVELS PLUS
2 FREE GIFTS!

HARLEQUIN®

super romance®

More Story...More Romance

HSRLP15

LARGER-PRINT BOOKS!
GET 2 FREE LARGER-PRINT NOVELS PLUS
2 FREE GIFTS!

HARLEQUIN®

Romance

From the Heart, For the Heart

YES! Please send me 2 FREE LARGER-PRINT Harlequin® Romance novels and my 2 FREE gifts (gifts are worth about $10). After receiving them, if I don't wish to receive any more books, I can return the shipping statement marked "cancel." If I don't cancel, I will receive 4 brand-new novels every month and be billed just $5.09 per book in the U.S. or $5.49 per book in Canada. That's a savings of at least 15% off the cover price! It's quite a bargain! Shipping and handling is just 50¢ per book in the U.S. and 75¢ per book in Canada.* I understand that accepting the 2 free books and gifts places me under no obligation to buy anything. I can always return a shipment and cancel at any time. Even if I never buy another book, the two free books and gifts are mine to keep forever.

119/319 HDN GHWC

Name	(PLEASE PRINT)	
Address		Apt. #
City	State/Prov.	Zip/Postal Code
Signature (if under 18, a parent or guardian must sign)		

Mail to the **Reader Service:**
IN U.S.A.: P.O. Box 1867, Buffalo, NY 14240-1867
IN CANADA: P.O. Box 609, Fort Erie, Ontario L2A 5X3

Want to try two free books from another line?
Call 1-800-873-8635 or visit www.ReaderService.com.

* Terms and prices subject to change without notice. Prices do not include applicable taxes. Sales tax applicable in N.Y. Canadian residents will be charged applicable taxes. Offer not valid in Quebec. This offer is limited to one order per household. Not valid for current subscribers to Harlequin Romance Larger-Print books. All orders subject to credit approval. Credit or debit balances in a customer's account(s) may be offset by any other outstanding balance owed by or to the customer. Please allow 4 to 6 weeks for delivery. Offer available while quantities last.

Your Privacy—The Reader Service is committed to protecting your privacy. Our Privacy Policy is available online at www.ReaderService.com or upon request from the Reader Service.

We make a portion of our mailing list available to reputable third parties that offer products we believe may interest you. If you prefer that we not exchange your name with third parties, or if you wish to clarify or modify your communication preferences, please visit us at www.ReaderService.com/consumerchoice or write to us at Reader Service Preference Service, P.O. Box 9062, Buffalo, NY 14240-9062. Include your complete name and address.

HRLP15

READERSERVICE.COM

Manage your account online!

- Review your order history
- Manage your payments
- Update your address

> *We've designed the*
> *Reader Service website*
> *just for you.*

Enjoy all the features!

- Discover new series available to you, and read excerpts from any series.
- Respond to mailings and special monthly offers.
- Connect with favorite authors at the blog.
- Browse the Bonus Bucks catalog and online-only exculsives.
- Share your feedback.

Visit us at:
ReaderService.com

RS15